The Path
to the
Last House
Before
the Sea

BOOKS BY LIZ EELES

HEAVEN'S COVE SERIES

Secrets at the Last House Before the Sea

A Letter to the Last House Before the Sea

The Girl at the Last House Before the Sea

The Key to the Last House Before the Sea

THE COSY KETTLE SERIES

New Starts and Cherry Tarts at the Cosy Kettle

A Summer Escape and Strawberry Cake at the Cosy Kettle

A Christmas Wish and a Cranberry Kiss at the Cosy Kettle

SALT BAY SERIES

Annie's Holiday by the Sea

Annie's Christmas by the Sea

Annie's Summer by the Sea

LIZ EELES

The Path
to the
Last House
Before
the Sea

bookouture

Published by Bookouture in 2023

An imprint of Storyfire Ltd.
Carmelite House
50 Victoria Embankment
London EC4Y 0DZ

www.bookouture.com

ISBN: 978-1-83790-436-5
eBook ISBN: 978-1-83790-434-1

PROLOGUE

Charity hurried down the path, trying not to stumble as the sun slid beneath the horizon and shadows lengthened. The day had hardly begun, it seemed, before it was slipping towards sleep. But there would be no sleep for Charity tonight.

She glanced back at Driftwood House, which sat alone on the clifftop. Its windows were sparking gold in the setting sun and, for a moment, her resolve faltered. What if she was caught and this was her last sight of home? What if she would never again watch a storm roll in across the sea or feel a salt breeze cool her cheeks?

'Hush,' she murmured to herself, turning away from the house and moving on down the cliff path. 'All will be well once I find Josiah.'

She felt in her pocket for the gift she had for him. A precious gift, once given to her, that would be passed on to the man she loved. A man who didn't realise that his life tonight was hanging by a thread.

Charity quickened her pace and, leaving the cliff path behind, soon reached Heaven's Cove. Candles flickered in cottage windows and the village seemed full of secrets as she passed through the streets, like a ghost.

Past the church and graveyard. Past the quayside where the hard slap of water hitting stone echoed her pounding heartbeat. On and on until she reached the beach that gave Heaven's Cove its name.

With a sigh of relief, Charity hurried towards the sea, her feet sinking into the cold sand. The sky was now inky and moonless, and cresting waves were pinpoints of white in the darkness that shielded her from prying eyes.

Charity hesitated when she reached the mouth of the cave that edged the cove. She pulled in a deep breath and felt her heart quicken at the thought of seeing Josiah. She would find him and warn him. She would give him the gift nestling in her pocket and keep him safe.

'All will be well,' she assured herself once more. Then she stepped into the cave. And disappeared.

ONE

ALYSSA

Why had he even bothered booking a tour? Alyssa wondered. It obviously wasn't his thing, if his hangdog expression was anything to go by. He looked terminally bored.

She sighed quietly when the man raised his hand, as if he was in a school classroom, rather than in an ancient stone circle on Dartmoor.

'Yes?' she asked with a smile, being careful to keep any hint of irritation out of her voice.

'These people,' he said, brushing dark hair from his eyes, 'these people who you claim would chant here at midnight to summon spirits from the deep – did they also sacrifice animals?' He raised an eyebrow. 'To enhance their summoning, perhaps, and bring forth... I don't know, elves or pixies...? Or Wombles?' he added, not quite under his breath.

Alyssa could feel the smile freezing on her face, but she kept her voice level. 'I have no idea. There are no myths or legends I'm aware of, regarding these stones, that mention any kind of animal sacrifice.'

No stories that mentioned human sacrifice, either. Though that could be remedied, right here and now.

The man raised his other eyebrow, and the corner of his mouth twitched upwards, as though he could read Alyssa's mind. Then, he went back to scuffing his feet in the grass.

There was no point in letting him get under her skin, Alyssa decided, turning to the seven other members of the group she'd brought with her from Heaven's Cove. They were an enthusiastic bunch: two middle-aged couples on holiday, a twenty-something student fascinated by the paranormal, and two elderly ladies carrying huge rucksacks. All of them seemed enthralled by the fantastical stories that laced Dartmoor's rich history.

'Let me tell you about that tor over there,' said Alyssa, pointing out where the land rose into a high peak of dark granite. 'That's where the so-called "Devilish Duke" lost his life in the late seventeenth century.'

She described a particularly gruesome legend involving a lost nobleman on the moors who refused to pay the beggar who was showing him the way home. A bad mistake, as it turned out, when the duke was dragged to the depths of hell for being such a skinflint.

The group gasped, entering into the spirit of Alyssa's myths and legends tour, and enjoying the wild beauty of the moorland around them. It was hard not to be awestruck by the towering tors and vast swathes of countryside stretching into the purple distance.

But the man – Jack, she thought his name was – seemed to be managing it.

Oh, well. There was always one.

She did her best to ignore him and concentrate on the others during the rest of the two-hour tour. He followed at a distance as she told of ghouls and ghosts, huge stones cracked open by demons, and rolling mists that obscured footpaths and swallowed people forever.

And he sat alone, at the back of the minibus, during their forty-five-minute return journey to Heaven's Cove.

Alyssa stared out of the window as the bus, driven by Claude, bumped along Devon's high-hedged lanes towards the village. Claude, well into his seventies, was a fisherman by trade, but happy to act as a driver when she needed him. He was also an oddball, which was why Alyssa – seen as something of an oddball herself – particularly liked him.

He and the other villagers had, in the main, welcomed Alyssa when she'd first arrived in Heaven's Cove six months ago. And they'd been encouraging about her plan to set up myths and legends tours of the area. Devon was awash with old stories, and she was happy to tell them to tourists. Her customers were entertained, she made money to help her get by and, crucially, no one got hurt as she went about her job.

Alyssa had a sudden flashback to what she'd fled from – the reason she was now living alone in Heaven's Cove. That was no fantastical story, made up to make sense of what had happened centuries ago.

Her story was all too real, and the traumatic past that she was hiding from in Heaven's Cove was available for people to discover on the internet. If they knew where to look. If she hadn't changed her surname and her whole life after *it* had happened.

Back then, she had had a career and peace of mind. Now, she lived alone in a caravan at the end of a Heaven's Cove garden, and she peddled old stories to tourists.

Alyssa shook her head to banish the distressing images flooding her mind. 'That was then and this is now,' she murmured, then glanced at Claude in case he'd heard her. But he was too busy trying to avoid a rabbit with a death wish to take any notice.

That was then and this is now, she repeated in her head, over and over.

At least here she was far from constant reminders. Though arrogant tourists, like the man at the back of the bus, didn't help.

'Don't forget the dragon,' hissed Claude out of the corner of his mouth, as the minibus trundled along the lane that edged the beach.

Alyssa grinned. Claude was starting to know her spiel better than she did.

'Thank you,' she mouthed to him, getting to her feet and grabbing the back of the seat as the bus hit a pothole. 'I expect you've all been to the beach already,' she said, in a raised voice, to her group who were now gazing out of the window at the pretty cove they were passing by. A chilly breeze outside meant the curve of sand was empty, but sunlight was dancing on the sea. 'So you'll know how lovely it is. But what you might not know is that there's a cave, at the far end of the cove, which locals claim is the lair of a fierce sea dragon.'

Alyssa noticed the man at the back of the bus roll his eyes.

'The legend of the sea dragon was born after a young couple disappeared off the face of the earth two hundred and seventy years ago, on the fifteenth of October, 1753,' she continued, deliberately not looking at him. 'Charity, the daughter of a local landowner, and Josiah, a farm labourer, both vanished on the same night. Locals said they heard a roaring sound coming from the cave, which was the sea dragon pulling poor Charity and Josiah into the depths of the ocean.'

The student's eyes opened wide, and Alyssa smiled. It was always good to have a believer on her tours – even though she was about to bring her down to earth with a bump.

'The reality is rather different,' Alyssa told the group. 'Josiah is thought to have murdered Charity for a jewelled brooch she was wearing, and then fled the scene. There's a memorial stone to her on Heaven's Cove green, near the church. You might have seen it. That's the far less fantastical story.

Though I prefer to believe that Charity and Josiah were forbidden lovers who ran away together.'

'You're just an old romantic, Alyssa,' called one of the elderly women, and the rest of the group smiled in agreement. All bar the man at the back, who continued staring resolutely out of the window.

He was studious-looking, with brown hair that flopped across his forehead and he was wearing a grey polo shirt and jeans. He'd be quite good looking if he toned down the brooding vibe going on and smiled, Alyssa decided, giving him a cold stare – that went quite unnoticed – before dropping back into her seat.

Five minutes later, Claude pulled the minibus into a parking bay near the quay and sat quietly while the tourists filed off. Alyssa stood at the foot of the steps, saying goodbye and wishing members of the group a very happy holiday, whatever their plans for the rest of their time in Heaven's Cove.

'Thanks a mill, Alyssa,' the student replied with a grin, blinking in the sunshine and flicking hair over her shoulder. 'That was, like, *totally* awesome.'

The man was the last to leave the bus. He gave Alyssa a brief nod and murmured 'Thank you' before walking off.

Alyssa stretched her arms above her head and sucked in a deep breath of briny air. 'I don't think *he* thought the tour was awesome,' she told Claude, who'd unfolded himself from the driving seat and joined her outside the minibus.

Claude, a man of few words, patted Alyssa's arm in sympathy and ambled off towards his cottage. He stopped suddenly and turned. 'He's got a familiar face, that one, though I can't for the life of me remember why. But don't let him worry you, is my advice. Some people don't want to be pleased.'

He was right. Some people simply enjoyed being miserable.

Alyssa watched the rude man stride past the ice-cream parlour. He also reminded her of someone she once knew.

Someone she was desperate to forget.

She shook her head and pictured a sea dragon towering over the rude tourist before devouring him in a single gulp. It was a childish but satisfying fantasy, she decided, before turning back to the bus and counting the tips she'd received.

Twenty-two pounds. That would pay for a decent meal or two this weekend, at least.

And talking of food... Alyssa glanced at her watch. Her second job began in an hour's time – she'd have to get back to her caravan and rustle up beans on toast to keep her going.

But she paused at the quay for a moment to gaze across the sea. Having been brought up in landlocked Leicestershire, she'd never tire of the view. At one edge of the village, a headland stretched into the water, its lower slope dotted with the ruins of an ancient castle. Heaven's Cove itself was a picturesque muddle of white-washed cottages and narrow lanes. And, at the other edge of the village, a high cliff rose out of the sea into the sky. On top of the cliff, standing watch over Heaven's Cove, stood Driftwood House.

Driftwood House was where Rosie lived; Rosie, who was getting married soon. Honestly, you'd think it was a royal wedding, with all the fuss there was about it. Magda, Alyssa's landlady, was in charge of catering at the reception, and talked about little else.

Alyssa breathed out slowly and let her shoulders slump. There was no point in being grumpy about other people's good fortune, simply because her own life was going nowhere. Rosie seemed like a lovely woman, and she wished her all the happiness in the world.

With one last look at blue-grey water stretching to the horizon, Alyssa turned away from the view and headed for her caravan. This was her life now, and she should make the best of it.

TWO

JACK

Demonic dukes, ghosts and sea dragons? For goodness' sake! Jack snorted out loud as he strode past the ice-cream parlour, swiftly turning his snort into a cough when people turned to stare.

He'd been keen to escape Heaven's Cove for a while, to see some countryside and forget the troubles that had pursued him to this familiar village. Dartmoor had seemed the perfect place, but he hadn't realised how ridiculous that woman's stories would be. Though the other people on the tour had lapped them up.

Jack sighed. He should never have listened to his father. 'Join the tour,' he'd said. 'People speak highly of it, and it'll do you good,' he'd promised.

Well, it hadn't done him any good at all.

His dad's car was off the road with a dodgy exhaust pipe, but he should have gone to the moor by public transport rather than rely on that silly tour. Then he could have stomped about, feeling miserable on his own.

Jack's brisk walking pace faltered. Perhaps he'd been a bit over-the-top grumpy with the tour guide? He was upset and worried, and had taken it out on her when she was only doing her job.

A hot wash of shame flooded through him. When had he become so...? He turned into the lane that led past the village green, unable to settle on the right word for his behaviour. Arrogant, maybe? Ignorant? Boorish?

Perhaps all three, he decided, wondering if he'd become harder since the break-up. He'd certainly become more bad-tempered – and more likely to resort to rudeness with a stranger. Though her perky bonhomie had been irritating, he told himself, trying to quash down the guilt that only made things worse. He had too much on his mind to worry about upsetting some bizarre woman for whom the rules of scientific evidence obviously didn't apply.

How she could live without the rules that got him through the day was beyond him. He couldn't cope with the chaos of life without definites – cold, hard, undisputable facts – to hold on to.

Even as a child he'd needed to know what was happening around him and why. Being in the know had provided a level of detachment as the health of John, his brother, had slowly declined. But it was also the reason why the recent break-up with Miri had hit him so badly. He hadn't realised what was happening – and he still didn't really know why it had happened.

'Three point one four one five nine...' he began to mutter under his breath. Reciting the mathematical constant pi from memory, as far as he could go, always calmed him down. The number was beautiful. It was fixed and unchanging – unlike his life right now.

He could remember reciting pi many years ago, soon after he'd heard about it in maths class at school, in his brother's hospital ward. Over and over again, until it did the trick and blocked out harsh reality.

'Two six five three...' he continued, trying to banish the thought of the tour guide in her baggy trousers and bright pink top that matched the streaks in her hair. Trying to block out her disappointed expression that had swiftly turned to irritation.

Jack ducked when a screeching seagull flew too close. It wasn't that he was a bad person. At least, that's what Miri had told him as he'd sat there, drowning in incomprehension. She just didn't feel the same way about him any more.

How long had her feelings been ebbing away? Jack wondered, spotting Magda on the other side of the village green. A few months? A year? From the moment they'd married six years ago?

Jack plastered on a smile and waved at Magda, who was walking towards him, a bunch of vibrant daffodils cradled in the crook of her arm.

'Hello, Jack! It's good to see you. Your dad said you were coming down for a visit.'

'Yeah, I arrived a couple of days ago. How are you?'

'I'm keeping well, thank you.'

He closed his eyes briefly when she leaned forward to peck him on the cheek. Magda always smelled of vanilla and caramelised sugar, and comfort. She was a family friend rather than a blood relative, but he knew her as Aunt Magda and she'd been a part of his life forever. Safe, stable, secure.

'And how are you doing?' she asked, stepping back.

'I'm OK, mostly. Yeah, I'm all right.'

'I'm glad to hear it.'

Magda knew exactly what was going on in his life and she gave him a sympathetic smile. But she knew better than to press him on the matter, which was one reason why Jack liked her so much.

'I'm sure your father is enjoying having you around. How is he?' Magda picked a piece of fluff from the sleeve of his jacket and let it fly into the wind.

'Still busy, and keeping the shop open all hours.'

'Too many hours.' Magda frowned. 'He's not as young as he once was, you know, and he's not in the best of health. He never says he's under the weather, of course, but you know what he's like.'

Jack nodded – he knew exactly what his father was like. Stan Gathergill was built of stern stuff. As a younger man he'd lost one of his sons, and, eighteen months ago, he'd lost his wife to cancer. But searing, crushing sadness was no reason, in Stan's mind, to cut down on the hours he spent running his business – the mini supermarket he'd opened in the village three decades earlier.

'So how long are you staying?' asked Magda, pushing grey hair behind her ears.

'I'm not sure. It's open-ended because I want to give Dad a hand. I'm on my way to the shop now, to see if I can help.'

'Then I won't keep you. But you must call in when you have time and have a cup of coffee with me. It's so lovely to see you.'

Magda's bright smile warmed Jack's heart and he thought, not for the first time, what a shame it was that she'd never married and had children of her own. She'd have been an excellent mum, just as his own had been.

He swallowed, suddenly feeling close to tears, and Magda put her hand on his arm.

'You take it easy, Jack, and look after yourself. And don't forget to come and see me.'

Jack tried to smile. 'I won't. I promise.'

'And say hello to Stan from me and tell him not to work so hard.' She gave a wry grin. 'I tell him all the time but he never listens. Maybe he'll listen to you.'

'I doubt it, but I'll do my best.'

'That's all we can do. He can be a stubborn old fool, sometimes.'

With another smile, Magda walked away and Jack stooped

down to do up the lace on his trainer. When he glanced up, he realised he was at eye level with the Mourning Stone, a small chunk of dark grey slate that sat on the edge of the green. The stone had been erected almost three hundred years ago, by a grieving family, to mourn the loss of Charity Hawkins.

The inscription was worn by centuries of wind and rain, but it was still legible. And – unfortunately – Jack knew it by heart:

In memory of Charity Hawkins, aged eighteen years and three months. Cruelly murdered on the 15th of October in the year of our Lord 1753 by Josiah Gathergill.

Why they'd included the name of Charity's murderer escaped him, though if it had been to shame the Gathergill family, it had done the trick. The Gathergills were persona non grata in the village for years afterwards, according to his dad, who'd heard old family tales from his great-grandfather.

That level of shame had long since dissipated but Jack would still rather not be related to a murderer. Especially a murderer whose deeds were still so public, thanks to the Mourning Stone – and tour guides spouting fanciful tales of sea dragons.

Which brought him back to the woman on Dartmoor and his bad behaviour. Jack sighed and started walking back to Gathergill's Mini Mart, leaving the ancient, accusatory stone behind.

THREE
MAGDA

Magda stepped into the churchyard and watched Jack until he disappeared from sight. He cut a lonely figure as he skirted the green and, though he wasn't her son, she worried about him these days. She worried on Penny's behalf, now her friend was no longer around to protect her family.

Poor Penny. Magda approached the grave that stood in the shadow of the yew tree, and laid down her daffodils. The flowers were a splash of yellow against the headstone, which was so shiny and new next to the older stones in the graveyard.

Penelope Jane Gathergill. Her name was picked out in silver lettering. *Beloved wife of Stan and loving mother to Jack, and John* (1985–1999).

It could also truthfully have said *Profoundly missed best friend of Magda. Surrogate sister,* even, as the two of them had been so close. But Magda was glad that her name was missing from this public memorial because Penny had not known what was in her heart. And if she had...

Magda stooped down and deliberately busied herself, pulling stray weeds from the graveside and brushing dirt from the headstone with her hand. 'Hey, Penny,' she said softly, glancing around to make sure she'd not be overheard talking to the dead. 'The cliffs are dotted with spring flowers and the first mackerel catches are coming in. The village is filling up with tourists and the lifeboat's already been launched a couple of times to rescue people who strayed too far out on the rocks. When will they ever learn?'

She paused, feeling foolish. Giving Penny a round-up of life in the village was probably pointless, but she liked to give it, nonetheless. Just in case Penny was watching from some kind of afterlife.

Though, if she was, she'd know very well what was really happening in Heaven's Cove – her husband working long hours to banish his grief, her son lost after the breakdown of his marriage, and her best friend running the village ice-cream parlour while trying so hard to squash down her emotions.

'Sorry,' said Magda, just in case Penny could hear. 'I'm really sorry. I'm sorry you're not here and I'm sorry that I was never as good a friend as I should have been.'

She straightened up, rubbed her aching back and wandered over to the wooden bench beneath the church tower. She had lots to do – running a business was time-consuming – but she would sit for a moment and gather her thoughts.

Heaven's Cove was bustling with visitors today but the graveyard was an oasis of peace. She loved this graveyard – which Stan referred to as the dead centre of the village, his humour often verging on black – and today the calm was broken only by chirping birds and bees humming past.

As the sun warmed her body, Magda's eyelids grew heavy and her mind began spooling back through the decades. Back to a bright autumn day in 1974, when she stood in this very grave-yard, dressed in blue satin.

Back then, a chill breeze caught her bare arms as she followed Penny into the ancient church. People stood and watched them walk past, Penny's white gown rustling when it brushed the pews. And there, waiting for his bride, was Stan, handsome in a dark suit.

He looked nervous, standing at the altar. He was biting his lip – always a sure sign of discomfort beneath his usual bravado. But his face lit up when he caught sight of Penny and he smiled at Magda too, following behind.

Memories of the wedding ceremony had faded over the years, but one remained clear: the vicar booming, '*Should anyone present know of any reason that this couple should not be joined in holy matrimony, speak now or forever hold your peace.*' And a deathly hush falling across the church.

Magda had imagined speaking up so many times since. 'It should be me! I love Stan more than Penny does.'

But what an awful, spiteful thing that would have been to say. And patently untrue, because Penny had been a loving and faithful wife until the day she died. It was only right that Magda had forever held her peace.

But she hadn't hung around in Heaven's Cove after that. She'd lived in Scotland for years and enjoyed her share of love affairs. One man, long ago, had asked her to marry him and she'd seriously considered it. But it wouldn't have been fair on him, because no one ever quite measured up to Stan.

Magda had never told anyone how she felt, including Penny. She *hadn't* known, had she? The panic fluttering in Magda's heart smashed through her memories, and her eyes flew open. She took a few deep breaths, trying to calm herself.

She and Penny had been the best of friends who told each other everything. Almost. So how could she not have realised that Magda was in love with her husband?

She didn't know, said the voice in her head that had reassured her constantly since Penny's death. It was probably empty reassurance. A trick of her subconscious. But she chose to believe it anyway, and Penny had never given any inkling that she suspected Magda's pathetic, unrequited passion.

It had remained both pathetic and pointless, because Stan was an honourable man who loved his wife, and Magda could never have done anything to hurt Penny.

But now her best friend was dead, and the longing Magda had worked so hard to extinguish had flared once more. What a wicked woman she was.

The creaking of the churchyard gate cut through Magda's thoughts and she waved automatically at Florence, one of Heaven's Cove's oldest residents, who'd just appeared with an armful of bright spring blooms. The flower shop by the quay had to be doing a roaring trade in graveyard daffodils today.

'Good afternoon, Magda. We're lucky with the weather,' called Florence, her voice hard to hear above the screeching of a seagull overhead.

'It's nice to see the back of the rain,' Magda agreed, getting to her feet. Usually she'd stop and chat with Florence. But right now she wasn't in the mood for making cheerful conversation – and she feared that Florence, over ninety but still sharp as a knife, would see through any fake jollity. She'd probably ask what was wrong and Magda would have to lie, because she could never tell anyone the shameful truth.

'Sorry to dash,' she added, 'but I need to get back to the parlour.'

'I dare say you're busy selling ice creams now the sun's come out,' said Florence, leaning on her walking stick. 'And Alyssa's tours will be picking up with the change in the weather. How's she doing living in that caravan at the bottom of your garden?'

'Fine. At least I think she is,' said Magda, her hand hovering above the gate.

'It can't be easy, living there on her own. Quite lonely, I'd have thought. She doesn't seem to have any family.'

'I really must go but I'll see you soon. Take care.'

That was rude of me, thought Magda as she hurried across

the village green. She'd not so much taken her leave of Florence as fled, and heaven knows what the elderly lady would think of her.

But she'd been thrown by painful memories. Memories and feelings that needed to stay put in the past.

FOUR
ALYSSA

Alyssa stepped inside the caravan and dumped her bag on the table, next to a large brown envelope that had arrived that morning in the post but she'd yet to open.

Her feet were killing her, but she put baked beans into the microwave and two slices of bread in the toaster before collapsing onto the bench-seat with a loud *oof*. It had been quite a morning, thanks to the sneery tourist, but food would revive her, ready for her second job of the day.

She pulled her feet up beneath her and felt herself relax in the warm sunshine streaming through the windows. The caravan had become home over the last few months, though why it had ended up sitting at the end of Magda's garden in the first place was still a mystery.

'It was already here when I moved into the cottage,' Magda had told her. 'I used it for storage initially, when I opened the ice-cream parlour, and I'd started converting it into accommodation when you arrived, although it's pretty old.'

The caravan certainly was old, and made of wood. It was more, Alyssa thought, like a large shepherd's hut than the mobile metal boxes that clogged village roads in the summer, infuriating the locals.

But it was fine for her. There was a tiny room, containing a toilet and basin, that was so small you had to back into it; a cooking area with an electric hob and sink; a fold-down table; and the seat she was sitting on, which opened out into a bed.

The only thing missing was a shower, but Alyssa nipped into Magda's cottage and used hers. That had been the agreement when she moved in, and it seemed to be working well. Though crossing a snowy winter garden in a dressing gown hadn't been much fun.

Overall, the caravan was short on space but it was homely and cosy, and it provided a welcome bolthole from the world outside.

Alyssa was trying to work out how a shower might fit into the caravan when there was a knock on the door and Magda poked her head inside.

'Sorry to disturb you. I wondered if I might have a quick word?'

'Yes, of course. Come in.' Alyssa swung her legs off the seat, curious about the reason for Magda's visit. She was a kind woman whom Alyssa admired – seventy-one years old and still working hard on two businesses she'd built from scratch showed tenacity and flair. But Magda kept herself to herself and rarely made house calls, even to the caravan at the bottom of her own garden.

'I don't want to interrupt your lunch,' Magda insisted when the microwave pinged.

Alyssa shook her head. 'You're not. It's only beans on toast, which I can have in a minute. Please, take a seat. Would you like a cup of tea?'

'No, thank you. I won't be long.' Magda sat down and smoothed a hand across her grey hair. 'I just wanted to check that everything's all right with you.'

'Why?' asked Alyssa, her heart starting to hammer. What had Magda heard about her? Had she stumbled across something on the internet?

'No reason.' Magda shook her head. 'Well, it was something that Florence said, actually. She asked how you were doing in the caravan and I said "Fine" but it made me realise that I haven't properly checked in with you for ages. Oh, I know we make small talk on the landing when you're heading for the shower, but I wanted to make sure that you *are* all right out here.'

Alyssa breathed out slowly, feeling her shoulders drop. 'That's kind of you, but there's no need to be concerned about me. I'm totally fine.'

When she smiled, Magda caught her eye and held her gaze.

She doesn't believe me, thought Alyssa.

But then Magda looked away. 'I love the bunting you've put up in here, and the art posters. They make the place look very cheerful.'

'Thanks. I found the bunting in a charity shop a while ago.'

'How long have you been here now?'

'Six months, give or take a few days. And, um... how long have *you* been here?' Alyssa asked in a rush, keen to ward off any questions about what she'd been doing before arriving in the village.

She felt bad for not knowing more about Magda's life already. They made pleasant conversation when they bumped into one another – 'How are you today?' and 'Isn't it cold?' or 'Did you hear the lifeboat was launched last night?' – but that was it. Alyssa, desperate to avoid searching questions about her past, had kept her emotional distance.

'How long have I been in Heaven's Cove?' Magda thought for a moment. 'It must be close to seven years now, since I moved into my cottage. I set up the ice-cream parlour six years ago, when the building next door to me came up for sale and I was able to buy it. And then, as if that wasn't enough to keep me busy, I set up my catering business a year after that.'

'Did you move to Heaven's Cove because of Stan?'

When Magda suddenly began to cough violently, Alyssa fetched her a glass of water and watched anxiously as the older woman took a few sips. 'Are you all right?'

Magda nodded, her cheeks red. 'Sorry. I've had this cough for a while and it's driving me mad.' She took another sip. 'What makes you think I moved here for Stan?'

'Just that... I know you're both good friends and I heard that you'd been friends with him and his wife for years.' Had she touched a nerve, somehow? wondered Alyssa, mentally kicking herself for being intrusive. Magda didn't look well at all.

'Sorry, I didn't mean to—' she began, but Magda interrupted her.

'That's right. Penny and I were best friends for four decades, so I already knew Heaven's Cove well. When she was first diagnosed with cancer seven years ago, I decided to move here, to give the family a hand and some moral support.'

'That was really kind of you. It sounds like you were a brilliant friend to Penny.'

'Mmm. It certainly sounds like it...'

As Magda stared glumly into her glass, Alyssa realised she'd definitely put her foot in it. Perhaps Magda and Penny had fallen out, or Magda was still too grief-stricken to talk about her friend? Either way, it was time to change the subject.

'How are preparations for Rosie's wedding going?' she asked brightly. 'It's quite a responsibility, making her wedding cake.'

Magda looked up from her drink. 'I've made a fair few in my time so it's not so bad, and the food for the reception is all planned and ordered.'

'Are you sorting out the marquee too?'

'No, that's Rosie and Liam's job, thank goodness. I'm not sure I'd have had the time to organise that as well. They've arranged for it to be erected outside Driftwood House, a few days before the ceremony. The views from the clifftop should be stunning, just so long as the weather behaves.' Magda crossed her fingers. 'Do you know Rosie?'

'Sort of. We say hello when we see each other in the village, and she comes into Stan's shop sometimes. Everyone seems very excited about her wedding.'

'Everyone likes Rosie and they're delighted that she and Liam have found each other and are getting married. Happy endings aren't always a given. Anyway...' Magda got to her feet so quickly, water slopped onto the floor. She placed the glass on the table. 'I mustn't keep you from your lunch a moment longer. I'm glad you're doing OK out here, Alyssa, and you know where I am if there are any problems.'

Alyssa watched Magda pick her way across the garden and disappear into the back door of her cottage. She had the feeling there was more to Magda's visit than met the eye. But it had been kind of her landlady to check up on her. In fact, everyone she'd met in the village had been kind to her – except for the sneery tourist, who, she decided as she spooned beans onto her toast, didn't count.

She sat at the tiny table and ate her lunch, all the while eyeing the brown envelope which had arrived earlier that morning. She could open it now and get it over with, or do it later, once the day's work was done.

'Now,' said Alyssa, making up her mind and pulling the envelope closer, even though it was tempting to wait until she had a large glass of wine in her hand.

When she ripped the envelope open and tipped it upside down, half a dozen smaller envelopes tumbled onto the table – remnants of her old life before Heaven's Cove – along with a piece of paper.

It was a note, she realised, as she picked the paper up. A note that simply said: *Missing you, Baby – Ben x*

FIVE

JACK

A blend of aromas hit Jack when he pushed open the door to Gathergill's Mini Mart: sharp citrus, chemical overtones of plastic packaging, and a meaty waft of dog chews. The smells were familiar – another constant in an ever-changing world – and even the faint whiff of damp rising from the cellar was soothing.

'The prodigal son returns from Dartmoor,' declared Stan, who was standing at the till. He closed the *Radio Times* he'd been looking at and smiled. 'How was the tour?'

'It was OK, thanks. Have you been busy?'

'Not really. There was a rush about an hour ago – a bunch of tourists in search of beer – but it's been quiet ever since.'

Not so much quiet as dead. The mini-supermarket that provided Heaven's Cove residents with everything from fresh fruit and breakfast cereal to hair grips and pet food was often rammed with customers. But right now, it was completely empty.

Jack picked up a fallen bar of Dairy Milk and put it back on the shelf, alongside a vast array of confectionery. As well as beer, tourists bought a huge amount of chocolate and sweets –

any diets apparently abandoned the moment they set foot in the village. Which was beneficial for Stan's profits, and very good news for Magda and her ice-cream parlour.

'I saw Auntie Mags in the village, on my way back, who said to say hello.'

Stan nodded. 'She's invited me round tomorrow morning to sit by the sea with a few scoops of salted caramel.'

'She knows the way to your heart. Actually...' Jack hesitated. He'd usually ease into a health-related conversation with his father, but talk of Magda had provided a shortcut. 'She's worried about you, Dad. She thinks you're working too hard and need a break.'

'That woman worries too much, just like your mother did.'

'They only worry because they care,' said Jack mildly, putting the *Radio Times* back into the magazine rack. 'And you do seem a bit out of sorts these days – not quite yourself.'

'What rubbish! I really don't want to discuss it,' declared Stan, closing down any prospect of a heart-to-heart conversation. 'There's no need to waste your time, because I'm perfectly fine.'

That was a lie, obviously. His dad worked far too hard for a widower with health issues, and he seemed less mobile these days. He was often overcome with a lethargy that made him sleep for hours, and Jack had noticed tremors beneath his skin – twitches, like small electric shocks.

But Stan wouldn't be told, which was why Jack was here – to help out for a while, and persuade him to have a check-up with his GP. The enforced break from work was also giving Jack time to consider his own impending divorce, but he was doing his best not to think about that.

'Anyway. The tour,' said Stan, putting a stray penny into the till and slamming it shut. 'You said it was OK, but did you enjoy it?'

Jack wrinkled his nose. 'It was great to be out on Dartmoor

again but devils, dragons and spirits? The myths and legends part was too bonkers for me.'

'That's a shame.' Stan ran a hand through his thinning hair. 'I thought you might enjoy something different, and I've heard good things about those tours.' He gave Jack a sideways glance. 'Plus, it's good to get away from facts and figures for a while. To expand your mind and embrace the unknown.'

'Facts and figures *do* expand my mind, thank you very much.'

Stan sniffed. 'So, how did you get on with the tour guide? She's a nice young woman, don't you think? Pretty and personable.'

'Mmm,' said Jack noncommittally.

'Did she tell you where she's living?'

'No, we didn't chat much,' answered Jack, dipping his head so his father wouldn't notice the flush on his cheeks. He hadn't chatted to the tour guide at all and, hopefully, after his less than stellar behaviour, he'd manage to avoid her until he left Heaven's Cove.

'She's moved into the caravan at the end of Magda's garden.'

'Really?' Jack lifted his head. 'The old wooden one? I didn't think it had any electricity or running water.'

'A few improvements have been made so it's not as ramshackle, and she uses the shower at Magda's, who's a soft touch.'

'Always has been,' said Jack, already trying to work out how he might call in on Magda without bumping into her garden guest. 'How long has she been living—?'

He stopped talking when the colour suddenly drained from his father's face and the old man sat down heavily on the stool nearby. There was a half-drunk cup of tea on the counter, which Jack pushed towards him. 'Are you OK, Dad? Have a drink.'

Stan pushed the tea away, impatiently. 'That's stone-cold.

And I'm a bit tired, that's all, and fancied a sit-down. I'm fine and dandy.'

'That's good then,' said Jack, although if his father were fine and dandy, he wouldn't be here, in the wilds of Devon, taking time out from his job.

Sharon, his boss, had taken pity on him – mother recently deceased, marriage breaking down, and father unwell. How much more could one man take? At least, that's what Sharon's expression had suggested when she'd insisted that he take time off: *Have a break before you collapse in a snivelling heap and cock up the research data we've been working on for months.*

Not that he would lose concentration and mess things up. Not when focusing on clinical data kept the rest of the world at bay and the darkness confined to the edges of his mind.

'Be a good lad and make me a nice hot cup of tea,' said Stan, fishing a handkerchief from his pocket and rubbing it across his mouth. 'I could murder a fresh cuppa.'

Jack went into the tiny kitchenette just off the shop floor, pulled the teapot from a cupboard and switched on the kettle. A cold draught hit his neck while he waited for the kettle to boil and he glanced around, almost expecting his mother to walk into the room.

'Don't be daft,' he murmured, dropping two teabags into the pot. 'You don't believe in all that. Mum's gone.'

The vicar at Heaven's Cove church had insisted his mother had gone to a 'better place' at her funeral and was still watching over her family. It was a lovely fairy story, but not one that brought Jack any solace. The only thing that brought comfort to his aching heart was his belief that energy could be transformed but never destroyed.

Which surely meant that his mum, always fizzing with life, would exist forever in some form or other: as atoms flying across the universe towards myriad suns; in the smell of baked earth dampened by summer rain; or in the waves breaking on Heaven's Cove beach.

That's what brought him solace in the dead of night, when even pi lost its healing power and he lay awake wondering how his life had gone so badly wrong.

'Is that tea going to be ready any time soon?' asked Stan, walking into the kitchen, one foot dragging slightly. 'A man could die of thirst around here.'

'Sorry. I got distracted. It's on its way, and shouldn't you be sitting down?'

Stan grimaced. 'Oh, don't fuss! I'll go back to my stool and try not to dehydrate while I'm waiting.'

'Very funny.' Jack returned to his tea-making and was just carrying two mugs into the shop when the front door opened and a customer walked into the store. 'Oh, hell!'

He ducked down behind a shelf of biscuits, trying not to spill the drinks. A flash of pink top was visible between the bourbons and digestives as the customer walked to the till and announced: 'Hello, Stan. I'm reporting for duty.'

Reporting for what? Jack carefully placed both mugs on the floor and poked his head around the end of the shelf. It was definitely the tour guide from this morning – Anna, Ava, or whatever her name was. She'd pulled her dark hair into a ponytail, but a pink-streaked tendril had escaped its tie and was twisting past her shoulder.

'Hello, Alyssa. It's good to see you.'

Alyssa! That was it. With any luck, she'd buy what she wanted and get the hell out, thought Jack, feeling ridiculous behind his shelf, and vaguely cowardly. But his father's next words shattered his hopes.

'Nip down to the cellar, will you, love, and bring up the box of crisps on the table. Then, you can get to work.'

'Will do.'

When Alyssa had disappeared down the cellar steps, Jack

picked up the mugs and approached the till. 'What's going on, Dad?'

'Didn't I tell you?' Stan gave an awkward laugh. 'You and Magda are always saying I work too hard, so I've taken on some additional help. Alyssa Jones is my new assistant.'

'Which you didn't mention before you suggested I take her tour.'

'I thought it would be a nice surprise to see her here, after you'd got to know each other elsewhere. Once you'd seen what else she can do.' Stan glanced at him then looked away. 'Magda says she's a lovely young woman, and she lives alone in that caravan. No partner at all, apparently.'

Jack felt like a grumpy teenager when he rolled his eyes. But if this was his father's clumsy attempt at matchmaking, he didn't know his son at all. Jack would rather stick pins in his eyes than spend time with a woman who peddled stories of demons and dragons. And after his ungallant behaviour this morning, he was sure she felt the same way about him.

'She'll be back upstairs in a minute, so why don't you go and make another cup of tea?' urged Stan. 'Then the two of you can watch the shop while I go and have a rest – like you keep saying I should.'

Jack stomped back to the kitchen, poured another cup of tea and took a deep breath. This was going to be awkward.

SIX

ALYSSA

Stan had disappeared by the time Alyssa brought the crisps up from the cellar. She could hear him clomping up the stairs to the flat above – a thud on each step, with the time between each thud getting longer as he neared the top.

Alyssa sighed. She'd known Stan for a few months – not very well, admittedly, but it was obvious, even to her, that he'd slowed down recently. Though still mourning his wife, he'd once had a spring in his step, but that was now missing. And last week in the shop, when he'd dropped a bag full of change, he had remarked that his hands didn't seem to be moving as they should.

Fatigue in a grieving widower nearing seventy-five, along with stiff joints, was pretty circumstantial evidence of serious ill-health. And Stan had told her not to fuss when she'd asked how he was. But Alyssa couldn't shake the feeling that something really wasn't right. 'Once a nurse, always a nurse,' she murmured, ripping open the box of salt and vinegar crisps.

Although that wasn't literally true, because she would never nurse again. And while she felt the occasional pang for what she'd lost – the camaraderie of staff at the hospital, the friendship of patients, and the satisfaction of a job well done – it was always swamped by a rush of traumatic memories. Memories of one man, in particular, who had needed her help.

'Would you like a cup of tea?'

A man's deep voice behind her made Alyssa jump, and she swung round, almost knocking the mug from his hand.

'Whoa! Watch it!' He stepped back as Alyssa, still wrapped in remembrances of the past, tried to make sense of what was happening: the snarky tourist from that morning's tour – the man she'd hoped never to see again – was standing in the shop, offering her a drink.

'It's you,' she managed.

'My thoughts exactly,' said the man, staring at her, blank-faced. 'Anyway, my dad reckoned you might like this.' He walked to the till and put the mug on the counter. 'If you'd like sugar, it's in the kitchen,' he added, as a curl of steam wafted towards the ceiling.

'Your dad?' said Alyssa, still feeling completely wrong-footed.

'That's right.'

'So, *you*'re the wonderful Jack who Magda's mentioned?' It came out more sarcastically than Alyssa had intended, and Jack's eyebrow shot up towards his hairline. 'What I mean is, I didn't realise when I saw you this morning. I thought you were a tourist.'

'I kind of am because I'm only here temporarily. I'm helping Dad while he's under the weather.'

'That's good news. Your dad's not been one hundred per cent for a while.'

Jack frowned and folded his arms. 'I know, but I've been too busy at work to get away.'

Did he think she was having a go at him for not being here earlier? 'I'm not criticising,' she said, putting down the three bags of crisps she'd only just realised she was holding.

'It sounded like—' Jack took a deep breath and breathed out slowly. 'Look, I think we probably got off on the wrong foot, and I may have been a little brusque. On your tour, I mean.'

You think? But Alyssa bit back her words and waited for Jack to continue.

He looked at her and gave his head a shake. 'I'm sorry if I was at all dismissive or a pain, only I'm a scientist, and myths and legends aren't really my thing.'

'OK, that's fine. I get it's not for everyone. But why did you sign up for the tour in the first place?'

'My father suggested it.'

'And do you do everything your father suggests?' asked Alyssa, smiling to make it perfectly clear that she was joking. Kind of.

Jack gave a smile back, though it didn't quite reach his eyes. 'Of course not, but I didn't realise how untethered from reality your tour was going to be.'

Untethered was a strong word, thought Alyssa. But she let it go because he *had* apologised, and she didn't want to be the kind of person who held a grudge. So all she muttered was, 'Reality isn't always everything it's cracked up to be.'

Jack shot her a baffled look before gesturing at her drink. 'Anyway, you'd better have that while it's hot.' He watched while she picked up the mug and took a sip. 'How long have you been working here?'

'Only a couple of weeks,' Alyssa replied, cursing inside as a bead of dark liquid fell from her lips and trailed down her sweatshirt. How hard was it to drink without dribbling? Scientist Jack Gathergill, with his brooding presence and insincere apologies, was making her flustered. 'I do mostly afternoon shifts,' she told him, carefully putting the mug down.

'Are you proficient with using the till?'

She nodded.

'And what were you doing before you came to Heaven's Cove?'

Alyssa frowned. This felt like a job interview, after the position had been filled. 'I worked in an office, in customer relations,' she said, surprised by how easily she lied these days.

'And now you live in Magda's caravan?'

'That's right. What about you?' she asked, keen to deflect attention from herself. 'You said you're a scientist.'

'I work in medical research in London, where I live.'

'With your family?' Alyssa assumed there was a family somewhere because he was sporting a wedding ring, so she was taken aback by the shudder of pain that crossed his face. 'I'm... I'm sorry,' she stuttered. 'I didn't mean to pry.'

'It's fine,' he said gruffly, glancing at the door as a customer came in. 'Anyway, I'd better leave you to it.'

Alyssa helped the customer find the breakfast cereals he was looking for and took his money. Then she started emptying the box of salt and vinegar crisps, all the while trying to remember what she'd heard about Jack Gathergill.

Snippets of gossip started coming back to her, until she suddenly realised her faux pas in bringing up his family. Jack was divorced or in the process of getting divorced. She'd overheard Magda talking to Stan about it. And they'd mentioned a young boy called Archie, who, she presumed, was Jack's son. Poor lad. His bedtime story, with a dad whose mind was so closed to magic and mystery, was more likely to be encyclopaedia extracts than Harry Potter.

Alyssa glanced at Jack across the shop floor. Perhaps she was being mean and he was a fun-loving father who missed his son. Maybe that was the reason behind his grumpiness, because being separated from your child was a terrible thing. She closed her eyes, suddenly overwhelmed with guilt and remorse – though not for thinking badly of the man who, let's be honest, *had* been a pain on the tour. Her mind was reeling back to a loss that she was determined not to revisit.

Alyssa kept the memories at bay by working flat-out all afternoon, while Jack appeared to be doing his best to avoid her. He spent ages stock-taking in the cellar, or nipping upstairs to check on Stan, and only emerged from the basement as Alyssa's shift drew to a close and Stan clumped back down the stairs.

'How are you doing, Dad?' Jack asked, pushing his fingers through his fringe. 'When I nipped up to check on you a while ago, you were dozing.'

'I'm fine, and you should have woken me up. I can't believe how long I slept.' Stan gave a slow yawn. 'However much sleep I get these days, I'm still worn out,' he added, setting off another klaxon in Alyssa's brain. Though if Stan was truly unwell, at least Jack was here now to sort him out.

'How have you two been getting along?' asked Stan, looking between Alyssa and Jack, who was loitering by the tinned tomatoes.

'Good,' said Alyssa brightly.

'Yeah, good,' Jack agreed.

'I'm glad to hear it,' said Stan, helping Alyssa into her jacket. 'Jack said he enjoyed your tour this morning.'

'Did he?' Alyssa caught Jack's eye and a frisson of amusement passed between them. He looked younger when he wasn't being so serious. 'That's good, then.'

'Do you have any more tours planned?' Stan asked, picking up a handful of bananas from the fruit display. 'Here you go, Alyssa. Take these home with you.'

'Are you sure?'

'Absolutely. They're starting to turn and need to be eaten. So, what about the tours?'

'Tomorrow's tour is fully booked and a couple next week are half full already.' Alyssa opened her canvas bag and dropped the bananas into it. 'I have a new project that I've been wanting to talk to you about, actually, Stan. I'm thinking of expanding into smuggling.'

'An unusual business decision,' murmured Jack, but he was silenced by a wave of Stan's hand.

'Shush! I want to hear what Alyssa's got in mind.'

'It's nothing definite yet because I'm at the research stage, but I'm thinking of setting up a new tour that focuses on the village's rich smuggling heritage. I had the idea when I was telling tourists about the sea dragon.' She glanced at Jack, anticipating his derision, but he gave her a straight stare back. 'I was googling about Charity and Josiah, whose disappearance sparked the dragon legend, and I discovered there was a secret smuggling ring in Heaven's Cove at the time.'

'Not so secret that you couldn't find it on the internet,' Jack butted in.

Stan gave his son a disapproving look. 'The whole world is on the internet. Nothing ever stays a secret.'

Alyssa crossed her fingers behind her back, hoping that Stan was wrong and her secret was safe.

'The new tour sounds very exciting,' Stan continued. 'But why did you want to talk to me about it?'

'Because of your surname. I saw it on the Mourning Stone.'

Jack took a step forward. 'Let me guess. You want to know if we're related to the thief and murderer Josiah Gathergill?'

When he put it like that, Alyssa could see that it might not have been the most sensitive of subjects to bring up.

But Stan simply rolled his eyes at his son. 'Yes, he's an ancestor of ours. It doesn't matter if Alyssa knows, Jack. It was a long time ago.'

'Not so long ago that I didn't get bullied at school about it. Even after John died.'

'John?' asked Alyssa, glancing at Stan, whose mouth had drawn into a tight line.

'My brother,' said Jack, his tone measured and low. 'He died when he was fourteen and I was twelve.'

'I'm so sorry. I didn't know.'

'Why would you?' said Stan, his eyes suddenly bright. He turned to Jack. 'I didn't realise the bullying went on even after John's death.'

Jack shrugged. 'You're right, Dad. It doesn't matter now and I don't live round here any more so who cares what my surname is?'

'Perhaps Josiah wasn't a thief and murderer anyway.' Alyssa bit her lip, cursing herself for getting even more involved in what was obviously a touchy subject for Jack. When neither he nor Stan said anything, she added weakly, 'Perhaps he and Charity ran away together.'

'Because they were in love?' Jack's lip lifted in one corner. It looked very much like a sneer. 'What's your evidence in support of that theory?'

'What's your evidence against it?' replied Alyssa, suddenly wearied by Jack's black and white view of life. She'd known another man like that: an arrogant man whose unbending opinion had caused chaos. 'Her body was never found and Josiah disappeared, too, so who's to say what the real truth is?'

'You're searching for fairy-tale endings, and I can assure you that they, just like the sea dragon, are a myth.' Jack glanced at his mobile phone, which had just beeped with a message. Deep lines scored his forehead when he frowned.

'Is everything all right?' asked Stan.

'Fine,' Jack replied, his voice clipped. 'But I need to reply to this, so if you'll excuse me...'

As he walked to the stairs, Alyssa pondered what it was with Gathergill men that they said 'fine' when things patently weren't.

Was Josiah the same? she wondered. Did he ignore his true feelings for Charity until the two of them could deny them no longer? Or was she being a hopeless romantic, as Jack obviously believed, and love hadn't come into it? His ancestor was simply a thief and a murderer.

'Sorry about Jack,' said Stan. 'He's not always so negative, but he's going through a few things at the moment.'

'That's OK. Life can be hard sometimes.'

Stan smiled and dropped another banana into Alyssa's bag. 'You could always try the village library, if you're looking for information about olden-days smuggling.'

'Heaven's Cove has a library?' This was news to Alyssa, who thought she knew the village inside out by now.

'It opened relatively recently, not far from the cultural centre,' Stan told her, curling and uncurling his fingers as if he was checking they still worked.

'Have you ever tried to find out more about your infamous ancestor?'

Stan shook his head. 'I remember my great-grandad telling me that the family's name was mud for generations after Charity disappeared. And it's persisted down the years – Jack was bullied, as he said. You know what kids can be like. But as I get older, I do wonder if letting sleeping dogs lie is always the best policy. The truth matters, don't you think, Alyssa?'

She nodded, even though her whole life in Heaven's Cove was built on nothing but lies.

'I knew Penny was unwell – very unwell,' Stan continued, gazing into the distance, 'but she never told me the truth about her prognosis. She was trying to protect me and Jack, you see. But it didn't protect me at all when the truth became so blindingly obvious in her final days. It was a huge shock and, though I hate to admit it, I was angry that she'd kept it quiet. Looking back, how I could be angry with Penny for simply doing what she thought was best for all of us is beyond me. But I still wish that she'd told me earlier.'

He blinked, his eyes bright with unshed tears, and gave

Alyssa a wobbly smile. 'Anyway, enough about my family and our sad and chequered past. I wish you the best of luck with your new smuggling tour. I'm sure visitors to Heaven's Cove will love it.'

Alyssa thought about Stan as she walked home, past the village green and the Mourning Stone with its blunt inscription. She was glad that he had his son and Magda to look after him. They could mourn the loss of Penny together.

She wished she'd known Penny, who sounded like a lovely woman, and wondered, rather morosely, who would mourn her if she unexpectedly shuffled off her mortal coil. Ben would, she decided, crossing the garden that led to her caravan. Ben would be heartbroken to lose her after all that they'd shared.

Alyssa sat down on the caravan steps, her chin in her hands, and gazed across the grass that was sprinkled with daisies. Purple clematis festooned the wall of Magda's cottage and, beyond it, Driftwood House was a white smudge on top of the cliff.

This was a beautiful village that had provided her with sanctuary, but Heaven's Cove kept secrets, just as she did: secrets about the smugglers who had once trodden its paths, laden down with contraband; and secrets about Charity and Josiah, whose disappearance still echoed down the centuries.

'Secrets, secrets everywhere,' murmured Alyssa, closing her eyes and listening to the soothing whoosh of waves lapping against the sea wall nearby.

SEVEN

JACK

Jack sat on a wooden crate in the cellar, cradling his mobile phone in his hand. He would have to open Miri's message sooner or later, but he felt bizarrely churned up at the prospect. This was the woman he'd married, the woman he'd promised to love for all eternity – and here he was, nervous about what she had to say.

Though he supposed, all things considered, that his angst was understandable. His soon-to-be ex-wife rarely messaged these days, unless it was to give him an update on Archie, which felt bittersweet. Or to berate him for some failing that she'd suddenly remembered.

She'd recently informed him that he never put the dustbin back where it should be – did it *really* matter if it wasn't standing directly opposite the garden tap? – and that he stole the duvet during the night. He was sure he had far more serious faults than these, but impending divorce appeared to distil complaints down to the minutiae.

Jack hated the breakdown of his relationship descending into pettiness. And the last thing he'd needed, after Alyssa had just come up with some fairy-tale ending for his ancestor who was, in reality, a total thug, were more imagined slights from Miri.

That was the reason for telling his dad everything was fine, and beating a hasty retreat when Miri's text had arrived and made his heart pound. He wasn't about to reveal his marriage woes to anyone, and in particular not to inquisitive Alyssa.

OK, he was going in! Jack clicked on Miri's message and smiled when he saw it was a photo of Archie, beaming as he zoomed down the slide at their local park in North London. Jack was relieved that Archie looked so happy. Of course he was. But a sliver of ice lodged in his heart at the thought that his son was happy without him.

Jack shook his head, feeling ashamed. He didn't want Archie to be miserable. But the suspicion that Archie was forgetting him made him feel like weeping. Not that he would, with his dad around, and Alyssa liable to appear at any minute with more outlandish fairy tales.

Jack shifted on the crate and recited pi to calm himself down. He could reel it off to at least thirty figures from memory, which was a party trick he occasionally performed for his more nerdy friends. It didn't go down too well at 'normal' gatherings – Sunday lunch with family, Christmas Day and the like.

Not for the first time, Jack wondered if he was insufferably boring. He sighed and went back to the photo on his phone.

Beneath it, Miri had written: *Archie yesterday. I'm in Devon in a fortnight's time and will come to see you in Heaven's Cove if that's acceptable. Just me. Archie will be with my mum.*

Jack read the message again. Why was Miri coming to Devon? And why was she going out of her way to see him? They only met these days when he collected Archie for a weekend visit. And though they worked hard to ensure those meetings were civil, the two of them were emotionally distant and spoke as little as possible.

Perhaps Miri wanted to meet now because she had a form

that needed signing for the divorce. Or she'd remembered another of Jack's failings that required a face-to-face row.

Or maybe... the thought slithered into his brain. Maybe she wanted to see him because she was missing him and had decided that the divorce was a mistake.

He sat for a while, wondering how he felt about that possibility. If, indeed, it was one.

Then he picked up his phone and typed a reply: *That works for me. Let me know where and when.*

He went to add a kiss, out of habit, but pressed 'Send' before he could make such a crass mistake.

Though perhaps Miri would quite like an *x* at the end of his message?

Shaking his head, Jack pushed the phone back into his pocket and got to his feet. He could drive himself crazy with speculation, but there was no point. Because soon, he would find out for sure what lay behind Miri's urge to see him.

EIGHT
MAGDA

Magda surveyed the rainbow array of ice creams and smiled. Mounds of Banana, Coffee and Cream, Raspberry Soufflé, Strawberry, and Chocolate Fudge glistened invitingly in their stainless-steel tubs.

The tubs were filled to the brim, ready for the first customers to arrive when the parlour opened in ten minutes' time. It never ceased to amaze Magda how early in the day people were willing to eat ice cream.

And later that morning, Stan would arrive for a chat by the sea and Magda would talk and smile and pretend that her heart wasn't breaking.

Her smile faded and she pushed a spoon full of Butter Pecan into her mouth. Eating her own merchandise wasn't recommended: there were only so many scoops of frozen dessert her hips could accommodate. But after a restless night tormented by unanswerable questions, a calorie-laden hit of flavour was the only way forward.

She was deliberating whether to dip into the Mint Choc Chip as well when Alyssa knocked on the shop door and waved at her. Magda walked over, turned the key and poked her head outside. The air was laced with the briny smell of the sea.

'Hello. Do you want to come in?' she asked.

Alyssa pushed a bundle of ten-pound notes into her hand. 'No, thanks, but I wanted to catch you to give you this month's rent. I can't stop because I'm heading for the library to check out smuggling.' She laughed at Magda's puzzled expression. 'Don't worry, I'm not contemplating a career change. I'd like to expand the range of tours I offer and apparently smuggling was once a booming local industry. I'm hoping tourists will lap up tales of derring-do in the eighteenth century.'

'What a great idea! I reckon they'll love it.'

'Fingers crossed. Anyway, have a great day and I'll see you soon.'

Alyssa waved and walked away, closely watched by Magda. The younger woman was wearing a muddle of brightly coloured clothes as usual – probably bargains she'd found in local charity shops – and the same trainers she'd worn ever since Magda had first known her.

There was nothing extravagant about Alyssa, or indulgent. But there was something that marked her out as different. Magda twisted her mouth, trying to narrow it down. Maybe it was the pink streaks in her hair; or the mysterious fat, brown envelopes that arrived for her; or her insistence on paying the rent in cash, rather than by cheque or bank transfer.

In truth, Alyssa had been an enigma since first arriving in Heaven's Cove six months ago and coming into the ice-cream parlour, looking for a job.

Magda hadn't had any work available, but her caravan was sitting in the garden, and she'd let Alyssa move in. She still wasn't quite sure why. She'd known nothing about the woman, but had felt sorry for her nonetheless.

Alyssa had never told Magda specifically what had brought

her to the village. She'd claimed she was simply looking for a different kind of life: a slower pace and seaside views.

But Magda had recognised the pain in her eyes and knew there was more to it than that. Alyssa was a damaged soul, which struck a chord with Magda, who felt rather damaged herself.

Fetching a clean spoon, she pushed it into the Mint Choc Chip and gave herself another soothing hit of chilly sweetness.

Two hours later, Magda and Stan were sitting on a bench near the quay. Tiny fish darted through clear water lapping gently against the stone wall.

'Are you sure you don't want an ice cream?' asked Stan, waving his cone so vigorously the double scoop of salted caramel on top almost went flying.

'Quite sure. I had some earlier.'

'I feel honoured that you're giving me half an hour of your time, seeing as you're caterer-in-chief to the royal wedding, which is only just over a fortnight away.'

When Stan gave her a wink, Magda felt her heart flip and she dug her fingers into her palm. This was ridiculous. She'd recently celebrated her seventy-first birthday and was far too old for these inconvenient feelings.

'So, how's the catering going?' asked Stan, catching a chunk of falling ice cream in his palm. He flattened his hand and pushed the sticky mess into his mouth.

'OK, I think,' said Magda, fishing a clean tissue from her pocket and dabbing Stan's chin. 'Everything's more or less organised, apart from the cake, but I only need to finish the icing and add a few final decorations. Rosie seems happy with the arrangements.'

'It's going to be a wonderful wedding, by all accounts.'

'Is Jack still going with you?'

'Yes, he's promised he'll still be in Heaven's Cove then.'

'How's he doing?'

Stan's face clouded over. 'He's not himself, Magda. Well, he's exactly himself in many ways – still straight-down-the-line logical, serious and sensible. He didn't much approve of Alyssa's myths and legends tours.'

'Did he go on that? Alyssa didn't mention it.'

'I don't think he and Alyssa quite know what to make of each other. I was hoping they might get on. They're both young and single, but they actually have very little else in common.'

'Do you think? They're both wounded souls.'

Stan gave Magda a sideways look. 'If you say so. Oh, talking of wounded souls, Jack got a text from Miri yesterday that threw him.'

'Saying what?'

'He wouldn't say much about it, only that Miri's coming to Heaven's Cove in a couple of weeks' time to see him.'

'Is that right? I wonder why.' Magda tried very hard not to purse her lips but it was impossible. She'd never really liked Miri, who was focused and successful but sometimes came across as bossy and cold. She knew that Penny had found her difficult.

However, Magda told herself, Jack loved his wife so Miri must have many good qualities that she had yet to discover. Though loyalty to her husband didn't appear to be one of them: the pending divorce had knocked poor Jack for six.

'I hope she's not messing him about, Magda. I wish he'd had a marriage like mine. I miss Penny.'

'I know you do. Me, too.'

When Stan stared out across the water, his jaw tight, Magda had an urge to rest her head on his shoulder, a comforting gesture offering support to a dear friend in pain. Only the whole situation was now too fraught for comforting gestures: now that Penny had died and Stan was no longer 'out of bounds', the easy familiarity with Stan that she'd managed to foster over the years had been replaced by a torrent of second-guessing her every move.

The questions that tormented her in the early hours sprang into her mind: *Should I tell Stan how I feel? How would he react to such news?* And the most upsetting question of all: *Why would he love someone like me?*

She and Penny had been great friends but, in many ways, they were chalk and cheese. Magda was a tall woman, angular, with a long nose, high cheekbones and a state of mind that tended towards the negative. Even her name, chosen by her Polish mother, sounded harsh and hard. Whereas Penny... that name sounded gentle and sweet, which is what her friend had been: all soft curves and a sweet nature.

That was why Stan had first fallen in love with his beloved wife. So what made Magda think he could love a woman like her?

Beside her on the bench, Stan took a lick of ice cream and began to cough. 'Sorry, sorry,' he spluttered. 'It went down the wrong way. You'd think at my age I'd know how to swallow my food.'

Magda patted him on the back, which seemed an appropriate, non-romantic gesture, until his spluttering eased. Then she steered the conversation into safer waters – village life, and the weather – until Stan tapped his watch and said he had to get back to the shop.

A sea mist had started to roll in and Magda shivered as she watched him walk away, his figure blurring in the encroaching fog. She could see the man he had been almost fifty years ago – youthful, energetic and strong – rather than the more stooped, silver-haired figure he'd become. Not that his changed looks made any difference. She loved him whatever.

It sounded like a TV drama, Magda suddenly realised, tendrils of mist curling around her. Something she'd watch on a

Sunday night, to relax before the week to come. The tale of a poor, deluded woman madly in love with a man who thought of her as nothing other than his wife's best friend.

But this was no TV drama. It was real life. Her life.

Magda sighed as she got to her feet. *What bad luck.*

NINE

ALYSSA

It had to be the smallest library in the world.

Alyssa was no stranger to large municipal libraries, laden with books and smelling of ink, dust and floor polish. She'd spent hours in them, studying for her nursing exams. But Heaven's Cove Library was very different. Not only was it crammed into a room above a boutique that sold clothing Alyssa couldn't afford, it also smelled of – Alyssa sniffed – the sea. A bracing aroma of fish and seaweed cancelled out any other smells, thanks to the open window facing the quay.

Alyssa glanced around the room, at the full shelves and paperbacks piled everywhere, many of them with battered covers. It was less a library and more a muddle of books that people no longer wanted.

But there might be something amongst the chaos that shed light on the old village smuggling ring. Though it was hard to know where to start.

'Are you looking for anything in particular?' asked Belinda, bustling over. According to the rota of volunteers pinned to the wall, she was on duty that morning.

'Yes, I—' began Alyssa.

'Only it's a complete jumble at the moment,' Belinda continued. 'Everything's donated, you know. People kept complaining there was no library in the village, so I spearheaded this project.'

'That's very impressive.'

'Thank you. If you need something doing, do it yourself. That's my motto.' Belinda smiled. She was a sturdy woman with grey hair pulled into a tight bun. 'So, what are you looking for? We have fiction, a number of biographies and a small health section. Does any of that interest you?'

Definitely not the health section, thought Alyssa, remembering wading through nursing textbooks. 'Do you have anything on local history?' she asked.

But Belinda was still talking. 'How are you getting on living in that caravan? It's rather unconventional.'

'I suppose it is,' said Alyssa, not wanting to get into a long conversation with the woman renowned as the village gossip.

Belinda had apparently become far less inquisitive since her sister had come to live in the village. But even so, the last thing Alyssa needed was someone asking her lots of questions. She'd had quite enough of that before her life in Heaven's Cove – gossip and rumour perpetuated by people who didn't have a clue about what had really gone on.

What she'd really done.

Alyssa felt her chest begin to tighten. Belinda was staring at her. 'S-sorry,' Alyssa stuttered. 'Did you say something?'

'I asked how Magda's doing,' said Belinda, taking off her glasses and letting them dangle on the gilt chain around her neck. 'She works so hard, running the ice-cream parlour and her little catering business. And did I hear that she's made Rosie's wedding cake herself?'

'She has. I think she just needs to add the finishing touches to it.'

'Marvellous. Any news of Rosie's dress, and how is Stan

doing?' Belinda continued, hardly pausing for breath. 'I know you're doing some shifts in the shop now, which is helpful, I'm sure. And I see that Jack is back in the village. He's having a tough time, what with the divorce and him not seeing his son, though he's a stepson, I understand. Do you know how long Jack's staying?'

'No,' said Alyssa, wilting under a Belinda barrage. 'Actually,' she said quickly, before Belinda could start talking again, 'I was looking for any books you might have on the history of Heaven's Cove.'

'Interested in the past, are you?'

'I'm particularly interested in the seventeen hundreds. I'm trying to find out more about the smuggling ring that existed in the village back then.'

'How exciting! Have you tried the village cultural centre?'

'Yes, I nipped in there a couple of days ago, but the information they hold on local smuggling is limited and I could do with more.'

'I see. Well, I know we have some books that might interest you over there.' Belinda waved her arm at a teetering pile in the corner. 'As I say, though, they're all donated and, between you and me, some of the donations leave a lot to be desired. Honestly, the books that some people read!'

Belinda leaned in closer, her floral perfume mingling with the briny scent. 'Ernie, who lived near the lifeboat station, passed away two months ago and his family donated all of his books. I went through them and, though I'd never speak ill of the dead, Ernie had a rather...' She paused. '... *eclectic* taste in fiction, shall we say. Some of the novels weren't fit to be in a family library. Erotica, I think you'd call it. Even the covers were... well...' She wrinkled her nose before smiling brightly. 'However, he was a man of varied tastes, and he had a wealth of local history books too, which I've added to that pile. There's also a potted local history, written by Gerald who lives past the bakery.' She leaned closer. 'But if I'm being honest, he rambles on a bit. He could have done with an editor.'

'Thanks. I'll have a look,' said Alyssa, stifling a grin at Belinda's blindness to her own tendency to ramble on.

Mercifully, Belinda wandered off and Alyssa began sorting through Ernie's collection.

Twenty minutes later, she was sitting cross-legged on the floor, making notes.

Most of the books were ancient hardbacks that focused on Devon's rich history and gave an overview of Heaven's Cove. The village was a fascinating place. Once a community of great importance, with a castle overlooking the stretch of water between England and France, it had then fallen into poverty, with fishing and farming the main occupations keeping the locals from starving. It had continued that way for centuries, with its inhabitants eking out a living as best they could, before the village found favour with tourists who couldn't get enough of its quaint cottages and beautiful scenery. The castle had also become a visitor attraction and was overrun by tourists in the summer, although it was now little more than a ruin.

At the bottom of the pile, Alyssa found a narrow volume entitled *Heaven's Cove: Past and Present*. Published in the 1950s, its 'present' was now long past but there was a chapter about smuggling in the village.

The village had been a clandestine smuggling hot-spot in the mid eighteenth century, Alyssa read. A local gang had brought in goods from the Continent, operating under a code of such secrecy that many residents were unaware of what was happening right under their noses.

There were even said to be smugglers' tunnels that ran beneath some of the old buildings.

Alyssa shifted to ease her aching back and imagined a

network of tunnels beneath her feet, as the germ of an idea took root in her brain. What if some of the tunnels had survived? Visiting one could be the highlight of the new tour.

Fired with enthusiasm, she carried on reading, hardly noticing the sounds of boats chugging into harbour and seagulls screeching outside.

The information about local smugglers was fascinating, and surely worth a tourist tour of its own. She could imagine telling the tales of people long gone. Men like local Jobe Cartwright, only twenty-eight years old in 1753, who was hanged for smuggling rum, tea and fine lace from the Continent.

'Harsh,' said Alyssa out loud, reading that Jobe had been caught and the gang broken up when the king's customs men raided the village on the fifteenth of October that year. She peered again at the date. Fifteenth of October 1753. Wasn't that the same day that Charity and Josiah had vanished?

She quickly scanned the rest of the chapter and her suspicion was soon confirmed.

Adding to the high drama of that night, Charity Hawkins of Driftwood House and Josiah Gathergill of Weavers Lane went missing and were never seen again.

There was no evidence that Josiah, an impoverished labourer, was a member of the smuggling gang. Instead, it's surmised that he murdered Charity that night after she came across him burgling her home – a valuable family heirloom, a jewelled brooch, went missing at the same time. He then disposed of Charity's body, probably by throwing it from a cliff into the sea, and fled the area, never to return. A memorial (known locally as the Mourning Stone) was erected to Charity on the village green.

The disappearance of the couple led to a myth that survives to this day. It recounts that a sea dragon, living in a cave on Heaven's Cove beach, dragged both Charity and Josiah to their deaths.

Alyssa jotted 'Charity lived at Driftwood House' into her notebook before re-reading what was written about the young woman's mysterious disappearance.

She put down the book and frowned. There was a huge amount of supposition involved around the couple's disappearance. And a complete dearth of the evidence that Jack had insisted was so important. Perhaps what had actually happened was that Josiah and Charity had been killed by customs men? And those men would surely have covered their tracks after realising they'd killed a local woman in error?

Whatever had happened to them, thought Alyssa, getting to her feet – murder, happy-ever-after or death by sea dragon – the young couple deserved to be more than just a footnote in history, or an enduring mystery that painted one of them in a dreadful light.

'All done?' Belinda's voice sounded in her ear. 'Did you find anything interesting?'

'I did, thank you,' said Alyssa. 'I didn't realise there were old smugglers' tunnels underneath Heaven's Cove.'

'There were, but they're all gone now, of course. Filled in or fallen in over the years. Though Ernie, God rest his erotic-fiction-loving soul, claimed one or two remained. There apparently used to be one leading from the Smugglers Haunt. Fred, the landlord, reckons his cellar was once a smugglers' store-room.' She sniffed. 'Now, is there anything else I can help you with?'

'No, thank you' – Alyssa pushed her notebook into her bag – 'though... I read that Charity Hawkins, the local woman who disappeared in 1753, lived at Driftwood House.'

'Really? I didn't know that was the case, but Rosie might because her mother was interested in the house's history.'

Belinda folded her arms across her large bosom. 'Now, Drift-wood House... all sorts have gone on there. Far more than we know about. Rosie, who now owns the house and runs her B and B up there, can be very secretive and—' She stopped abruptly and bit her lip. 'But I mustn't gossip, or my sister will have my guts for garters. Why don't you ask Rosie about that poor murdered woman?'

'She'll be too busy focusing on her upcoming wedding to answer my questions.'

Belinda beamed. 'I'm so looking forward to her wedding! Do you know that she and Liam first met at school and didn't get on at all? Let me tell you all about it.'

Five minutes later, by which time Belinda had recounted everything about Rosie and Liam's romance, Alyssa mumbled something about a dental appointment and beat a hasty retreat.

The village's main promenade was thronging with tourists dressed optimistically in shorts, in spite of the glowering sky. So Alyssa made her way home via narrow back streets, imagining smugglers in the shadows and Charity slipping unseen through Heaven's Cove on the day that she disappeared.

High above the village, Driftwood House stood on the clifftop, looking sinister thanks to a black storm cloud behind it. What secrets did that house hold? Alyssa wondered, as the first spots of rain began to fall.

Its secrets might be impossible to uncover, but Alyssa knew she had to try to find out what had really happened to Charity and Josiah. In her heart of hearts, she hoped that she might clear Josiah's name – not just to prove Jack wrong, though that might be satisfying, but because she felt a kinship with the maligned labourer. She'd been on the receiving end of supposition herself and it wasn't pleasant. Josiah Gathergill deserved better.

TEN
JACK

Jack stared out of the shop window at the cottages opposite, with their white-washed walls and thatched roofs. He liked the antiquity of Heaven's Cove: the sense of history co-existing with the present day. Whereas Miri, his wife – his soon-to-be ex-wife, he corrected himself – hated it.

'This place is stuck in a time warp,' she'd told Jack the first time he'd brought her home to meet his parents. 'There's no way I could ever live anywhere like this.'

Regularly visiting his parents had been a no-no – she was usually 'too busy at work' to accompany him to Devon. So why she was going out of her way to see Jack on his home turf was a complete mystery.

He pulled out his phone and read her text again: *I'm in Devon in a fortnight's time and will come to see you in Heaven's Cove if that's acceptable.*

No clues there and he didn't want to ask, worried it might make him sound anxious or needy. He'd been trying to cultivate an air of detached insouciance recently, although it was killing him. Especially when it came to Archie.

If Jack had his way, he would talk to his son every day. But

Miri had claimed that was too unsettling for a child in the midst of divorce, so his calls were currently rationed to three per week.

Jack clicked onto a photo of Archie and stared at the brown-haired youngster smiling back at him. Breaking up with Miri had taken his breath away. But not seeing his child was breaking his heart.

Three point one four one five nine...

'Is everything all right?' asked Alyssa, behind him. 'Is that your stepson? He looks sweet. How old is he?'

'Archie's eight,' said Jack, turning off his phone and putting it down.

'Nice age,' said Alyssa, plugging a gap on the dried goods shelf with half a dozen packets of brown rice. 'I remember being obsessed with Steps and Britney Spears when I was eight. Happy days!'

When she sighed, Jack's irritation dissipated. There was something about Alyssa that he glimpsed occasionally: a sadness that bled through when she wasn't spouting rubbish about demons and sea dragons; a sorrow and vulnerability that swept across her face.

The woman was still a pain, though. She'd come into work talking about smuggling tunnels and missing jewels, as if she were in an adventure movie – *Alyssa Jones and the Caravan of Doom*. And she was planning a visit to Driftwood House, apparently, to see if Rosie knew anything about Charity Hawkins. Obsessed with pop stars at eight and, a couple of decades later, obsessed with people who'd been dead for centuries.

However, she had just asked if he was all right. And she'd also shown an interest in Archie.

'Um, do you have kids?' he said, doing his best to be amenable.

'Me?' She turned from her shelf-stacking. 'No, though it's

not that I don't want kids. It's just that my life hasn't turned out the way I thought it would.'

'Tell me about it,' Jack muttered, picking up a packet of noodles that had fallen to the floor and handing it back to her.

'I'm assuming that's a rhetorical "Tell me about it", rather than a genuine wish to know more about my life?' said Alyssa, twisting her mouth into a wry smile.

Jack blinked. 'No, I'm interested,' he lied. 'Interested in what brought you to Heaven's Cove in the first place.'

Alyssa appeared to hesitate, and then folded her arms. 'Actually, I was born in Devon and brought up not far from here, until I was five and my parents divorced. My dad went to Scotland and I went to Leicestershire with my mum. I grew up in suburbia, worked in admin until I got bored and decided to move back to Devon where I'd been happy. Then, I moved into Magda's caravan.'

Jack nodded. She'd given him quite the whistle-stop tour of her life and living arrangements. 'What's it like living in the caravan?' he asked. 'I've always thought it should be hitched to a horse and dragged off to the tip. No offence.'

Damn. He hadn't meant to be rude, but Alyssa stifled a grin, seemingly unbothered by his opinion.

'I think Magda might take offence at that. But I like living there. Have you seen the caravan since she's made lots of improvements to it?'

Jack shook his head, feeling guilty that he still hadn't visited Magda, even though he'd promised.

'The caravan's got running water and electricity. There's no shower, but I nip across the garden and use Magda's.'

'That's nice.'

An image of Alyssa in a dressing gown, her face soft with sleep, slid into his mind but he batted it away.

'Your family seems very close to Magda,' Alyssa said gently.

'We are. She was Mum's best friend for years and she's

always taken an interest in me and my life. Even when she was living in Scotland.' Jack hesitated. There was a question he was now longing to ask Alyssa but it was very personal. Though she had asked questions about his great-great-great-something uncle being a murderer. How much more personal could you get?

'How did your parents' divorce affect you?' he blurted out, before he could change his mind.

Alyssa frowned. 'Why? Oh!' Comprehension dawned in her big blue eyes. 'Are you thinking of your stepson? I know... well, I mean, I heard on the village grapevine that you're divorced.'

'Not yet,' said Jack quickly. 'Miri and I are separated, but you're right. I am thinking of Archie.'

'Well.' Alyssa paused. 'It was hard at the time. I remember missing my dad and not wanting to leave Devon. I loved my life here. But, hey!' She grinned and held her arms out wide. 'I've turned out to be a perfect human being, as you can see!'

Jack realised she was trying to lighten the atmosphere and make him feel better, so he nodded – all the while fervently hoping that Archie wouldn't end up living in a caravan, spouting nonsense to gullible customers.

He suddenly realised that Alyssa had referred to Archie as his stepson. The village grapevine was obviously in overdrive regarding his marital and familial relationships – gossip that he'd usually ignore, even though it was annoying. And yet, for some reason, it felt important that Alyssa knew the truth about his son, and what was at stake when it came to Jack's heart.

'You appear to know that Archie isn't biologically mine,' he said, keeping his voice level.

'Sorry, I-I...' Alyssa stuttered, going pink. She stopped and swallowed. 'I heard someone refer to him as your stepson.'

'He was, for a while, but now he's my adopted son. Archie was a talkative toddler when we first met and I...' His voice caught in his throat. 'I fell in love with him as well as his mother.

I became his dad, to all intents and purposes, and I made that official when I adopted him three years ago. He's very precious to me.'

Alyssa put a hand on his arm. 'As long as you see your son as often as you can and he knows that you love him, I'm sure that Archie will be just fine.'

And her eyes, when they met his, were so filled with warmth and understanding, gratitude washed over him. Gratitude that she cared – and shame at his general boorishness since they'd first met. He felt like crying but he wouldn't. Not in front of this unusual, unreadable woman who was being unnecessarily kind.

'How are the tours going?' he asked, desperate to change the subject before his self-composure shattered.

Alyssa removed her hand from his arm. 'Really well, thank you, and I'm gathering information together for the new smuggling tour. The castle's fascinating, too. I've been reading about its history and impact on the village, and wondering if I could maybe work that up into a tour as well.'

'Perhaps you could include a few spectres floating amongst the castle ruins.'

Jack groaned to himself when Alyssa's face fell, and wished he'd kept his mouth shut. Alyssa had just been kind and his immediate response was to be snarky. What was wrong with him?

'I'm sorry. That wasn't—' he began, but his apology was interrupted by an almighty crash from above their heads. 'What the hell?' he blurted out, feeling sick as a question popped into his head: *Where's Dad?*

He sprinted towards the back of the shop. And as he raced up the stairs, two at a time, he was aware of Alyssa close behind him.

ELEVEN
ALYSSA

Stan was on the floor. He was lying on his back in the kitchen, next to the fridge, with the ingredients of his lunch spread around him. The fridge door was open and the light inside was casting a ghostly glow over his still figure.

'Dad!' Jack knelt down and started stroking his father's face. 'Are you all right? Speak to me!'

Alyssa stepped forward as Jack began to slip his arm beneath his dad's neck. 'No. Don't move him.'

'I'm making him more comfortable.'

'We can do that in a moment. But let's see what's happened first.'

Alyssa kicked aside a tomato and stooped down beside Stan, who was breathing heavily with his eyes closed.

She gently shook his shoulders. 'Can you hear me, Stan?'

'Coursh I can,' he murmured, opening his eyes. 'I'm unshteady on my feet, not deaf.'

Jack, kneeling beside her, sighed with relief at his father's cantankerousness. 'Thank goodness, he's all right.' He glanced at Alyssa. 'He is all right, isn't he?'

'Probably,' Alyssa answered, noting the slight catch in Stan's speech. 'But you'd better ring for an ambulance, to be on the safe side. And mention that his speech is a little slurred. Go on, you make the call and I'll keep an eye on your dad,' she urged when he hesitated. 'Don't worry, I know what I'm doing.'

'I think I've left my mobile downstairs.'

'Here, take mine,' she said, pulling her phone from her pocket and stabbing in her passcode.

She turned back to Stan while Jack stood in the corner, her phone clamped to his ear.

'Do you have any pain anywhere?'

'Don't think so.'

'Can you smile at me, Stan?'

'Don't much feel like it,' he told her, but he smiled all the same.

'That's good.' No sign of facial weakness. 'Can you raise both your arms?'

Alyssa was relieved when he did so without any apparent trouble.

'So, what happened? Do you know why you fell?'

'Tripped over my own feet.'

'I've noticed you've been dragging your foot a bit lately,' said Jack, the mobile phone still glued to his ear. He frowned at Alyssa when she glanced up. 'What's the problem? What does that mean?'

'Probably nothing,' said Alyssa, though Jack's words had set off even more alarm bells in her head.

'He said he was just tired. Didn't you, Dad?'

'And that's probably the case,' Alyssa reassured him, not wanting to make the situation more alarming than it currently was. She turned back to Stan. 'But I'd mention your foot, and anything else about your mobility or health that's changed recently, when you're checked over in hospital. Now, did you hit your head when you fell?' Her fingertips gently explored his scalp. There was no blood and no obvious bumps. 'What about your hips and your back? Any pain there? Try not to move while I'm checking you over.'

'You've turned into a sergeant major,' said Stan, but he lay as still as a statue while she checked his limbs and abdomen. After a few more checks, to ensure Stan wasn't in immediate danger, Alyssa sat back on her heels.

'Is everything OK?' Jack handed the mobile back to her. 'There's an ambulance nearby, apparently, so it shouldn't be long.' He knelt down beside Alyssa and stroked his father's shoulder. 'You daft old bugger. Maybe have more water with your whisky next time?' he joked, trying to ease the tension in the room. But when he looked at Alyssa, his face was strained and pale.

'Thank you,' he said. 'I'm glad you were here when this happened.' His hand briefly rested on hers and gave it a squeeze.

'Me, too.'

'You said you know what you're doing, and you certainly seem to.'

'I was a Girl Guide,' said Alyssa, feeling slightly sick from the rush of adrenaline that had carried her through the last five minutes. She patted Stan's arm. 'You'll be back on your feet in no time.'

Alyssa shielded her eyes from the sun and watched the ambulance drive off, tourists moving out of its way like a wave. A group of local residents stood on the corner, murmuring to each other as the vehicle went past.

Alyssa hoped Stan would be all right. He didn't appear to have broken anything in his fall, but she feared there was more going on than a simple stumble and loss of balance. It was only eighteen months since his wife had died and grief could hollow you out. She knew that. But her nursing training and intuition told her he was not a well man.

'What's happened to Stan?' demanded Magda, rushing up to Alyssa. Strands of grey hair were sticking to her shiny face. She looked as if she'd run from home without stopping.

'He's had a fall, Magda.' Alyssa put her hand on her landlady's arm. She was breathing heavily and looked about to collapse herself. 'I don't think the fall has done a lot of damage, but they'll give him a check-over at the hospital, to make sure.'

'So he's all right?'

'I think so.'

Magda put her hands on her thighs and leaned over. 'Thank goodness.' She straightened up. 'I know I'm in a state, but Claude said an ambulance had stopped outside the shop and they were putting Stan in it. I was so worried. He means such a lot to me, you see.' She bit her lip, her eyes glistening with tears.

'Sit down for a minute,' Alyssa commanded, steering Magda to the chair that Stan had placed near the front door of his shop for his more elderly customers. 'Can I get you some water?'

Magda shook her head. 'No, thank you. I'm fine, honestly. Stan's not on his own, is he?'

'No, he's got Jack with him.'

'Is Jack coping all right?'

'Yes,' Alyssa assured her, though he'd seemed lost and panicky before the ambulance arrived, completely knocked off kilter by his father's collapse. Almost as if his logical brain had been thrown by something it could not compute.

Magda breathed out slowly. 'I'm glad to hear that. Poor Stan. I'm so relieved that you and Jack were here when he fell.'

'Me, too. It was all a bit of a shock.'

Alyssa leaned against the shop window, with its eclectic display of baked beans, nappies and buckets and spades. Her legs suddenly felt wobbly.

Magda frowned and got to her feet. 'Look, why don't I give

you a hand with the store? The girls can manage without me at work for a while.'

'There's no need. I can cope on my own.' Alyssa smiled at her landlady, but her legs wouldn't stop trembling.

'I'm sure you can but you look done in with the stress of it all. Why don't you take a break and I'll mind the shop?'

Alyssa hesitated, filled with emotion. She should stay really, but Magda's breathing had steadied and the unshed tears had vanished.

'Go on,' Magda urged. 'I can manage the hordes who'll no doubt descend to find out what's going on. Talking of which...' She nodded towards Belinda, who had just turned the corner and was hurrying in their direction.

Alyssa winced. The last thing she needed was inquisitive Belinda asking lots of questions. 'If you're sure that's all right, Magda, I won't be long.'

'There's no rush. I'm always happy to help Stan out, and I'll only be pacing at home otherwise, waiting to hear from the hospital.'

Alyssa slipped out of the shop and headed in the opposite direction from Belinda, grateful to be on her own for a while in the fresh air. She did need a breather, but not for the reasons that Magda imagined.

Alyssa walked briskly along the street until she reached the sea wall, following it along until she got to the lifeboat station. Corey, one of the volunteer lifeboat crew, waved and she waved back.

She'd made a new life for herself in Heaven's Cove. She liked the people here and they seemed to like her. Mostly they didn't pry, and they accepted her for who she was – apart from Jack, who obviously had issues of his own. Her carefully constructed new existence was holding up.

Except when something out of the ordinary happened and the past came flooding back.

It had been a shock to find Stan on the floor, but she'd coped with far worse when working as a nurse. She'd switched straight back into medical mode the moment she'd seen him lying there, and she was glad that her old job had given her the skills and confidence to help.

But switching back had brought up bad memories. Memories of a man she'd cared about. A man who was now dead. Images swam into her mind, along with emotions she'd tried so hard to bury – sorrow, anger, guilt.

Alyssa leaned against the wall and looked out to sea. A stiff breeze was blowing and huge rolling waves were crashing against the shore. Her mind must be playing tricks because the sea air seemed laced with the sharp tang of hospital antiseptic.

She took some deep breaths in time with the water rising and falling.

Her new life was going well, she told herself, in spite of people like Jack pouring cold water on her efforts to set up tours that visitors to Heaven's Cove would enjoy. She was gradually becoming Alyssa Jones and the old Alyssa was starting to fade away.

Thinking of Jack prompted a recent memory to surface – the warmth of Jack's skin when he'd briefly squeezed her hand as they knelt beside Stan. And his words, 'I'm glad you were here.'

Alyssa pushed herself away from the wall and squinted at the cliff topped by Driftwood House. She'd walk up there when she got a chance, she decided. Not to bother Rosie, who would be up to her eyes with last-minute wedding plans, but to have a good look at the house where Charity had once lived.

And if she was lucky, focusing her efforts on solving a mystery from the past would prove a distraction from her present-day troubles.

TWELVE
MAGDA

The bar of the Smugglers Haunt wasn't busy in the early afternoon. Most tourists had finished their pub lunch and headed off to see the sights, and locals who'd called in for a pint at lunchtime had gone back to work.

Magda had almost the pick of the pub when it came to choosing where to sit. She decided on a window seat in the corner. It was far enough from the bar to be quiet, and there was a fabulous view across the sea, which, today, was like an aquamarine mill pond.

Nursing her second drink in the space of ten minutes, she stared through the window at the headland that jutted out into the water. She rarely visited the pub during the day, and she hardly ever drank alcohol, but today she needed a break – time away from her cottage where the silence only magnified her thoughts. The Smugglers Haunt had seemed the perfect place to while away an hour, and the thought of a stiff drink, even though it wasn't long gone two o'clock, had been inviting. A vodka or two might take the edge off her anxiety which had ramped up to the max in the days since Stan's fall.

Rosie's wedding was keeping her awake at nights. Catering

small events was easy: she'd made elaborate iced cakes and provided buffets for plenty of village birthday parties and anniversary celebrations before. But this was different. The reception had grown to include almost everyone in Heaven's Cove, it seemed, and Magda desperately didn't want to let Rosie down.

Her nerves hadn't been helped by Soraya, a local girl who'd agreed to help at the wedding, suddenly deciding to go off travelling. Which meant she'd be understaffed at the reception.

And then there was Stan. The main focus of her anxiety.

'Oh, Stan,' she murmured, running her finger around the rim of her glass. 'What's to become of us?'

His fall, several days ago now, had frightened the life out of her. He was home after having 'investigations' carried out. But as Jack hadn't been there when the investigations were done, and Stan was being vague about them, neither Jack nor she were much the wiser.

Magda was staring into her drink, feeling uncharacteristically sorry for herself, when a shadow fell across her table. When she looked up, Alyssa was standing there, her dark hair shining in the sunlight streaming through the window.

'The sun's obviously over the yardarm already,' said Alyssa. She raised her eyebrows at Magda's drink and grinned. 'One of those days, is it?'

'You could say that.' Magda tried very hard to smile. 'So, what are you doing in here? Are you meeting someone?'

'I've been talking local history with Fred.' She waved at the pub's rotund landlord, who was pulling pints. 'Did you know smugglers used to meet here, in the cellar, in the seventeen hundreds? I guess the name of the pub is a giveaway.' She grinned. 'Though I believe it was called something else at the time. They didn't want to make life too easy for the king's customs men.'

Magda gestured at the chair opposite. 'Sit down, and you can tell me how your smuggling research is going.'

'If you don't mind me interrupting your session.'

'One vodka and lime is hardly a session,' Magda assured her, deciding not to mention the previous one she'd drunk in a few gulps. 'Can I get you a drink?'

Alyssa dropped into the chair, her arm brushing against the gleaming horse brasses on the wall. 'No, thanks. I'm off to Dartmoor with a tour later this afternoon, and I don't think my customers would appreciate me being anything other than boringly sober. Though Jack might have enjoyed his tour more if I'd been three sheets to the wind.'

'I didn't realise he'd been on one of your tours until Stan mentioned it.'

Alyssa wrinkled her nose. 'Let's just say it didn't go brilliantly.'

'Not his thing?'

'I don't think my myths and legends were either scientific or evidence-based enough for him.'

'Ah, that sounds like Jack.' Magda took another sip of her drink. 'He was once quite a boisterous child, but he became a very serious boy after his brother died.'

'It must have been terribly traumatic for him.'

'It was a dreadful time for the family, but' – Magda drained her drink – 'let's focus on something more cheerful. I saw Rosie this morning, and she's looking forward to the Big Day.'

'It looks as if they've started putting up the marquee. I was thinking of taking a walk up there, actually, before my tour, but I don't want to get in the way.'

Magda shrugged. 'It's a big clifftop so I don't think it would be a problem.'

'Are your plans for the Big Day all in hand?'

'They were, until Soraya decided to go off travelling and left me short-staffed.'

'Oh, no.' Alyssa pushed a strand of hair behind her ear. 'Would you like me to help instead? I'm a dab hand at putting cake and doilies on plates.'

When she grinned, Magda couldn't help but smile back. That would solve one problem she could tick off her anxiety list.

'That would be extremely helpful, a real life-saver. Thank you so much. So, when will you start your smuggling tours?'

'Soon, I hope. I've uncovered some fascinating tales of smuggling in the village. It was all hush-hush at the time but there was a lot of it going on. And I've been reading up about the castle, and I'm thinking of running a tour that focuses on its history.'

'Smugglers and castles! It sounds like you're keen to expand.'

'Absolutely. Today, an extra tour or two in Heaven's Cove, tomorrow...' – Alyssa widened her blue-green eyes – 'global domination.'

'And all masterminded from the caravan at the bottom of my garden.'

'Definitely. I've got nowhere else to go.'

Magda frowned. She'd grown fond of Alyssa over the last few months. She was the perfect tenant who paid her rent on time, kept noise to a minimum and always had a friendly smile. But she knew as little about her now as she had on their first meeting.

Why had this personable young woman's life shrunk to a wooden caravan in a village garden? She was obviously keeping secrets. No one was that buttoned up about their past without having something to hide.

But then she, Magda, had her own secrets too.

It was only when Alyssa reached across the table and gently touched her arm that Magda realised she'd been staring morosely into her empty glass.

'Earth to Magda! Are you OK? You don't seem yourself today.'

'I'm fine,' said Magda automatically, realising as the words left her mouth that she was never truly fine. And she never could be, not while she loved a man who remained oblivious to her devotion.

'The seventeen hundreds were a prime smuggling time, were they?' she asked, to deflect attention from herself.

Surprise at Magda's swift change of subject flickered across Alyssa's face. 'It seems so,' she said, settling back in her chair. 'There was a raid by customs men in 1753 that broke apart the secret smuggling ring in the village. Actually, the raid was on the same night that Charity and Josiah went missing.'

'The sea-dragon couple? That's quite a coincidence.'

'I think so. I'd love to find out what really happened to them, but I'm not sure that Jack is too keen on me playing detective. He says Josiah is a thief and a murderer and that's that.'

Magda noticed a faint flush rising across Alyssa's cheeks. It was the second time, she noticed, that she'd mentioned Jack in as many minutes.

'Jack's view of life can be very black and white. How are you two youngsters getting on? You must be together in the shop sometimes.'

'I'm not sure we have a lot in common. In fact' – Alyssa leaned forward – 'I don't think he likes me very much.'

Magda smiled. 'Don't be fooled by Jack's manner. His bark is worse than his bite. He's a sweetheart really and he's been through a lot, like you.'

Alyssa jumped as if Magda had reached across the table and slapped her. 'What do you mean? What have I been through?'

Magda spread her arms wide. 'I don't know. But we've all been through something, haven't we? Some pain that's brought us to where we are. Some terrible heartache that's left scars.

Some secret we can never tell, however much we might wish we could.'

Oh, for goodness' sake, was she crying? Magda touched her face, alarmed by the tears snaking down her cheeks. This wouldn't do, crying in public. She was a respected local businesswoman with a reputation to uphold. She dipped her head and searched in her handbag for her handkerchief.

Alyssa passed a clean tissue across the table. 'I don't want to pry but if I can help in any way, I hope you'll let me know.'

Magda took the tissue but shook her head, too scared to speak. What if she started sobbing in the pub? How long would it take for Belinda to hear about it and bustle into the ice-cream parlour, bristling with curiosity?

Alyssa said nothing for a while, which Magda appreciated as she pulled herself together. After a few minutes, she pushed the tissue into her pocket and raised her head. 'Thank you.'

'For the tissue?'

'For not asking lots of questions.'

'It's none of my business. But if it would help to talk, you know where I live. And don't worry, I can keep a secret.'

'Because you have a few of your own?'

Alyssa paused, as if she was about to deny it. But then she shrugged. 'One or two, so I know all about the importance of confidentiality.'

Magda nodded but stayed silent and, after a while, Alyssa got to her feet. 'I'd better go. I'm meeting someone from the tourist information office in five minutes – before I walk up to the clifftop – to see if I can do some work with them. But will you be OK?'

Magda sniffed, feeling wrung out. 'I'll be all right. I always am. It's just...'

Looking back, Magda wondered if it was the concern radiating from Alyssa that made her say it. Or the fact that the secret seemed to be growing with each passing day and was eating her alive.

'It's just... Stan,' she blurted out.

Alyssa sat back down again. 'He's home from hospital now.'

'I know. It's not that.' She closed her mouth as a thrill ran through her. She was so close to saying it out loud. So close to telling the secret that was throttling her. And she wasn't sure if the prospect was filling her with horror or excitement.

'You don't have to tell me anything,' said Alyssa.

'I know, but I've reached a point where I have to tell someone and there's no one else. I mean, that sounds insulting but—'

Alyssa gave her such a sympathetic smile, Magda felt the prickle of tears again. 'I know what you mean and I'm not insulted.'

Was it the alcohol she'd drunk so quickly that was making Magda feel light-headed? Or the company of a woman who guarded her own secrets so well?

Alyssa waited and Magda took a deep breath. 'I care about Stan. Really care about him. In fact, I think... well, I know that I—'

She stopped, disappointed she'd been unable to say it out loud after all. But Alyssa had heard enough. 'You're in love with him,' she said softly.

'Shh!' Magda looked around but there was no one within earshot.

'How long?' asked Alyssa simply.

'Years.'

'And does he know?'

'No, and it has to stay that way.' Magda picked up her glass, wishing it wasn't empty. If there was ever a time for vodka, it was now. 'It's ridiculous, really. He was married to my best friend and she never knew. I was so careful not to let her know. I just got on with my life.' She paused. 'Sort of.'

'And you still haven't told him, although Penny's gone now?' Magda shook her head. 'Even though you're so upset?'

Magda opened her mouth to protest that she wasn't really upset. It was the drink talking because she was fine with the status quo. But all she could manage was a nod of the head.

'Oh, Magda. I'm so sorry.' Alyssa reached out and took hold of her hand. 'It must have been such a difficult secret to keep over the years.'

Difficult? Alyssa had no idea. No appreciation of the daily toll of loving someone who could never love you in return. Because if he had, by some miracle, felt the same way, it would have broken Penny's heart. And how could she have respected a man who hurt her best friend? It had been an impossible conundrum.

Magda gently pulled her hand away. 'I can't tell him.'

She'd never contemplated telling him. Not even after Penny had died. Though now... the truth of it rolled around her brain. Now, Magda's passion couldn't hurt her oldest friend.

'What would *you* do?' she asked Alyssa. 'If you were in my position?'

Perhaps Alyssa *was* in the same position and it was a doomed love affair that had brought her to Heaven's Cove.

Alyssa thought for a moment. 'I'm not sure what I'd do. But I can see that keeping this secret is causing you pain.' She looked into Magda's eyes and held her gaze. 'In your heart of hearts, do you want to tell Stan? Do you want him to know how you feel?'

'Truthfully? I'm not sure.'

The secret had become so entwined with Magda's everyday life and who she was, it was almost impossible to prise it apart and consider it clearly.

'Do you have a gut feeling about what you'd like to do?' Alyssa asked. 'You must have trusted your instincts when you set up your businesses and moved from one part of the country to another.'

Magda gazed out of the window, at the sea endlessly striving to reach land. She trusted her instincts when it came to work and property, but when it came to her heart, that was a different matter. 'I guess the truth is I'd like Stan to know how I feel, but I'm scared.'

'Of course you are. Who wouldn't be?' Alyssa took a deep breath. 'Look, I'm not the right person to give you advice. Stan did tell me recently that the truth is important to him...' She paused. 'But, to be honest, I've made a hash of my own life, so I think you should do whatever you feel is best for the two of you.'

That wouldn't cut it, thought Magda fiercely. She needed to know what to do. If only her mum were here, to give her a hug and tell her how to sort out this mess. But her mother was long gone.

Magda caught hold of Alyssa's arm. 'I've never been able to ask anyone about this before. I've never had anyone else's opinion, so I'd really like yours. *Please.*'

The pub door slammed, making the tables shake, but Alyssa's eyes didn't leave hers. Then, she sighed. 'All right. My view is, if you really want to tell Stan, I think it's a shame if fear holds you back. I was scared once, when I had a gut feeling about something important and I let my fear win because I didn't follow my instincts. I believed someone who told me my instincts were wrong, and I've regretted it ever since.'

'And now, like me, you have secrets that eat you up inside?'

'And now, like you, I have secrets that I'd rather not have.' Alyssa pushed her chair back and stood up. 'I'm sorry but I really do have to go or I'll be late for my meeting.'

Magda nodded, her stomach churning with emotion. 'Of course, and thank you for listening. You won't tell anyone what I've said, will you?'

'My lips are sealed, I promise.'

Magda watched Alyssa leave the pub before heading to the bar to order another vodka. And as Fred cut a fresh lime into slices, she thought about the woman she'd entrusted with her secret. What had Alyssa failed to do? she wondered. What was it that had brought her to Heaven's Cove, to hide in a caravan at the bottom of her garden?

Secrets could be toxic so perhaps it would be best if her feelings for Stan were out in the open. She so wanted to say the words out loud to Stan, even if only once: 'I love you.' But was she brave enough to risk rejection?

Maybe it was the last of the vodka hitting her bloodstream but Magda suddenly felt courageous. She'd kept a tight rein on this secret for almost fifty years but it was time to set it free. To set herself free. 'Sorry, Fred. Can I cancel that drink? I need to go.'

Magda almost ran out of the pub and stood for a moment, taking in the view. Then, she walked briskly towards Gathergill's Mini Mart, before she could change her mind.

THIRTEEN
ALYSSA

The meeting at the tourist information office had gone well. The woman she'd spoken to was keen to promote a new smuggling tour, and she'd also expressed interest in a tour focusing on the castle's history.

It was exciting stuff, but all Alyssa could think about as she climbed the cliff path was Magda. That poor woman had lived with a secret for almost half a century. Alyssa had managed just six months so far, which seemed like forever.

Would she still be running from her past in another forty-nine years' time? Alyssa firmly pushed that thought from her mind and tried to focus on her surroundings.

It was a beautiful day in Heaven's Cove and the sun was dancing on the ocean far below. The water rippled green close to shore, and fishing boats bobbed on the waves.

'It's totally glorious,' said Alyssa out loud to a passing seagull, stopping for a breather with her hands on her hips. It felt like nothing bad could happen when the world was so filled with wonder. Was that what Charity had thought when she saw this spectacular view on the day she died? Had she felt protected from dangers lurking nearby?

Alyssa climbed higher and had almost reached the clifftop when she spotted a hive of activity. A huge white marquee was being erected – an elegant structure with a domed roof and arched windows that reminded her of the Pavilion in Brighton. She'd visited Brighton with Ben a few years ago, a day that had been filled with laughter. Though the memories were now tainted by what had come after.

How bizarre and unsettling that something as seemingly innocuous as a large tent could catapult her into the past, thought Alyssa, her attention caught by a woman who was waving at her.

'Hello, there!' the woman said, when Alyssa got closer.

It was Rosie, who owned Driftwood house. Rosie, who would soon be marrying Liam and didn't need unexpected visitors.

'Sorry,' said Alyssa. 'I don't mean to intrude on your preparations.'

'You're not.' Rosie smiled. 'So, what brings you up here?'

Alyssa couldn't help but smile back – Rosie was glowing and, even in jeans and a baggy jumper, looked every inch the radiant bride-to-be. 'It's such a beautiful day, I felt like a walk and I was interested in seeing Driftwood House again. I'm putting together a tour about smuggling in Heaven's Cove and I've discovered a possible link to the disappearance of Charity Hawkins and Josiah Gathergill in 1753. I found out that Charity once lived up here so I thought...' Alyssa pressed her lips together. She was burbling on, when Rosie didn't care what she thought, not while her head was filled with wedding plans.

But Rosie gave her a wide grin. 'That sounds fascinating. I love a bit of history. Would you like a cup of tea, and I can tell you what I know about Charity, which, I warn you, isn't much?'

'I don't want to take up your time when you're busy.'

Rosie smiled again, her russet-brown eyes twinkling. 'I'm

only getting in everyone's way, and I could do with a cup of tea myself.'

'In that case, thank you, that would be great.'

Alyssa looked around her curiously after walking into Driftwood House. You could see the house, perched high on the cliff, from most places in Heaven's Cove. But she'd never been inside before.

Her first impression was of light and space. The walls in the large square hallway were painted a soft yellow that seemed to bring the sunshine indoors. And the black and white floor tiles were gleaming.

A curved staircase with polished banister rail led upstairs. And in the corner stood a small wooden desk, presumably for checking in guests when they arrived. Alyssa had learned soon after arriving in Heaven's Cove that Rosie had turned Driftwood into a successful guesthouse.

'Do you have many guests staying at the moment?'

'No, thank goodness.' Rosie laughed. 'I blocked out a couple of weeks around the wedding. I couldn't cope with demanding guests on top of pre-wedding nerves. Come on into the kitchen.'

Rosie didn't seem nervous. She seemed completely at ease with herself and the approaching ceremony. She was happy, Alyssa realised as she sat at the kitchen table. Completely and utterly happy with the way her life was panning out.

Lucky woman.

'So, you live in Magda's caravan. What's that like?' asked Rosie, placing a steaming mug of tea onto the table. 'I've been dying to ask but our paths have hardly crossed since you moved in.'

'I like living there. It's very small, obviously, but that means there's hardly any housework to do.'

'Which,' said Rosie, dropping into the chair opposite, 'sounds fantastic. You wouldn't believe how long I spend cleaning this place, changing beds and cooking.'

'Don't you have any help?'

'Some, and Liam is as helpful as he can be, though he's got a farm to run. Do you know Liam?'

'I've met your fiancé a couple of times, when he's come into Stan's shop. He seems like a very nice man.'

'He is a very, *very* nice man.' Rosie's smile was brighter than the sunbeams dappling the flagstone floor.

'I need to thank you, actually,' said Alyssa, curling her fingers around her mug.

'Why?'

'For sending some of your guests my way. They said you'd recommended my myths and legends tour.'

'You're welcome. I've heard lots of good things about it, and I'm delighted you might be expanding your tour repertoire.' Rosie picked up her own drink and cradled it in her hands. 'So, you're particularly interested in poor Charity.'

'That's right. I'd love to find out what really happened to her. I realise that's probably impossible because it was so long ago, but I thought I'd try.'

'You don't believe she was dragged into the ocean by a sea monster, then?'

Alyssa wrinkled her nose. 'Probably not.'

'And you don't think Josiah killed her?'

Alyssa shrugged. 'Maybe he did, but it seems to me that he's been found guilty without a trial.'

'Are you trying to save his reputation?'

She hadn't been able to save her own, but Alyssa nodded. 'Something like that.'

Rosie took a sip of tea and put her mug down on the table. 'I know a bit about Charity because my mum was interested in the history of Devon and this house. Not that Driftwood House was like this when Charity lived here. It's been altered and extended over the years, but a few parts of the old building remain. People say the poor woman was actually murdered here, though I haven't mentioned that to any of my guests. "Gruesome murder scene" isn't quite the vibe I'm aiming for.'

'I bet.'

'All I know is that Charity was living here with her father, after her mother died, when she was mur— well, when she vanished, on the same day as Josiah. She was an only child and was in the house on her own when whatever happened, happened. That's what my mum reckoned anyway, from her research.' Rosie began to drum her fingers on the table top. 'I'm pretty sure the books and documents that Mum collected about Driftwood House are in a box under my bed. I was thinking of donating the books to the new library that Belinda's set up. I've no idea if there's anything more in there about Charity, but would you like to see them?'

'That would be wonderful, if you don't mind.'

'I'll go and grab them, and you can have a look while I make drinks for the tent team.'

Rosie got to her feet and headed out of the kitchen. Soon, she reappeared with a large cardboard box and settled Alyssa in a bright, airy sitting room. Shouts of the men putting up the marquee drifted in through the open window that overlooked the sea.

There were a dozen books in the box and a couple of A4 folders filled with a treasure trove of photocopied documents about the house's history. Alyssa also found a handful of scrawled notes, presumably jotted down by Rosie's mother during her search for information.

Kicking off her sandals, Alyssa began to leaf through the books. Most of them were general history books about Devon and only mentioned Driftwood House in passing. But a couple gave more details about the house and one, in particular, caught Alyssa's eye.

This one claimed, as if it were proven, that Josiah had

murdered Charity. But it gave more details of the family heirloom that had vanished at the same time: a jewelled brooch that Charity had been bequeathed by her mother.

Alyssa pulled her notebook from her bag and copied down the sketch and description of the missing jewellery. Her artistic skills were appalling – she was the first to admit it. But her drawing looked fairly brooch-like by the time she'd finished.

She put down her pen and stared at what she'd done. Even her rudimentary drawing revealed how stunning the real artefact must have been: an oval-shaped brooch made of gold, with a ruby at its centre and small diamonds and emeralds around it. Seed pearls hung from the bottom of the brooch, like tear drops.

It must have been worth a good deal of money, back in 1753. Enough money to tempt an impoverished Josiah to commit murder? wondered Alyssa, pushing her notebook back into her bag.

She glanced at her watch. Time was getting on, she had a tour to run, and she didn't want to impose on Rosie's good nature any longer. So, she began to put the books and documents back into the box.

'All done?' asked Rosie, standing in the doorway. When Alyssa jumped, Rosie laughed. 'Sorry, I didn't mean to creep up on you. Did you find anything interesting?'

'I found a description of the brooch that went missing when Charity disappeared.' She held up her notebook for Rosie to take a look.

'That must have been a beautiful piece of jewellery. I wonder what happened to it?'

'Hopefully, Charity and Josiah used it to fund their new life together.'

'You really want them to have had a happy-ever-after, don't you?' Rosie looked at her, curiously.

Alyssa nodded, still unsure why it mattered to her so

much. These people were long gone, whatever had happened to them. But Josiah's redemption – possible redemption – was becoming almost an obsession. She wanted to clear his name for herself and also, she realised, for Jack and Stan. The thought of the then newly bereaved Jack being bullied as a child because of his black-sheep ancestor had stuck in her mind.

'We can all learn from history, don't you think?' said Rosie, leading Alyssa back into the hall. 'I like to think of all the people who've lived up here at Driftwood House over the years. I wonder what made them laugh and cry? Who they hated and who they loved?'

'And what mistakes they made so we can try not to repeat them.'

Rosie grinned. 'If only it were that simple.' She opened the front door and a shaft of sunlight fell into the hallway and striped across the grandfather clock in the corner.

'Thank you so much for letting me see your mum's books and documents. I really appreciate it, especially so close to the wedding – which I hope will go brilliantly.'

'Why don't you come?' urged Rosie. 'To be honest, I've lost track of who's been officially invited to the reception. It'll be a bit of a free-for-all, but that's what Liam and I want – a real village affair. And you're a part of the village now.'

What a lovely thing to say! Alyssa couldn't help beaming. 'That's so kind of you, but I'll be at the reception anyway because I've promised to help Magda with the catering.'

'That's great! I'll see you there, then.'

'And the best of luck with running your guesthouse. This really is a very special place.'

'It is, but you should have seen it before the renovations were done. It was in a sorry state, with damp, damaged wood-work, and holes in the roof. The renovation team did a great job and uncovered lots of history along the way.'

'What kind of history?' asked Alyssa, her interest piqued despite the fact she knew she ought to be going.

'Old lath and plaster on interior walls and ceilings, and we found a couple of craftsmen's signatures on the plaster beneath old wallpaper.'

'That sounds amazing.'

'It was a real link to the past. We found some boarded-up fireplaces as well, and a hidden box in one of them.'

'Wow! Was it filled with treasure?'

Rosie wrinkled her nose. 'Sadly not. I'd forgotten all about the box, to be honest, but it's interesting, and very sweet. Would you like to see it?'

Alyssa hesitated, concerned about taking up more of Rosie's time. But the chance of handling a mysterious hidden box was hard to turn down, so she nodded. 'I'd love to, if you don't mind.'

'Not at all. Wait here a tick. I won't be long.'

Rosie hurried upstairs while Alyssa tried to imagine Charity walking through this hallway. The tap of her feet on the floor and the swish of her long skirts against the walls. Could this beautiful place really be the scene of her gruesome murder?

'Here it is!' Rosie was coming back down the stairs, a small wooden box in her hand. 'My renovators found this in a room at the back of the house. That's the only part of the house that remains from the really old building that once stood here.'

She handed the box to Alyssa, who turned it over in her hands. It must have been beautiful once but now it was scuffed and worn. One corner was black, as if it had been burned. 'Where exactly did they find it?'

'There was a covered fireplace and this was behind a loose stone in the chimney breast. You can open it if you like.'

Alyssa opened the lid and peeped inside. A faint smell of mildew rose into the air as she ran her finger across pieces of folded, yellowing paper.

'No ruby brooches, I'm afraid.' Rosie laughed. 'Just paper, and some of it disintegrated when I handled it. But this is what's left.'

Alyssa pulled her finger away. 'Is it OK for me to touch it?'

'Yes. There are two pieces of paper, and you can unfold them if you're careful.'

Alyssa gingerly took out the papers and unfolded the first one. It was small, only the size of an envelope, and bore faded ink marks. There were faint black lines, small shaded-in boxes and, at the paper's centre, a cross. Beneath, there was a small circle with an 'x' inside it. She squinted at the spidery lines that looked like arteries, trying to make sense of them. 'Do you know what it is?' she asked Rosie.

'No idea. The box was found when this place was in uproar, and I've been so busy with getting the guesthouse up and running that I just shoved it in a drawer and have hardly looked at it. I'd love to know more, though. Open the other piece of paper.'

Alyssa carefully unfolded it and her jaw dropped at what lay inside. 'Oh, my goodness!'

A lock of red hair, the colour of straw bathed in the rays of the setting sun, was curled against the paper. And at the bottom of the page was one word, written in blue ink: *Beloved.*

'How romantic is that?' Rosie grinned.

'It's beautiful,' Alyssa agreed, surprised by the prickle of tears the lock of hair had prompted. It seemed almost unbearably poignant that something so personal, so important to someone now gone, had lain undiscovered in this house for so long.

She carefully put the box down on the key shelf next to the front door and pulled her mobile phone from her bag.

'Do you mind if I take a couple of photos?'

'Of course not. I would let you borrow the box, if you're

interested, to see if you can find out any more about it. But it's been in this house for years and I feel it needs to stay here. Does that sound daft?'

'Not at all. It's been a part of Driftwood House, possibly for centuries.'

Alyssa took a couple of pictures, of the spidery markings on the piece of paper, and the lock of hair. Then she carefully returned them to the box and closed the lid.

You're a part of the village now. Rosie's words warmed Alyssa's heart as she walked down the cliff path. The inhabitants of Heaven's Cove had accepted her for who she was. Or rather, who they thought she was.

Did anyone truly know anyone else? Alyssa mused, before berating herself for navel-gazing. People simply did the best they could in the circumstances, even if that meant keeping some things to themselves. People like Magda, who'd done her best to live with unrequited love. Where was Magda? Alyssa wondered. Had she made up her mind about telling Stan? Or was she still in the pub, drinking her sorrows away? Alyssa hoped not.

She stopped walking and shielded her eyes to look at Heaven's Cove laid out far below. She could just make out the thatched roof of the Smugglers Haunt and cars navigating the narrow streets nearby. There was the village green, a verdant patch surrounded by white-washed cottages. And close to the church was Gathergill's Mini Mart, which would be busy with shoppers. Perhaps Magda was there right now, telling Stan that she loved him and waiting for his response.

Alyssa crossed her fingers, just in case, and watched seagulls – tiny white dots – swooping over cottage roofs, and a child's lost red balloon floating into the sky. The village looked like a spider's web from up here, with paths going in all directions and the church in the centre.

It reminded her of something. Alyssa thought for a moment and then reached for her phone. She brought up the photos she'd just taken at Driftwood House and stared at the spidery markings on the yellowed paper. If the cross denoted the church, that curved mark there could be a rough outline of the cove, and those faint lines were roads.

Could it really be an old map? She held her phone at arm's length, turning it this way and that until – bingo! – the lines on the photo mirrored the view.

'Good grief! It *is* a map,' she breathed, wondering if the shaded boxes could be buildings.

She traced her finger along the roads that led from the church. One of the boxes might arguably be the Smugglers Haunt, and another, the castle. And there was one in what looked like Weavers Lane – the lane that housed Stan's shop, along with a dozen old cottages.

Alyssa glanced around, desperate to share her excitement, but there was no one in sight. So she went back to studying the map and frowned because there was something strange going on.

The clearest two lines on the paper didn't appear to match any of the streets that were laid out before her. She stared again at the bustling village far below and shook her head. These two lines crossed streets and linked buildings until they merged into one line that led to the cove, almost as if they were drawing energy towards the beach. *Or*, said a little voice in Alyssa's brain, *taking goods from it*.

Her mind raced ahead. This was a smuggling map, revealing the tunnels that had once criss-crossed deep beneath Heaven's Cove. It had to show the hidden paths that smugglers had trodden with contraband from the Continent almost three centuries earlier. Or... Alyssa took a deep, steadying breath. Or was she merely seeing what she wanted to see?

Alyssa clicked off the photo and stuffed the phone back into her bag. She needed to think about this before sharing what was probably a hare-brained idea with anyone else. But her mind was filled with thoughts of the past as she started walking once more towards Heaven's Cove.

FOURTEEN
MAGDA

'I was going to bring grapes but that's like coals to Newcastle, seeing as you sell them here. So I brought you this instead.'

Magda stopped talking. Her voice was too loud, her speech too fast, but Stan didn't seem to have noticed. He was sitting in his favourite chair, in his first-floor sitting room that had a view of the sea in the distance.

He studied his hands in his lap and hardly looked up as Magda pulled foil off the bowl she'd carried from home.

She'd left the pub all fired up to tell Stan the truth. But she'd stopped off on the way for three scoops of ice cream. It seemed important to bring him a gift – a way of saying 'I love you' in frozen cream and sugar, before saying it for real.

Was she really going to say it after all this time?

Magda swallowed and pushed the bowl into Stan's lap.

'Your favourites – Salted Caramel, obviously, Vanilla Cream and Blueberry Crush.' She paused. 'That's not against doctors' orders, is it?'

He looked up at that and smiled. 'Definitely not.'

Magda fetched him a spoon and he tried the Salted

Caramel first, as she'd known he would. She watched him eat, savouring every mouthful as if it was the first ice cream he'd ever tasted.

And as she watched, she paced the room – past the TV and the sofa and the glass cabinet filled with Penny's treasures. She glanced at her best friend's photo on the mantelpiece and her resolve to be truthful began to falter.

Here, in Penny's home, it felt as if the woman she'd known for decades had never left.

Magda shivered. She wasn't sure she believed in an afterlife. But what if Penny *was* watching her, reading her mind and judging her?

How disappointed would she be in her best friend? How surprised by her decades-long duplicity? Magda had never acted on her feelings for Stan, but she'd had them, nonetheless.

'You're going to wear a groove in that carpet,' said Stan, placing his half-eaten ice cream on the table next to his chair. 'Are you going to sit down?'

'Yes.' Magda sat in the chair opposite Stan and immediately got back to her feet. 'No.' She swallowed again. 'I came round because I have something to tell you. And I really need to say it.'

She could feel her heart hammering in her chest, and Alyssa's words sounding in her head: *I let my fear win... and I've regretted it ever since.*

'I've been wanting to tell you for a while but it was never the right time. But now—'

'I have something to tell you too,' interrupted Stan, gazing out of the window. 'Can I go first?'

'I'd rather say—'

'Please,' Stan interrupted, turning his head and staring straight at her. 'I think you need to know.'

Magda's breath caught in her throat at Stan's expression. She thought she'd seen every side of him – loving father, bereaved husband, kind friend. But he looked vacant, as if the light in his eyes had gone out.

'Know what?' she asked, a hollow feeling in her chest.

'I don't quite know how to say this so I'll just say it straight.' He wiped a hand across his face. 'I'm dying.'

Magda couldn't breathe. She stared at him mutely.

'Not immediately, but sooner rather than later. Certainly sooner than I'd anticipated. They call it a neurological disorder. I ignored the signs because I was so sad after Penny died. I didn't really care if...'

He petered off and a hush fell over the room. Below them, Magda could hear a hum of conversation as people came into the shop and were served by Jack. People whose lives hadn't just been turned upside down.

'Is that why you fell over the other day?' she managed.

He nodded. 'My balance has been off for a while and I've been finding it harder to walk. My joints have stiffened up and sometimes my speech seems affected. Anyway, they've done some tests and investigations which have confirmed what they suspected.'

'But there must be treatment you can have,' insisted Magda, her head reeling.

'There's no cure. I might have a couple of years – more, if I'm lucky. Though I'm not sure luck comes into it,' he said, a hint of bitterness creeping into his voice. 'I can pursue what treatments there are but I'm not sure I want to overly prolong things, to be honest. Longer isn't always better. I saw that with our John. He had a few extra months of life but the treatments that gave him that took their toll.' For the first time, tears sprang into his eyes. 'Anyway, that's what I wanted to tell you.'

He went back to staring at his hands in his lap as another hush descended.

'And what does Jack say about you not wanting to *prolong*

things?' spluttered Magda, her words coming out more sharply than she'd intended.

'Jack doesn't know yet. He's got enough on his plate with his mother's death and then his marriage breaking up. He's lost right now, Magda.'

'But he needs to know!' Magda glared at Stan, suddenly angry. 'Penny kept everything quiet and it didn't help in the long run. You can't keep this from Jack, and he might be able to bash some sense into your head about treatments.'

'I doubt it. He saw what happened with John, and you know what Jack is like. He'll work out the cost-benefit ratio and probably come to the conclusion that I'm right. But I will tell him.' Stan sighed. 'Everyone faced with this makes their own decisions based on their own circumstances, and this is my decision. I'll be joining Penny, so I'm at peace with it.'

'I'm not.' Magda began pacing again as red-hot fury coursed through her body. This wasn't fair on any level. Not for Stan, not for Jack, and not for her.

'Thank you for caring.' Stan's words were level and polite. 'But decisions about my health aren't yours to take. They're mine and I will make them.'

He ate another mouthful of ice cream and closed his eyes to savour the taste. Not as if it was the first ice cream he'd ever tasted, Magda realised. But as if it might be the last.

Selfish, she wanted to yell. *You selfish man! This isn't just your life you're talking about. You need to fight.*

But she couldn't make a fuss. Not here and not now, when Stan was coping with such devastating news himself. What kind of heartless woman would that make her?

So Magda did what she always did when visited by pain, sorrow and anger. She took a deep breath and tried to put herself in the other person's shoes. It *was* his life, she told herself. His life to do with whatever he wished.

'The fact of the matter is, I don't have enough to live for,' he said suddenly, dropping his spoon with a clang into the bowl. 'Not any more.'

'You have a son and a grandson.'

You have me, echoed through Magda's head.

'And they'll be fine without me. Jack is going through a tough patch but he'll come out the other side, and I know he'll always have you to look out for him.' Stan stopped and gave her a questioning look. 'You will look out for him, won't you?'

'Of course I will. Why do you even need to ask?' Though she'd damped down her anger, she still sounded irritated and cross. 'But they need *you*.'

'No, they don't.' He shrugged. 'They just need each other.'

'I need you,' Magda blurted out, unable to contain her true emotions a moment longer.

'What? When I spend most of my time moaning about the weather?' He chuckled. 'No, you don't, Magda. And I can't go on forever. That, as Jack would say, is not a scientifically valid proposition.' He glanced at the photo of his dead wife and shook his head. 'So, cut me some slack, Magda. Stop looking so cross with me for being ill and let's have that cup of tea you promised when you came in.'

'And Jack?'

'Jack *will* be told, this evening. I promise.'

'Poor Jack,' Magda murmured, banging cupboard doors in the kitchen as she searched for the teapot. She knew where it was kept. She knew this first-floor flat inside out, but her brain didn't seem to be working. She couldn't think straight.

'Poor Jack,' she murmured again. 'Poor Stan.'

Poor Magda, said the little voice in her head but she ignored it. This was Stan's and Jack's tragedy. Not hers.

Teapot found, she somehow made a passable drink and then sat with Stan while they made small talk, as if nothing had happened.

And all the while, Magda's heart was breaking.

At last, unable to bear the surreal atmosphere any longer, she got to her feet and said goodbye.

She'd reached the door before Stan called out to her: 'You said you had something to tell me, too, Magda.'

Magda opened her mouth and then shook her head. 'Don't worry. It was nothing important.'

FIFTEEN
JACK

Even reciting pi under his breath wasn't working this evening. Jack gave up mumbling the mathematical constant and took a deep, shuddering breath. He was standing on the quayside and everything smelled of fish.

A small fishing boat was setting out for the night, and he watched it pass by, stepping back as a wash of water topped the wall and puddled on the stone.

It must be wonderful to be alone on the ocean, under a dark sky – netting fish, staring at the stars and escaping the harsh reality that waited on shore.

He was filled with a sudden urge to throw himself onto the deck and beg the fishermen to take him with them. Perhaps an expedition on the high seas would drown out the news that his father had just shared. The news that seemed to be strangling him.

Jack swallowed painfully and glanced at Driftwood House, sitting high on the cliff. It was glowing in the light of the dying sun and next to it stood a smudge of white, the marquee that on Saturday would host Rosie's reception.

People would celebrate while he mourned the impending loss of his father, and the end of his marriage.

Why *was* Miri coming to see him? Jack wondered for the umpteenth time. Might she really be having second thoughts about their separation?

Losing Miri and Archie was so hard and now he was losing his father too. He would, in effect, be abandoned.

'Oh, for goodness' sake,' Jack murmured, aware he was being over-dramatic. 'You're born, you live, you die.'

Cells were generated and cells broke down. His father was ill and his father was going to die. Just as Jack would die one day, and Archie.

He shook his head. Thinking of his son's demise really wasn't helping, even though dying was inevitable and, putting emotions aside, simply a scientific process that everyone had to go through.

Alyssa was right, he decided, pacing up and down the quay. Reality did suck at times so no wonder she immersed herself in fantastical tales of the past. Perhaps that was her escape? Though he had no idea what she'd be escaping from. He knew virtually nothing about her, except she'd lived in Devon for the first five years of her life, and she clearly had some sort of medical training. She'd taken charge after his father had fallen, as if she knew exactly what to do.

Jack stared across the sea, watching the fishing boat chug further away from land. Seagulls swooped and screeched above the churned water, following the vessel towards the horizon.

'Hello,' said a voice in his ear.

Jack looked around. Alyssa was standing behind him, in a pink sundress that she'd covered with a green cardigan. The cardi was baggy and misshapen, as though it had been washed a hundred times.

'Hello. Where did you come from?'

'Magda's.' She nodded towards his aunt's cottage that stood

next to the ice-cream parlour. 'I wanted to see her but the kitchen door was locked, so I'd nipped round to knock on her front door. Then I spotted you and you looked—' She stopped talking and bit her lip.

'I looked what?'

Alyssa's bright eyes met his. 'Troubled.'

'That's my usual expression these days.'

'I did wonder if you were wrestling with some baffling scientific dilemma?'

She smiled, but he stared back stony-faced, not in the mood for her ribbing. 'Nope. I was watching that boat set out to sea.'

'Oh. Right.'

An uncomfortable silence stretched between them. She was probably regretting coming down to check on him, thought Jack, feeling guilty for taking out his bad mood on someone who was only being kind.

When he turned to her, they both started talking at once and both stopped.

'You first,' said Jack.

Alyssa pulled her cardigan tightly around her body. 'I was just going to say that I'm about to climb the cliff and watch the sun set from Driftwood House.'

'Nice.' Jack flapped his hand at a fly that was buzzing around his head.

'You could come with me, if you like.'

Jack ignored the fly and gave Alyssa his full attention. 'To see the sun set? Why?'

Alyssa grinned. 'Because it's what people do. Every day, all around the world, thousands of people watch the sun set, simply because they can. It's glorious, especially on a clear day like today. Trust me.'

Trust her? Jack stared into her eyes. They were a peculiar shade of bluey-green, he realised. The colour of heated copper chloride.

'But don't worry if you need to get back to your day,' she added, looking away.

Jack did need to get back to his father. But first he needed time to assimilate his father's latest news. News that had set off an earthquake beneath his feet.

Perhaps Alyssa's sunset would do the trick, seeing as reciting pi had failed miserably.

'Yeah, I'll come with you,' he said, glancing at his watch.

Soon the sun would dip below the horizon and then he would go home to his father and say the right things.

'Oh. Right. OK.' Alyssa sounded surprised, as if she'd never truly believed he would agree to go with her. 'Let's go then. I'm glad I asked you.'

Was she? Jack wondered, as she set off at a cracking pace. Or was she already regretting her rash invitation?

SIXTEEN
ALYSSA

Sunsets in Heaven's Cove were magnificent. Alyssa wiped hair from her eyes and tried to focus on the panorama of colour that was splashed across the sky. Which was hard when Jack was standing close, arms folded and his mouth set in a thin line.

She should never have invited him to come up here with her. She never would have suggested it if he hadn't looked so upset. But now he was here so she'd better make the best of it.

'Look at that. Don't you think it's amazing?' she said, with as much enthusiasm as she could muster.

Jack squinted at the sky, which was burning red as the sun slid ever closer to the sea. Tendrils of orange and pink scored the heavens above them and, far below, the sea was a shimmering silver.

'Such glorious colours,' whispered Alyssa, feeling overcome with emotion. 'It's so beautiful, doesn't it almost make you believe in magic?'

'No.' Jack sounded puzzled. 'It's quite a sight but there's nothing magical about it. The colours are a natural phenomenon caused by the sun being low and rays of light being scattered. That means your eyes are more able to see sunset colours, such as red, orange and yellow.'

Alyssa sighed.

'In fact,' Jack continued, 'did you know that, when it comes to visible light, the longest wavelength belongs to red, which means—' He glanced at Alyssa, who had folded her arms. 'What?'

'Can't you simply appreciate the beauty of the sunset?'

Jack shrugged. 'I guess, but I find what causes it more interesting. Don't you?'

'Yes, I'm interested in the science behind what I can see. But I'd rather feel the sunset right now than analyse it.'

'*Feel* it?' Jack frowned. 'You're not about to start meditating or chanting, are you?'

Alyssa resisted the urge to drop to her knees, raise her hands to the heavens and start bellowing 'om'. It would serve him right. But she hadn't invited him for a walk on the clifftop to goad him.

She was curious to know why sadness was emanating from him in waves.

Was Stan all right? she wondered. He'd returned from hospital with nothing to show for his visit other than a compression bandage on his knee. And he'd been less than forthcoming when she'd been working in the shop and had asked about his health.

'I'm fit as a flea. There's no need to worry,' he'd insisted, though the ticcing muscle near his mouth and the hint of fear in his eyes had screamed otherwise.

She'd seen it before, that stunned, frightened expression. But she hoped that, this time, she was wrong.

'So, why have you dragged me up here?' Jack asked, waving his arm to take in the clifftop, scattered with spring flowers. In the distance, the windows of Driftwood House were glowing gold in the setting sun.

'I didn't *drag* you anywhere.'

'Sorry. Wrong word.' The corner of Jack's mouth lifted. 'You invited me, which was kind, but why, really?'

'I wanted to talk to you about something.'

'Let me guess... mysteriously vanished people? Ghouls and ghosts? Sea dragons?'

Alyssa gave him her best sardonic smile. 'I don't want to discuss anything you'd term "strange". I simply wanted to ask about your dad and how he's doing after his fall.'

The muscles in Jack's jaw tightened and he stared at the village spread out far below them. 'And here was me thinking you wanted to show me the sunset.'

'I wanted to show you that, too.'

'Why?'

Alyssa shrugged. 'Because I wasn't sure you ever looked at it.'

'Of course I look at it.'

'Yes, I know you do. But there's more to life than scientific fact. I mean, do you ever really *look* at a sunset, without all the science-y stuff watering down the... the... existential wonderment?'

'The existential wonderment?'

Jack's eyebrows had disappeared into his fringe. He was looking at her as if she was totally bonkers, which made Alyssa feel foolish. He also obviously didn't want to talk about his father, which was telling in itself.

'Do you feel sorry for me?' he asked suddenly.

'No, of course not,' Alyssa protested, thrown by the change in subject. When he shook his head, she added: 'Well, not really. It's just...'

'Just what?

She took a deep breath. 'You're here in Heaven's Cove on your own and I know your marriage has broken down and you must be worried about your dad but you seem a bit...'

She petered off again, wishing she'd stayed put in her caravan and hadn't ventured out in search of Magda at all.

'A bit what?' demanded Jack with a frown.

'A bit serious about life, in general.'

'There's nothing wrong with being serious.'

'I didn't say there was.'

Alyssa bit her lip. This wasn't going the way she'd planned, when she'd decided to slip out and enjoy the last rays of the sun. She'd planned to sit on the clifftop in perfect peace and think some more about the map – the possible map – that had been found at Driftwood House.

'A bit serious about life,' Jack repeated slowly. Alyssa thought he was about to throw a strop but, instead, he stared at the sunset for a moment and said: 'I suppose I am, yeah.'

'Oh.'

'Oh?' Jack shook his head, a faint smile on his lips. 'I admit that you're right and that's the best you can come up with? "Oh"?'

Alyssa shrugged. 'Sorry. In my defence it's getting late and it's been a long day. Plus, I've never heard you say I'm right before.'

'What about you?'

'Me? What do you mean?'

'We've ascertained that I'm not the life and soul of the party. So what's your character flaw?'

'I wasn't implying that being serious is a character flaw.' When Jack said nothing, Alyssa folded her arms. 'All right. My character flaw is... I don't know.' She was going to make something up. Give some trite response. But she was suddenly desperate to tell the truth for once. And why not to this man whose face was bathed in pink rays from the dying sun? 'My character flaw is that I'm a coward.'

Jack frowned. 'From what I know about you, I doubt that.'

What did he know? What had people said? It was a small

village and secrets were often uncovered. Though not hers. Please, never hers.

When Alyssa shuddered, Jack glanced at her. 'Are you cold?'

'Not really.' But he'd already taken off his jumper and was holding it out to her.

'The temperature's dropping, so take this,' he insisted, thrusting it into her hands. 'And we'd better be getting back before it gets too dark to see the path properly. I don't fancy taking a dive off the cliffs.'

When he started walking back down the path, Alyssa slipped his jumper over her head and put it on before following him. The soft grey wool swamped her, but she rolled up the sleeves.

She took a good look at Jack as he picked his way, ahead of her, down the steep path. He'd swapped his usual grey cord trousers for blue jeans and a grey polo shirt made of thin cotton. But if he was cold, he didn't show it.

Alyssa stared at his arms but no goosebumps were visible. His arms were surprising, actually. She'd expected him to have pale, skinny arms – the physique of a man who worked in a research lab and probably spent his weekends reading academic journals. But Jack's arms carried the hint of a faded tan. And he had muscles – not bulging I-work-out biceps, but his arms were nicely toned.

Overall, with his hair curling where it touched his collar, Alyssa had to admit he looked rather handsome. In a nerdy kind of way.

She was so deep in thought that when Jack stopped walking abruptly, she almost barrelled into the back of him.

He turned to her, the sun a blazing golden globe over his shoulder.

'There's something you should know,' he said gruffly.

'Seeing as you work in the shop now and will be around when I go back to London.'

'OK.'

Alyssa waited as the boom of waves hitting the cliffs reverberated around them.

'I've had some bad news about my dad.' He swallowed. 'Can you keep a secret?'

You have no freaking idea! Alyssa kept her expression neutral.

'I am very good at keeping secrets.'

'Only you were so good when Dad fell the other day and he's going to need support from the people around him.' Jack closed his eyes briefly. 'Dad told me this evening that he has a neurological disorder and his prognosis isn't good.'

'I'm so sorry,' said Alyssa, feeling overwhelmed with sadness for poor bereaved Stan but not surprised. She'd suspected as much from the hints his body was displaying.

'I can't believe it, after losing Mum so recently.'

Without thinking, Alyssa grabbed hold of Jack's hand. He seemed so lost and lonely, standing on the cliff with the dying sun behind him.

His hand was warm and she felt his fingers curl around hers.

'Has he been told of treatments that might help him?'

'What? Like crystals or something?'

She let go of his hand. 'No, like evidence-based treatments.'

Jack shook his head, his face a mask of misery. 'He doesn't seem keen to pursue the treatment route. He says he wants to leave this world on his own terms, as if he's resigned to letting nature take its course.'

'I can understand that. I've seen it before.'

'Have you?' Jack moved a step closer. 'I know so little about you, Alyssa. Yet here I am, telling you such personal news.'

He paused, as if he was waiting for Alyssa to reciprocate

with personal news of her own. And for a moment she was tempted to tell him everything about the mistake she'd made and the terrible consequence of her cowardice and weakness. But the words wouldn't come.

Jack held her gaze for a moment, his eyes bright with disappointment, before turning and walking away. He called over his shoulder: 'Dad doesn't want a fuss so please do keep it quiet. The last thing he needs is Belinda bustling round.'

'Of course.' A terrible thought struck Alyssa. 'Does Magda know?'

'Dad told her this afternoon because she's family.'

It was strange, thought Alyssa, how you could feel two strong emotions at exactly the same time: sorrow for Magda that she would lose the man she'd loved for so long, and relief for herself that she wouldn't have to keep that news from her landlady. This was one secret too many for Alyssa to bear.

'Thank you for trusting me with the news about your dad, and I'm so very sorry,' Alyssa called out.

But Jack was already so far ahead, she wasn't sure that her words were heard.

SEVENTEEN

JACK

The face staring back at him from the mirror was the same, and yet different. Older, thought Jack, puffing out his cheeks, to see if the lines around his eyes would disappear – they didn't. And sadder.

There was a definite air of melancholy about him, and with Miri arriving in Heaven's Cove in half an hour's time, it just wouldn't do. He gave himself a wide, cheesy grin in the mirror. Now he simply looked demented.

'Get a grip, Gathergill!' he muttered. 'Yes, your life is a car crash right now, but perhaps things are about to start looking up.'

He did up another button on his shirt, an old one that Miri had once remarked brought out the 'storm grey' in his eyes.

Jack presumed that was a good thing and that she liked his eyes. Or maybe she considered grey boring, which would be a shame seeing as a significant proportion of the clothes he owned were that colour.

This was in stark contrast to Alyssa, who, he imagined, would never allow anything so dowdy as grey into her wardrobe. It was bright colours all the way for Heaven's Cove's resident myth-teller. This morning she'd arrived at the shop in daffodil-yellow trousers, a white T-shirt and a purple cardigan several sizes too big.

He'd look like a clown in that outfit, but he had to admit it worked on her. She'd looked good today – more than good, actually. And she'd been very kind to his father, while not letting on that she now knew about his condition.

Jack had been on tenterhooks in case she let anything slip, and had berated himself for telling her during their walk the other night. Maybe the 'wonderment' of the sunset had loosened his tongue.

But Alyssa had been subtly supportive – insisting Stan sit at the till to work, fetching stock without his help, and making sure that he took breaks.

Jack shook his head, not sure why he was thinking about Alyssa when he should be concentrating on the woman he'd married six years ago. Miri would be here soon and if he didn't leave now he would be late for their meeting.

Jack grabbed a jumper that had been in his wardrobe for ages. It wasn't Alyssa-levels of eye-catching. It was dark green, the colour of hedgerows that lined Devon's lanes. But it wasn't grey, so it would do.

'Miri's coming here for a quick chat and that's all,' he told himself, noting that he seemed to be talking to himself a lot these days. But... why would she come all the way here just for a quick chat? What if it was more than that?

Jack sat down heavily on the bed, his thoughts crowding in on him. What if Miri was having second thoughts about the divorce? What if she'd decided that Archie would be better off with Jack, the only dad he'd ever known, living at home?

Thinking of Archie's trusting face brought tears to his eyes and he bit his lip to get himself under control. He couldn't turn up to this meeting a snivelling wreck.

'Come on, man,' he murmured. 'Be the dashing, debonair Jack Gathergill who Miri first fell in love with.'

Had he ever been dashing and debonair? Jack doubted it, but he needed to assume some semblance of it, for his own pride's sake, during Miri's visit. He also needed to stop thinking and get a move on because she wouldn't approve of him being late.

Taking a deep breath, Jack got to his feet, made sure he'd wiped all the toothpaste from around his mouth, and walked out into the spring sunshine.

Jack moved briskly through the village, which was waking up as April got into full swing. Tourists were thronging the narrow lanes, peering into gift shop windows, and licking ice cream, even though the watery sun held little heat.

The Heavenly Tea Shop came into view and – Jack's heart quickened – there was Miri sitting outside, waiting for him. She'd insisted they meet here, on 'neutral territory' rather than coming to his father's shop.

'Neutral' was a strange word to choose, Jack mused, walking towards the woman he'd once thought he knew so well. It was the sort of word used when discussing warfare. His hope that Miri was about to suggest some form of reconciliation began to wobble.

'Jack.' Miri got to her feet when he arrived. 'You came, then.'

Had she thought he might not? Jack paused, unsure of the etiquette when greeting a woman to whom he'd once pledged his undying devotion. A woman who now wanted to divorce him.

She solved the dilemma by leaning forward and brushing her lips briefly across his cheek. Her perfume was different – a heavy, musky aroma rather than the lighter, floral scent she usually favoured.

'Take a seat,' Miri told him, sitting back down. 'I've ordered you an espresso, if that's all right?'

'Perfect,' said Jack as he sat down too, though he'd have preferred a caffè latte. He already felt wired.

When Miri bent her head to pull a tissue from her handbag, he took the opportunity to look at her closely.

She was dressed in her signature black, in a skinny black polo neck and dark skirt that hugged her thighs. Her fair hair was pulled into a low bun that grazed the back of her neck, and a large silver pendant rested between her breasts. She looked amazing, thought Jack – relaxed, glowing, and nothing like a woman badly affected by a traumatic separation.

'So,' he said, keen to get their conversation started. 'It's good to see you. How are you, and how is Archie?'

'I'm all right, thank you.' She dabbed at her nose with the tissue. 'And Archie's doing well. He's staying with my mum for a few days while I'm away. Are you going to FaceTime him later?'

'Of course, seeing as it's one of my allowed "phone days",' retorted Jack, still smarting at Miri's imposed restriction on how often he could converse with his son.

Miri sighed. 'I'm only trying to stop Archie from being upset.'

'He always seems very happy to hear from me. Though the last time I tried to speak to him, at an allowed time, you said he was busy.'

'He was,' Miri replied tartly, a faint blush spreading across her cheeks. 'We had a house guest and Archie was playing with him in the garden.'

'Who was that?' Jack asked, but he was interrupted by Pauline, the café owner, arriving with their coffees. She smiled at them both but rested her hand lightly on Jack's shoulder before moving off.

Jack groaned inside. Everyone in Heaven's Cove knew he was getting divorced – his dad's shop was often a hubbub of gossip – and now he was an object of pity, sitting here with the woman who no longer wanted him.

Miri picked up her coffee and sat back in her chair, watching him.

'I'd like to see Archie soon because I miss him horribly. It's hard to go from seeing him every day to seeing him so infrequently.'

'I'm sure, and he misses you too. You can see him once you get back to London.'

'I was thinking, maybe I can have some time off in the summer and take him to France with me. For a holiday.'

Miri gave the ghost of a smile. 'Mmm, we'll have to sort something out. How's your dad, by the way?'

Jack hesitated, remembering how much Miri had complained about his frequent visits to see his dad, after his mum had died. Now didn't seem the time or place to tell her the truth.

'He's OK, considering. He's older, sadder and more tired. That's why I'm here for a while, to give him some support.'

'Poor old Stan,' Miri murmured.

'You could always nip in and say hello to him. He'd like to see you.'

'And I'd like to see him too but I'm on a tight schedule today.' She pursed her lips and blew gently across her steaming coffee. 'Also, it's a bit awkward, isn't it, with things being the way they are? I don't think I'm Stan's favourite person right now.'

Jack shrugged. 'He'd be perfectly civil.'

'I'm sure he would, and I'll definitely see him before I leave Devon.'

How long was she intending to stay? They lapsed into silence, tempered by the lapping of waves against the quayside and a soft buzz of conversation around them.

'So, Jack, what have you been up to?' Miri asked when the silence started becoming awkward.

'Work, helping Dad, that's it, really. What about you?'

'This and that. Work, Archie, you know.'

He nodded. 'And your parents? Are they all right?'

'Not too bad. Mum's arthritis is playing up a bit and Dad's driving her mad with his golf obsession.' She straightened her skirt and brushed her hands over her knees. 'Was it a problem, taking time off from your job to come down here?'

'Not really. I had some time owing.' Jack swallowed. 'Why did you want to see me?' He wanted to get to the nub of why they were both here, and making small talk was excruciating. 'Why have you come to Heaven's Cove? I know you don't like the place. We could have talked on the phone, or I'll be back in London soon enough.'

'I know, but I was in the area anyway and I wanted to tell you something as soon as possible.'

Jack was suddenly aware of his heartbeat sounding in his ears. Was Miri about to say she'd changed her mind? He stared at her, a vision in black with the blue sea behind her.

She leaned forward, running her tongue across her lips. 'The truth is...' Her hesitation was killing him. 'The truth is, I'm seeing someone, and I didn't want you to hear it from anyone else.'

'Oh.'

Jack hadn't been expecting that. He sat back in his chair, feeling winded and stupid. Of course Miri was moving on with her life – while he was stuck. Stuck here in Heaven's Cove with a dying father.

'Has Archie met him?' he managed.

The faint blush on Miri's cheeks flared brighter. 'Yes, a few days ago. We waited until we knew our relationship was serious.'

Our relationship. Jack was aware of a queasy feeling spreading upwards from his stomach. 'It got serious pretty quickly, then.'

'Mmm,' said Miri, vaguely, as Jack had a sudden realisation.

'That's why you told me Archie was busy the last time I called him.' Jack's laugh sounded hollow. 'The house guest you mentioned was actually your...' What should he call him? Boyfriend? Partner? Lover? 'Anyway, you didn't want Archie to speak to me in case he mentioned *him*.'

'As I said, I thought it was best that you heard it from me first,' said Miri, her face now pale and expressionless. 'And I didn't want to have to ask Archie to keep secrets.'

'What's his name?'

'Does it matter?'

When Jack nodded, she sighed. 'All right. His name is Damian and he's a computer programmer.'

Damian? What kind of *Omen*-y name was Damian? And how nerdy was a computer programmer? thought Jack, his mind whirling.

About as nerdy as a research scientist who sees scattered light rays rather than the wonders of a sunset.

'I'm so sorry, Jack.' Miri reached across the table and put her hand on his arm. 'I know you're still very upset about us splitting up, and now there's Damian for you to contend with. I feel so sorry for you and—'

'I've started seeing someone too,' Jack blurted out.

Miri's eyes opened wide. 'You're going out with someone?'

'Yeah, that's right. I was going to tell you today.'

She didn't believe him. He could see it in her eyes. And she pitied him for coming up with such a ridiculous falsehood.

'It's true,' he blustered, heaping lie on top of lie. 'So you don't need to worry about me.'

You don't need to pity me.

'What's her name?' asked Miri, folding her arms.

'What?'

'What's the name of the woman you've started seeing?'

Jack looked around him, at the sea and the sky and the wheeling seagulls circling overhead like vultures. Every woman's name he'd ever known had vanished from his head. Every single one, except for Penny. But he couldn't tell Miri he was seeing someone who happened to have the same name as his late mother. She'd see through that immediately.

Then he spotted her, standing at the quayside, chatting to Claude. A rainbow of colour against the pale stone.

'Alyssa,' he said quickly. 'Her name's Alyssa and she's recently moved to Heaven's Cove.'

'Alyssa?' Miri raised an eyebrow. 'And what does this Alyssa do?'

'She works in the tourism industry.'

'Right. So tell me about her.'

'Well, she's a bit younger than me.' Jack tried to concentrate on the lie he was spinning but, out of the corner of his eye, he had noticed that Alyssa had stopped chatting with Claude and was walking in their direction.

He blinked in alarm. There was no reason for Alyssa to come over. She didn't even like him that much.

But when he blinked again, she was definitely making a beeline straight for them.

EIGHTEEN
JACK

'Hello there,' Alyssa said when she reached them. She brushed her dark hair from her eyes before reaching into her canvas bag and pulling out Jack's jumper.

'I was going to drop this into the shop. I've had it since our walk and keep forgetting to give it back to you.'

'Thank you.'

Jack grabbed the jumper and dropped it across his knees. He gave Alyssa a tight smile, all the while his eyes urging: *Go away! Go away, please!*

But it was too late. Miri had leaned forward and was staring intently at her.

'Hello,' she said, holding out her hand. 'I'm Miri, and *you* are—?'

'I'm Alyssa. It's good to meet you.'

'Alyssa?' Miri's mouth twitched into a peculiar smile as they shook hands, her lips all twisted. 'Not *the* Alyssa, surely?'

'I guess so,' said Alyssa, confusion flitting across her face. 'The one and only.'

Jack slumped down in his chair, wishing he was anywhere but here.

'Well, that's fortunate because I've just been hearing all about you,' said Miri brightly.

'Have you?' Alyssa shot him a quizzical look. 'None of it good, I dare say.'

Jack groaned quietly. This was going from bad to worse. If Miri found out he'd been lying, he'd never live down the humiliation. Not only had he failed as a husband and been ousted by some idiot called Damian, but he was such a sad sap, he was now making up fantasy girlfriends.

Jack came to a sudden decision. Whatever it took, Miri must never find out the truth.

He grabbed hold of Alyssa's hand. 'None of it good? You're such a joker! Thank you so much for returning my jumper, Aly.' Alyssa glanced at her hand and gave a discreet pull, but Jack tightened his fingers around hers. 'I didn't realise you still had it after our walk on the cliffs. That was a beautiful sunset, wasn't it?'

He tried to smile at Alyssa but he could feel his mouth wobbling. What on earth was happening to him?

'Would you care to join us, Alyssa?' asked Miri with studied politeness. 'You can tell me all about yourself.'

For the love of all that's holy, please say no!

Jack's eyes met Alyssa's and she hesitated, her hair blowing in the breeze. 'Thank you for the invitation but I can't stop right now. I have a tour to organise.'

Jack breathed out slowly, his whole body tense.

'That's a shame.' Miri smiled. 'Jacky told me that you're involved in the tourism industry.'

Alyssa shrugged. 'I guess you could call it that. I run myths and legends tours around the village and across Dartmoor.'

'Myths and legends? What, ghouls and ghosts?'

Alyssa caught Miri's incredulous tone and her smile froze. 'That's right. Ghosts, ghouls, demons and dragons. Very large sea dragons.'

'Gosh.' Miri looked questioningly at him. 'I didn't think Jack was into that kind of thing, but they do say that opposites attract. So how long have you two been together?'

As Alyssa stiffened beside him, Jack closed his eyes. She was about to tell Miri there was no way in hell she'd ever go out with a man like him. Or she'd simply laugh and walk off. He wasn't sure which would be worse.

But when he opened his eyes, Alyssa was still standing there. She gave him a cool stare. 'How long is it, Jacky? Not that long, really. We met on a tour and just clicked. Isn't that right?'

'Mmm, that's right,' he mumbled, so grateful she hadn't outed him, he could have kissed her.

'So, are these tours the only work you do?' asked Miri.

'No, I also work part-time in Stan's store.'

'Do you? That's nice. You're becoming a part of the family.'

Miri sounded quite put out. But she had no right. Not when she'd just told him she was sleeping with someone else.

'I guess. Anyway, I'll leave you to it,' said Alyssa, gently pulling her hand from Jack's. He hadn't realised he was still holding on to it. 'It was lovely to meet you, Miri.'

'You too,' said Miri coolly, running a hand across her forehead. 'I hope to see you again soon.'

'That would be great,' said Alyssa, sounding as if she didn't mean what she was saying either.

Jack sighed as Alyssa walked off. She already thought he was boring and overly serious. Now she must think he was losing his mind.

'She seems... nice,' said Miri, watching Alyssa move away, the red scarf tied around her pink-streaked ponytail swinging with every step. 'She's not quite... well...'

'Not quite what?'

'Not quite the sort of woman I'd have expected you to go for.'

'Why's that?'

Miri wrinkled her nose. 'You know. Myths and legends? Eek! And she doesn't look your type, with her bangles and sandals and… unusual fashion sense.'

'She's a lovely person, actually,' said Jack, feeling protective towards the woman who'd just saved him from total humiliation. 'She's kind and competent and her tours are entertaining. They bring the rich history of Devon to life. And, after all' – he swallowed – 'there's more to life than scientific fact.'

'Do you think so?' Miri raised an eyebrow. 'She *is* pretty, I'll give you that.'

When Miri started drumming her nails on the café table, as she often did when thinking, Jack was reminded of how irritating this particular habit could be.

'Actually.' She stopped drumming. 'If I've moved on with a new partner and you've moved on too, maybe you should meet Damian, seeing as you're planning to still be a significant figure in Archie's life, and Damian will be as well.'

'I'm not sure meeting up would be—' Jack began, but Miri cut him off with an imperious wave of the hand. He remembered she could be bossy at times, too.

'It would be good for Archie's sake. I mean, if Damian is going to share some of the parenting with you, it's probably best that the two of you meet.'

Do you think? Jack could feel anger and despair bubbling up inside him at the thought of another man parenting Archie. What would Archie call him? Damian? Dad? Dickhead, maybe?

Miri sat up straighter in her chair. 'I've had a good idea. Are you going to Rosie's wedding, like me?'

'Yes, I'll be taking Dad.' He shook his head. 'Sorry, did you say you'd be at the wedding? I didn't realise that.'

'You and I were both invited.'

'Yeah, but that was ages ago. Back when we were together.'

'To be honest, I wasn't planning on going, but Damian fancied a short break in Devon so I thought I might combine the two, as long as you weren't going to be weird about it. And I've never got round to telling Rosie that I wouldn't be there.'

When Jack said nothing, Miri continued. 'The whole thing sounds very informal, with a marquee on the cliff and a buffet. I bet Rosie wouldn't mind if I brought an extra. Then, Damian and I, and you and Alyssa could all sit together and be very adult about the situation. What do you reckon?'

I reckon I'd rather pull out my own teeth without anaesthetic, thought Jack but, instead, he answered with: 'I'm afraid Alyssa's not going to be at the wedding.' He knew for sure she hadn't been invited because he'd overheard her and his dad discussing the guest list in the shop.

'Really?' Miri sniffed. 'Surely Rosie's invited her now you two are an item?'

'She did, but Alyssa has to work that day. She's got tours to run. Lots of them. They're very popular and she can't, um... let her public down.'

When Miri slowly replied 'Ohh-kay' with a sympathetic tilt of the head, Jack's heart sank even lower. She obviously doubted that the two of them truly were together. And why wouldn't she? Why would she believe that a woman like Alyssa would be interested in a strait-laced scientist like him?

Miri sighed, closed her handbag with a snap and got to her feet. 'Anyway, I've told you my news and I'd better be getting on. Perhaps Alyssa could join us at the wedding once her tours are done? I'd love to get to know her better.'

'I'll ask her but I expect she'll be busy for most of the day.'

Miri stared at him for a moment. 'I thought she might be, which is a shame but never mind. It's good to see you, Jacky.'

She gave him a perfunctory peck on the cheek and walked away, without offering to split the bill.

Jack waited until she was out of sight before putting his head in his hands. That had not gone the way he'd expected. Not only was his 'wife' seeing another man, he seemed to have gained a new, very unwilling, girlfriend.

Reciting pi wouldn't even touch the sides of this one.

NINETEEN

ALYSSA

What the hell was that all about? Alyssa hurried towards the centre of the village, past tourists putting on extra layers to protect themselves against the chilly wind blowing off the sea.

Miri, chic in her expensive-looking clothes, must be the imminent ex-wife. But why on earth had Jack implied to her that he and Alyssa were in some sort of relationship? No, he'd more than implied. He'd held her hand and almost crushed her fingers when she'd tried to pull away.

All she'd done was show him a glorious sunset and he'd gone all peculiar. Perhaps his science-y brain was overheating and about to crash.

Alyssa gently rubbed her palm across her cheek. It had been a long time since a good-looking man had held her hand. And although Jack was frustrating and had a *very* closed mind, it had felt nicer than she would have imagined.

He must have been point-scoring with Miri, or trying to win her back. But if that was the case, why choose Alyssa as his fake girlfriend? Was he that desperate?

Alyssa sighed. As Magda had pointed out, Jack was coping with a lot – a divorce in the making, the death of his mum, and now his father's illness. So, she'd cut him some slack. But it would still be awkward when they next met up at Stan's store.

Fortunately, her next shift wasn't for a couple of days and, fingers crossed, much of the awkwardness might have worn off by then. It would be old news, she told herself, heading through Magda's garden towards her caravan. Old news that, just like secrets, could be shoved under the carpet, never again to see the light of day.

Alyssa had reached her door when she heard the garden gate bang and someone calling her name. Swinging round, she groaned because Jack was running towards her, his long legs going nineteen to the dozen. He reached her and put his hands on his thighs, leaning over to catch his breath.

'Sorry,' he puffed. 'I haven't run that fast for ages. But I need to see you.'

'I've just got home and need to have some lunch,' said Alyssa, turning her key in the lock and pushing open the caravan door. Did this man know nothing about the concept of giving awkwardness some time to wear off?

'I won't take up much of your time.' Jack straightened up, his cheeks flushed. 'I only need to see you for a couple of minutes.'

Alyssa sighed. 'Why?'

'To say sorry. Can I come in?'

'Are you going to be peculiar again?'

When he shook his head, she glanced across the garden, aware that Magda was watching them from her kitchen window. 'OK,' said Alyssa, keeping in mind her decision to cut Jack some slack. 'Come in, but I haven't got long.'

'Thanks. I appreciate it.'

Alyssa stepped back and let Jack walk ahead of her into the caravan. And as he looked around, she saw the place through his eyes.

The caravan *was* tiny – there was no chance of swinging a

cat, even if you were that way inclined. But it was tidy, clean and cheerful, brightened with colourful throws she'd found in a charity shop.

'How long have you been living here?' he asked.

'Six months.'

'It must have been freezing in winter.'

'It did get a bit chilly.'

Actually, the caravan had been so cold when it snowed in January, Magda had let her sleep on her sofa bed for a few nights. But Alyssa didn't want to prolong this conversation. 'You wanted to say sorry?' she said, throwing her canvas bag into a corner. 'Is that for dragging me into some deception involving your wife?'

'Soon-to-be ex-wife,' mumbled Jack.

'*Ex*-wife – whatever. She seems to think we're an item.'

'I know. I panicked.' Jack ran his hand through his hair.

'You don't seem the panicky type.'

'Really? What type am I then?' Jack shook his head. 'Ignore that. It doesn't matter what you think of me. I just wanted to apologise for letting Miri believe that you and I are, well, you know, together.'

'Why did you panic?' asked Alyssa, suddenly feeling sorry for him. He looked done in.

'I'm not sure.' He hesitated, as though deliberating whether to tell her or not. Then, he shrugged. 'Oh, what the hell... I thought maybe Miri had come here to tell me she wanted to make another go of our marriage. But I was wrong. She came here to tell me that she's seeing another man.'

'Oh.' Alyssa winced, not sure what to say. In the end, she managed: 'That's sad. I'm very sorry.'

'He's called Damian,' declared Jack, putting his hands on his hips as if this was an appalling fact.

'Right.' Alyssa paused as he waited for her verdict on his love rival's name. 'Um, he sounds a bit... *Omen*-y?'

'Absolutely!' Jack raised his hands to the sky. 'That's exactly what I thought.'

'Good. Well, I don't mean good that she's got another man. I mean...' Alyssa stopped and took a breath before continuing. 'So, let me guess. After a shock like that, you didn't want Miri to think that you were still pining for her.'

Jack nodded, looking thoroughly miserable now. 'I didn't want her to think I'm a sad bloke with no life, even though I guess I am. So I told her I had a new partner, which, now I say it out loud, sounds completely ridiculous. Sorry.'

He seemed so vulnerable all of a sudden, Alyssa gestured to the seat below the window. 'You can sit down if you want.'

He sat, without a word.

'Look, I can understand you pretending that you had a girl-friend. It wasn't a great idea, but I get it. But why did you use *my* name, for goodness' sake?'

'I don't know. My mind went totally blank and I couldn't think of any women's names. Except for "Penny".'

'Wasn't that your mum's name?'

'Yep.'

'So you could hardly use that one.'

'Nope.'

'And then you spotted me talking to Claude.'

'Exactly. I saw you and said your name without thinking it through.'

Alyssa nodded. 'OK, I can see how that happened. But then, I came over.' She shook her head. 'Oh my God, you must have been dying inside.'

'I thought I might self-combust on the spot.'

Alyssa began to giggle and dug her nails into the palm of her hand to stop herself. 'I thought you went a funny colour as I got closer.'

'I was quietly hyperventilating and then, when I grabbed your hand, I was worried you were going to hit me.'

'I did consider it. I wonder what Miri would have thought if I'd slugged you with a left hook.' She pictured Miri's horrified expression and began to laugh. And try as she might, she couldn't stop. She hadn't laughed so inappropriately since she and a cousin had giggled during a great-uncle's funeral twenty years ago.

Jack stared at her, with his mouth open, as she tried to compose herself. The thought of him having kittens when she'd approached him and Miri *was* funny. But even so, she was laughing after he'd just told her that the woman he loved was seeing someone else. He was going to storm out and she didn't blame him.

But to her surprise, Jack's mouth began to twitch and suddenly he joined in. 'Of all the names I could have chosen!' he spluttered between guffaws, which only made her worse.

They both laughed until tears ran down their faces and Alyssa had to hold on to the wall to steady herself.

Her stomach was hurting by the time she stopped and took a deep breath. Jack had stopped laughing too and was wiping his eyes. 'I'm so sorry, Jack. I shouldn't have started laughing. Miri's news must have been hard for you to hear, especially as I know you worry about Archie?'

He sobered up immediately at the sound of his son's name. 'I worry about him all the time because I love him so much.' Jack swallowed. 'Do you know, I wanted Miri and me to have a child, a brother or sister for Archie? However, she told me she didn't want any more kids, which I accepted although I found it upsetting. But hey, maybe she'll want one with *Omen*-y Damian.'

He flinched, his face suddenly a mask of pain.

'I'm so sorry,' said Alyssa, kicking herself for being so ineffectual, though nothing she could say would make him feel any better.

When Jack shrugged and tried to smile, it broke her heart.

She knew how it felt to battle on through regret and pain. To desperately want to turn back the clock and make things turn out differently.

'Anyway.' He stood up and stretched his legs. 'Enough of my marital woes. I came round to apologise for dragging you into the whole mess and I'd be very grateful if you didn't mention any of it to my dad. He's got enough on his plate.'

'Of course I won't. Our make-believe relationship will remain our secret.'

Jack breathed out slowly. 'Thanks. That's very decent of you.'

'At least Miri's leaving Heaven's Cove now.'

'Yeah, about that.' Jack rubbed his hand across his mouth. 'It appears that she and Damian are going to Rosie's wedding.'

Alyssa stared at him, in shock. 'How come they've been invited?'

'Rosie invited me and Miri, when we were together, and Miri is wangling an extra invitation for her new boyfriend. Now I'm in a new relationship too, she thinks Damian and I should meet.' He winced. 'She's expecting you and me to go along together. But don't worry. I told her you're busy working so won't be there.'

'But I will be there,' said Alyssa, her heart sinking. 'Magda's short on catering staff and has asked me to help her out on Saturday. I've already said yes and can't let her down.'

Jack grimaced. 'No, of course you can't.' His shoulders slumped. 'In that case, I'll tell Miri that we've split up so you won't have to pretend to like me any more. In fact, you can keep your distance and glare at me the whole time. I don't suppose that'll be a hardship.'

'Do you have to go to the reception? From what Rosie says, it sounds more like a giant party and I doubt you're in a party mood.'

'Not really. My mum's dead, my wife's divorcing me, I

rarely see my son, and my dad's seriously ill. I can't promise I'll be the life and soul of Rosie's shindig.'

He shrugged and it was the shrug that did it. The colossal pain and heartache encompassed in such a small movement that made Alyssa want to hug him.

Her eyes met his and held his gaze. Outside, children going past were shouting to each other, and gears were grating as frazzled tourists made a hash of negotiating narrow lanes. But inside Alyssa's caravan, everything was silent.

'Anyway.' Jack was the first to break eye contact. 'I'd better leave you to have your lunch. And thanks again for not dropping me in it with Miri. I appreciate it.'

'That's OK and—' She winced. 'I'm so sorry about the laughing.'

He smiled at that. A proper smile that made the corners of his eyes crinkle. 'Don't worry about it. To be honest, that's the best laugh I've had in ages.'

His gaze strayed to the table, where the letters Alyssa had tipped from the large brown envelope she'd received a while ago were scattered. This was the trouble with people invading her personal space. There was always a risk they might find out too much about her.

She pushed the letters into a pile and stood in front of them, blocking his view.

'I'll see you in your dad's shop, then, when I'm in for my next shift.'

Alyssa glanced at the floor to make sure none of the incriminating letters had fallen from the table. And when she looked up again, Jack had gone.

She sank onto the window seat and nibbled at a hangnail. She should have sorted out the letters and got rid of them. But Jack had only glanced at them so there was no harm done, she told herself, trying to quell flutters of panic. He didn't know what she'd done, and he never would.

After several slow, deep breaths, she began to feel calmer. The last five minutes had been beyond awkward and yet the caravan felt empty without Jack taking up half the space.

She remembered him laughing, as if he didn't have a care in the world – their shared hilarity which made him seem less colourless and intimidating. And then his switch back to stark, serious reality.

Alyssa felt so sorry for Jack, coping with such heartache. And she wondered how his meeting with Damian at the wedding reception would go. He was right to expect it to be difficult.

But he was wrong about one thing: she wouldn't have had to pretend to like him if she'd gone to the wedding as his plus one. Not really.

Alyssa had begun to glimpse a different man beneath Jack's stuffy, pedantic exterior. And that man was someone she rather liked.

TWENTY

JACK

Jack strode through the village, feeling as if his insides were in a washing machine, on a fast-spin cycle.

Miri's bombshell was still sinking in. And he'd made an utter fool of himself in front of Alyssa. Though at least she'd been very decent about it.

Decent, and secretive. His mind flitted to the letters that he couldn't help but notice had been scattered across the table. The letters that she'd been so keen to hide from him.

However, whatever secrets she might be keeping, Alyssa had managed, just for a moment, to chase away all the sad things in his life. Her giggling was infectious and had led to the first good laugh he'd had in ages. The sort of laugh he sometimes had with Archie, where he'd find himself snorting so hard that coffee came down his nose.

Jack waved at bridegroom-to-be Liam in the distance and quickened his pace. He'd better get back to see how his dad was coping on his own.

He was so worried about his father. But he couldn't stop picturing Alyssa's face as he'd banged on about his heartache.

Her big blue eyes had filled with sympathy and warmth. *You could drown in eyes like that.*

'Oh, please! Don't be ridiculous,' he muttered, faintly disgusted with himself for having such a romantic notion. He'd be marvelling at Alyssa's 'full lips' next and 'longing to take her in his arms'.

Well, he'd tried that with Miri. He'd shown her the more romantic side of his nature and look where that had got him: divorced and replaced – as a husband and, probably, as a father, too.

He walked on, so deep in thought he hardly noticed the seagulls dive-bombing him from above, and tourists wandering nearby.

Rosie's wedding was going to be a living nightmare, but he couldn't cry off. His dad would need his support, and Miri was right – he and dismal Damian would need to forge a relationship if they were both going to be a part of Archie's life. But would he gradually be pushed to the margins of Archie's life as Damian took over? Jack so didn't want to lose his son.

Tears prickled as he strode on, past his dad's shop and up the cliff that led to Driftwood House. A quick glance into the store had shown his father deep in conversation with an old army buddy, so Jack wouldn't be missed for a few minutes more.

He walked higher and higher, stopping before he reached the clifftop. Then, he stood looking out over the sea.

Perhaps losing touch with Archie was inevitable. His son would grow up in the same house as Damian and start to call *him* 'Dad'. Spending the weekend with Jack would become a nuisance as he got older. And, eventually, he'd never want to come at all.

Perhaps he'd say the words that Jack dreaded hearing: 'I don't have to see you. You're not my real dad.'

Tears were blurring Jack's vision and he slipped on the

steep path. Stones tumbled off the side of the cliff and fell into the churning waves below.

'Stop it!' he shouted, suddenly feeling horribly out of control. He wasn't the kind of man who shouted into the wind. He sat down on a boulder that almost blocked the path.

If he didn't stop getting upset, he would fall, and Miri would probably assume that, completely heartbroken, he'd thrown himself from the cliff deliberately. Which he'd never do because it wouldn't be fair on Archie.

Jack brusquely wiped away tears with the back of his hand. It was all too much: Miri's news coming hard on the heels of his father's gloomy prognosis. And now he was dreading Rosie's wedding reception, which was a shame because part of him had been looking forward to it.

Parties weren't usually his thing. Talking quietly with a friend, face to face, was far more pleasant than yelling at acquaintances while a would-be DJ cranked up the music to top volume. But Rosie's wedding party would be different because Heaven's Cove villagers knew how to have a good time.

He would have enjoyed it, if it didn't now entail socialising with Damian, and lying to Miri that he and Alyssa had endured a spectacular and speedy break-up since they'd last met.

'Three point one four one five nine…' he began to recite out loud, startling a seagull feasting nearby on a dropped crisp packet. 'Two six five three five…'

Gradually the chaos inside him began to subside and was replaced with the unbending order he needed to hold himself together.

He would go to the wedding, and he would be civil to Damian, and he would spin a story so that Alyssa didn't have to pretend to like him. Miri probably wouldn't believe him: she'd twig that he'd made up the whole sorry story about being in a new relationship because he couldn't bear her pity.

But the sun would rise and the sun would set. He'd

continue to gather research data at work and see Archie as much as he could. And life would go on.

He gave a deep sigh, his thoughts returning to Alyssa, whose life had shrunk to a tiny caravan in Magda's garden. Alyssa, whom he knew almost nothing about.

She had tried her best to hide the envelopes spilling across the table and he'd only glimpsed them. But it had been enough to see they weren't addressed to Alyssa Jones – at least, not the letter that had been most visible. That had been sent to someone with the initials 'A.S.'. Alyssa had stepped in front of it before he'd had a chance to read the surname but it had definitely begun with an S, which was confusing. Might that be her maiden name? he wondered.

One item she hadn't been quick enough to hide was the handwritten note lying next to the envelopes, which had simply said: *Missing you, Baby – Ben x*

Was Ben her husband? And if Alyssa was married to a man who was missing her, why was she holed up in a caravan in the middle of nowhere, peddling myths to gullible tourists?

It was a mystery, and one that Jack was curious to solve. But he deliberately squashed down any thoughts about it. His life was complicated enough with adding Alyssa's secrets to the mix. They were hers to keep.

He stared out across the sea. It was beautiful today – the water shining as waves were caught in beams of sunlight. Alyssa would insist that it resembled quicksilver, he thought, before shaking his head. It didn't matter what Alyssa, with her own peculiar slant on life, would say. And he needed to get over himself and get back to his father, who needed him.

Jack started walking back down the path, picturing vials of quicksilver – liquid mercury, atomic number eighty in the periodic table, that moved as if it were alive.

TWENTY-ONE

MAGDA

Magda didn't normally dread seeing Stan. Far from it – she often went out of her way to call into the shop for a tin of beans or a packet of sugar. Her food cupboard was heaving with beans and sugar, but any opportunity to spend time with Stan was grabbed and relished.

But now things were different. Now she knew Stan's time on this earth was more limited than either of them had expected, and it was breaking her heart.

Not that she could show it. Not when Stan was dealing with so much and Jack, bless him, was doing his best to cope. They needed her to be capable and strong, even when she felt as if she couldn't go on.

'This isn't about you,' Magda muttered to herself, pushing open the shop door and standing aside to let a couple of teenagers out. 'So get over yourself and act normally.'

'Magda! You're out early this morning.'

Stan smiled and waved from across the store. He was sitting at the till, serving Florence with a large cabbage and a box of washing powder. Most people used laundry liquid these days but Stan, ever thoughtful, kept powder in for Heaven's Cove's older residents who were set in their ways.

'What brings you into the store?' he asked, after bidding Florence goodbye. 'Run out of beans again? I've never known someone get through so many.'

'No, actually, I don't need anything. I was passing and thought I'd call in to see how you are.'

'Checking up on me, are you?' A cloud flitted across Stan's face, then he smiled. 'There's no need to make a fuss about what I told you the other day, Mags. I'm feeling all right at the moment and might be for a while. There's no point anticipating trouble before it gets here, is there.'

'As Penny would say.'

'As Penny often did say.'

Magda smiled, remembering how Penny always knew which words to use when life got tricky, which words would bring comfort to the distressed. She swallowed, keenly feeling the absence of her good friend.

'Are you after a cuppa?' asked Stan, leaning forward to push the till drawer shut.

A muscle was moving beneath the skin of his upper arm, and Magda watched in horrified fascination as his arm began to ripple.

'Muscle twitches,' said Stan curtly, pulling down the sleeve of his jumper. 'One of the many symptoms I'm likely to encounter. Though I dare say you've googled it already.'

Magda shook her head. She'd deliberately stayed away from the internet for fear of coming across statistics about Stan's illness that she'd rather not know.

He tutted. 'Jack's been doing nothing *but* googling, of course, and coming up with various treatment options. He wants to know all the whys and wherefores, but that's always the way with him.'

'I'm glad you've told him.'

'I had no choice seeing as you bullied me into it, though it's best he knows.' He swallowed hard. 'You *will* look out for him, won't you, Mags? When I'm not here to drive him mad myself?'

'Uh-huh.' Magda pulled her lips tight to stop them from wobbling. 'I promise to drive him mad on your behalf.'

'You're a good friend, Mags. Penny would be so grateful.'

'Mum would be so grateful for what?' asked Jack, at the top of the cellar stairs, his arms straining beneath boxes of tinned soup.

Stan shot her a warning look before she replied. 'Grateful she didn't have to read the latest misery memoir suggested by the village book club. She always preferred a good psychological thriller.'

'She certainly did,' said Jack, looking between the two of them.

He wasn't daft and clearly knew she was lying. But Magda realised that this was how it would be from now on: people trying to protect one another from harsh reality. Secrets and subterfuge in the name of compassion.

Penny had taken it to extremes by not telling anyone, not even Stan, how ill she was until she could hide it no longer. But at least Jack knew the truth about his father's ultimate prognosis.

It was definitely better to know, thought Magda, so you had time to prepare. Though how could anyone ever be fully prepared for losing someone they loved?

'Cheer up, Mags,' said Stan, giving her shoulder a gentle shove. 'It might never happen, you know.'

He started chatting about Rosie's wedding, and Magda managed to make five minutes of small talk before a group of tourists came in and she made her escape.

She'd only gone a few yards down the road when Jack came running up behind her.

'Auntie Mags, hold on. Are you all right?'

'Me?'

'Yes, with Dad's news. I know you're good friends. He relies on you, to be honest, and it's all so' – he closed his eyes briefly – 'grim. It doesn't seem fair, does it? First John and then Mum, and now he gets ill.'

When Jack shoved his hands into his pockets and stared at the ground, twenty years fell away and Magda saw again the serious schoolboy attempting to make sense of his world as it fell apart. He'd had so much death and tragedy to navigate in his relatively short life.

Magda held out her arms and, after a moment's hesitation, Jack walked into her embrace. She held him tightly, murmuring into his ear: 'I'm so sorry, Jack. I'm so very, very sorry.'

Both of them were in tears by the time Jack stepped back. He scraped his hands roughly across his cheeks. 'Sorry. I don't usually go around sobbing on people's shoulders.'

'You've had a rubbish time recently.' Magda rubbed her hand up and down Jack's arm. 'And my shoulder is always available if you need it.'

He nodded, twisting his mouth and sniffing. 'Thanks, I've been meaning to call round to see you, to have a chat about Dad, but the shop's been busy and I don't like to leave him for too long.'

'Of course, I understand. I've been wondering how you are, but your dad always seems to be around whenever I call in to the shop.'

'He's keeping busy, like me. I'm actually all right most of the time but every now and again it hits me that Dad's time is running out.'

'I know. But he's here now and we can make the most of that.'

Jack pulled himself tall, all traces of the schoolboy gone. 'You're right. We've got time to tell him everything we need to and to make more memories. I'll arrange to bring Archie down as often as I can. Dad'll like that.'

She agreed that Stan would and stood watching as Jack went back to the shop. He waved from the door and disappeared inside.

Magda headed for home. She needed to put the finishing touches to Rosie's wedding cake, and a large order was due to arrive for the ice-cream parlour. But she couldn't get Jack's words out of her head: *We've got time to tell him everything we need to.*

For years she'd kept her counsel and her feelings for Stan to herself. It had been hard, yet she'd done it, and had managed to live a relatively peaceful life. But almost telling Stan the truth the other day, the truth about how she felt, seemed to have re-ignited those feelings she'd pushed down for so long.

The genie was out of the bottle and she wasn't sure how to shove it back in.

TWENTY-TWO

ALYSSA

'Hi.' Alyssa poked her head round Magda's back door. 'Sorry to disturb you but I wondered if you had a little bit of sugar I could have?'

When Magda looked up from the icing she was piping onto a large cake, Alyssa noticed an unaccustomed air of weariness about her landlady this morning.

'Yes, of course. If there's one thing I'm never short of, it's sugar. It's in that cupboard over there. Help yourself.'

'Thanks,' said Alyssa. 'I know it's not great for my teeth but I can't drink coffee without it.'

Actually, Alyssa always drank her coffee black and sugar-free, but she'd been worried about Magda for days. Their chat in the Smugglers Haunt was on her mind, and her concern had ramped up after hearing about Stan's illness – an illness she wasn't supposed to know anything about.

'Have you brought something to put the sugar in?' asked Magda, wiping the back of her hand across her forehead and leaving a smear of icing there.

Alyssa shook her head, her plan to covertly check on Magda falling at the first hurdle. 'I'm afraid not. I forgot.'

'No problem. I'm sure I've got a container you can borrow.' Magda put down her icing bag and pulled a small plastic pot from a cupboard. She poured sugar into it, snapped the lid on tight and handed it over.

'Thanks so much. You're a life saver.' Alyssa glanced at the table. 'How are you getting on with Rosie's wedding cake?'

'Have a closer look if you like.'

When Alyssa stepped nearer to the cake, a rich aroma of dried fruits and alcohol tickled her nose. 'Is there a fruit cake underneath that icing? It smells very alcoholic.'

Magda smiled. 'Rosie asked for a single tier, rich fruit cake, and I've been feeding it with whisky. The main icing was done a while ago and now I'm adding the final embellishments. What do you think?'

Alyssa put her hands on her hips and studied the enormous cake in front of her. It was a real work of art, its frost-white icing topped with a cascade of carefully crafted flowers in blue and yellow.

'It's absolutely beautiful. It looks like the clifftop in front of Driftwood House as it is right now, blooming with spring flowers.'

'Perfect! That's the look I'm going for. I just hope that Rosie and Liam will like it.'

'I'm sure they'll love it. Their wedding's going to be quite an event, isn't it?'

Magda frowned. 'You haven't come over to tell me you can't help on Saturday, have you? Only I'll be stuck trying to find someone else at this late stage.'

'No, don't worry. I said I'd help you and I will. I just needed some sugar, that was all.'

'Hmm.' Magda didn't sound convinced by Alyssa's white lie. Which was ironic since Alyssa had been lying to her since arriving in Heaven's Cove. Though that was more lying by omission, rather than directly to her face.

Alyssa sighed. 'OK, I'm rumbled. I don't really need sugar. The reason I came over is to see how you are.'

Magda picked up her icing bag and crafted another delicate petal. 'That's sweet of you,' she said, not looking up from the cake. 'But I'm absolutely fine and I'm sorry that I worried you. Ignore what I said in the pub the other day. I'd had a bit to drink, which isn't like me at all.' Her tone was light but a dark flush had begun to stain her cheeks.

'My lips are sealed, obviously. If you're sure you're OK.'

Magda's hand was shaking and she cursed as too much icing squirted out. She put the bag down on the table and breathed out deeply.

'Only...' Alyssa stopped, unsure if she should say more. It wasn't her business, and yet she felt close to Magda and concerned that she was facing a new bombshell on her own.

'Only what?'

'Only you must be upset about Stan's diagnosis. I'm so sorry about it.'

Magda's jaw dropped. 'How do you know about that?'

'Jack told me.'

'Did he? I'm surprised he confided in you. Jack's always been a reserved and private person.' Magda gave her a sideways look. 'He must think highly of you to tell you something so personal.'

'I doubt it. I came across him when he was upset. He'd just found out from his dad – he needed to talk and I was there.' Alyssa shrugged. 'He told me in confidence, and I won't tell a soul, but I knew that you'd heard the news too, and I was concerned about you.'

'You appear to be collecting people's secrets,' said Magda, an edge to her voice.

Alyssa winced, realising she'd misjudged the situation. Magda was a private person, like Jack, and didn't appreciate people sticking their noses in. 'Sorry. I shouldn't have said anything. I was worried about you, that's all. But I won't mention it again, and I'll leave you to finish Rosie's cake.'

Magda's face softened and she waved a hand at Alyssa, splattering bits of icing across the floor. 'Don't rush off. It was kind of you to think of me. I-I have been rather blindsided by Stan's latest health update.'

When she swallowed, as if she didn't have the strength to say any more, Alyssa recognised the expression in her eyes. She'd seen it many times before on the faces of mothers, fathers, partners trying to assimilate bad news about someone they loved. Alyssa had sat with them as they cried and railed against the world, against God, against fate, what or whoever they held responsible as their lives careered out of control.

'It's really tough, Magda, and if I can help in any way, I will. I have some experience of Stan's condition.'

Why had she said that? Alyssa cursed herself quietly when curiosity flared in Magda's eyes.

'What sort of experience do you have?'

'I was in a caring role, before coming here,' said Alyssa, hoping that would be enough for Magda, because it meant she wasn't giving away too much about her past life. There was a lot about her on the internet if people had enough information to find her.

Magda stared at her, as if trying to size her up. Then she nodded. 'Thank you for checking up on me, Alyssa. I am upset about Stan. Of course I am, but he, Jack and I will deal with it.' She shrugged. 'There's no other choice, is there?'

Alyssa agreed there wasn't and placed the pot of sugar on the table. 'Thanks for this but, as you so expertly deduced, I don't really need it.' She paused, wanting to ask Magda one more question but quite sure she shouldn't.

Magda sighed. 'Spit it out, Alyssa! I know what you want to ask.'

Was she so transparent? Alyssa cleared her throat. 'I wondered if you'd told Stan how you feel about him?'

Magda gazed past Alyssa, through the window towards the caravan and the cliffs beyond. 'No, I've decided not to tell him in the circumstances, so I'd be grateful if you could definitely keep what I said to yourself.'

'Of course I will. I promise.'

Magda nodded, seemingly satisfied, and turned back to the wedding cake.

It was such a shame, thought Alyssa, as Magda created another delicate petal from lemon-yellow icing. A terrible shame that Magda, a woman with a huge heart, would have to carry her secret forever, always wondering what might have been between her and Stan. But perhaps she was right, and it was for the best in the circumstances.

Alyssa stood for a few moments more, watching Magda finish a cake for a couple whose love story had a happy ending. Then she let herself out of the back door and hurried across the garden to her caravan.

TWENTY-THREE

JACK

It was awful, Jack decided, glancing round the marquee. Absolutely mind-numbingly awful.

Not the marquee, of course, which was resplendent with flowers, tables topped with white cloths, and silver bunting. And not the wedding, which had gone off without a hitch. Rosie and Liam had pledged their undying love within the historic walls of St Augustine's Church and were now cutting the impressive wedding cake made by Magda. Rosie looked beautiful in a flowing white dress with a circle of entwined spring flowers in her hair. And though Liam seemed slightly uncomfortable in his smart suit, he was beaming beside her.

That was all wonderful, and Jack wished the two of them many happy years of marriage.

What *was* awful was that he was sitting here, making inconsequential talk with the man who was now sleeping with the woman who was still technically his wife. And, to make matters worse, Jack couldn't even hate him.

He'd tried. Really hard. But *Omen*-y Damian seemed pretty decent, all things considered. He'd shaken Jack's hand and congratulated him on being such a 'brilliant dad' to Archie.

He'd asked about Jack's job and feigned interest in the data they were working on. And he hadn't once put his arm around Miri.

Miri, on the other hand, had spent the last three hours grabbing at the man who had replaced him: pushing her hand into his, slipping her arm around his waist, kissing him on the lips. It was almost as if she was goading Jack. As if she was trying to prove something that was already patently obvious.

You weren't good enough for me, so I've moved on.

Miri's behaviour had reminded Jack of the unkind streak she'd occasionally displayed during their marriage. While Miri could be loving and generous and fun – and she was a great mum to Archie – she could come across as unfeeling. He remembered when she hadn't cared a jot that he'd lost funding for a precious research project. Or the times she'd commented that Archie's pale colouring and looks were so different from his own.

Jack was no saint, either – he knew that. But while he'd obviously failed as a husband in many ways, he didn't think he'd ever been unkind.

But then his mind flitted back to the Dartmoor tour he'd taken with Alyssa. His lack of interest and sarcastic comments might be viewed as unkind, he realised anew, and another hot flush of shame flooded through him. No wonder she thought he was a boring weirdo.

'I'm so sorry about you and Alyssa,' said Miri beside him. Jack jumped. Could she read his mind? 'About the break-up,' she added, noticing his startled expression. 'Oh, look. Rosie and Liam are cutting the cake!' She applauded the happy couple, who were lit by the afternoon sun streaming into the marquee.

'Yeah, thanks,' he managed, once the cheering and applause had died down. Trust Miri to pick such a joyful moment to finally mention Alyssa. He'd been on tenterhooks all afternoon, expecting Miri to ask about her, but she'd been too busy chatting with Damian.

Miri glanced across the marquee at Alyssa, who was putting pieces of wedding cake onto paper plates. 'You didn't actually say in your text why you'd split up.'

Jack watched Alyssa wipe cake crumbs from her fingers. 'It was nothing in particular,' he said quietly. 'We simply grew apart.'

'I'm surprised you had time to grow apart,' said Miri, raising an eyebrow. 'It's such a shame. She didn't seem your type, but she seemed nice enough.'

'She's very nice.'

'I'm sure she is, and we hope you're not too broken-hearted about it.' Miri caught Damian's eye and gave him a look that Jack recognised.

They didn't believe him. Miri had probably discussed it with Damian as they lay together in bed. *Poor Jack. How pathetic to make up a fantasy girlfriend!*

Jack watched Alyssa cutting into the beautifully iced cake. She was wearing a pretty dress, in shades of pink and purple, and her dark hair was streaked today with peacock blue. She looked like an exotic bird with fancy plumage.

Miri was still talking, however, and he pulled his attention back to her as Alyssa and Magda started distributing wedding cake to the guests. 'Sorry, what did you say?'

Miri tilted her head and pushed out her bottom lip, her face a picture of sympathy and pity. 'We're worried about you, Jacky,' she said, resting her hand on his arm. 'We're worried that you're unhappy and not properly facing up to reality.'

The 'we' stung. Miri was worried, and so was Damian. The man he'd met only three hours ago. The man who would be replacing him in the family home, where Archie lived.

'There's no need to worry about me,' said Jack, through gritted teeth.

'But I do worry, Jacky.' Miri squeezed his arm. 'You don't

seem yourself and you're even—' She stopped speaking and shook her head.

'Even what?' asked Jack, trying to smile because people were watching them. They were an odd little grouping, and Belinda's eyes had been on stalks from the moment they'd sat together at the same table.

'Well.' Miri laughed self-consciously and, letting go of his arm, grabbed hold of Damian's hand instead. *From one man to another: one discarded, the other desired.* 'I mean, making up stuff about that Alyssa woman. I don't think she knew what you were talking about at the café the other day.'

'Of course she knew,' blustered Jack, feeling sick.

Miri made her 'Aw, bless you' face that she usually saved for her elderly grandmother. 'If you say so, Jacky. I'm sorry for you. I really am. But I'm afraid you have to learn to live without me. I know it's hard but there's no other way.'

'Cake, anyone?' asked Alyssa, suddenly appearing at his shoulder. She leaned across him and placed two plates on the table. The rich fruit cake had made grease marks on the paper.

To Jack's surprise, her hand slowly brushed his as she straightened up. Miri noticed it too. Her eyes opened wide when Alyssa leaned forward again, until her dark hair was against his cheek.

'Jack, I know this isn't the time or place, but can I have a quick word?' Her voice was low and breathy.

'Um...' His eyes met hers. What the hell was she doing?

'Please,' she urged. 'It's important. *Really* important.'

Miri stared at the two of them as Jack muttered, 'Yeah, sure.' And he was aware of her watching him when he got to his feet and followed Alyssa, who made a beeline through a crowd of villagers who'd taken to the dance floor.

When they reached a shadowy corner of the marquee, she stopped and pulled him behind a table stacked high with bottles of wine and beer.

'What is it?' asked Jack, feeling punch-drunk from the whole afternoon. 'I told them that we'd split up, so you don't have to have anything to do with me.'

Alyssa grabbed hold of his hand and squeezed his fingers so hard it almost brought tears to his eyes. 'Just stop talking,' she hissed, staring up into his face. 'I'm talking to you right now about how upset I am that we're finished, OK?' She ended with a loud sniff, her bottom lip wobbling. 'I know, Jacky,' she said, moving her mouth slowly so every word was crisp and clear. 'I know what you said but I just can't accept it.'

'What the hell?' muttered Jack.

'She's watching us, so shut up and kiss me,' hissed Alyssa.

'I don't know what—'

Before he could say any more, Alyssa threw her arms around his neck and pressed her lips against his. He recoiled in shock but Alyssa held on tight. Her lips were soft and warm and, once he got over the surprise, he had to admit that the kiss was pleasant.

More than pleasant, in fact. As the kiss went on, Jack put his arms around Alyssa's waist, closed his eyes and pulled her tightly against his body. He couldn't remember the last time he and Miri had kissed like this.

Alyssa shuffled him to the side, still holding on for dear life, and when Jack opened one eye, he realised why. Alyssa had played a blinder and positioned them so they were in Miri's direct line of sight.

Miri was watching them with a strange expression on her face. She looked annoyed, even jealous, maybe? Belinda, he noticed, was also watching, so there would be consequences later. But what the hell.

He closed his eye and went back to enjoying the kiss that was, metaphorically, two fingers up to his wife and her lover.

It was Alyssa who pulled away first, her face flushed and her ponytail falling down where he'd pushed his hands into her hair. He blinked, the spell broken and embarrassment rushing in.

Alyssa dabbed the back of her hand across her lips. 'There you go. That should do the trick. You can tell them that I desperately still want to go out with you.'

'Why did you do that?' asked Jack, but Alyssa had already turned and walked away, adjusting the skirt of her dress as she went.

Jack made his way back to his seat, watched every step by Miri, whose mouth had drawn into a tight line. He held himself taller as he walked, buoyed up by his self-esteem that Alyssa had just helped to drag out of the gutter.

'What was that all about?' Miri asked when he sat down.

'Alyssa's upset about our break-up and wants me to give our relationship another chance,' said Jack, struggling to keep his face impassive when he felt like punching the air.

Miri glanced at Alyssa, who was chatting to Rosie and Liam. 'Do you think you will get back together with her?'

'Possibly,' said Jack airily. 'Probably. We'll see.'

Miri pulled a chunk of icing from her cake and shoved it into her mouth. The icing was sweet; however her expression was anything but.

Jack, catching Alyssa's eye across the marquee, gave her a slight nod and the ghost of a smile.

TWENTY-FOUR

ALYSSA

The whole of Heaven's Cove was dancing. Or it appeared that way to Alyssa, who'd come out of the marquee for a breather.

She glanced inside the tent and smiled. The bride and groom were Gangnam-Styling in the centre of the dance floor, Rosie with the train of her long white dress tucked over her arm. Dozens of villagers were gyrating around them.

Everyone was happy and full to the brim with wine and cake. Even Jack was on his feet, after being dragged onto the floor by a young woman in scarlet whom Alyssa recognised.

She'd come into the shop three times during Alyssa's last shift and had engaged Jack in conversation each time. It was plain the Lady in Red fancied the dour scientist and, watching Jack do a passable hop from foot to foot, Alyssa could understand why.

He carried a suit well, the cut accentuating his tall, long-legged frame, and his hair looked chestnut brown against his crisp white shirt. There was a hint of stubble on his chin, not that Alyssa could see the shadow from where she stood – she'd felt the slight scratch of it when they'd kissed.

She ran a finger across her lips, hardly able to believe she'd been so forward. Though the astonishment on Miri's face made her impulsive action worthwhile.

'Here you are! I thought I saw you making a run for it.' Belinda had marched out of the marquee and come to stand beside Alyssa. She was dressed in salmon-pink from head to toe and carrying a diamanté clutch bag.

Alyssa gave her a smile. 'I needed some fresh air and there's plenty of it up here.'

'An abundance, I'd say.' Belinda took a deep breath, her bag twinkling in the sunshine. 'Everyone seems to be having a good time.' She gestured at the dance floor. 'Though some people will have sore heads tomorrow, I dare say. I must admit that I've had a few. Free Cava is hard to resist. But what about you?'

'I've been working, helping Magda with the food, and haven't touched a drop.'

'I don't mean drinking. I mean are you having a good time?'

'Yes, it's a wonderful wedding and Rosie and Liam will be very happy together, don't you think?'

Belinda glanced at the dancing couple. 'Yes, I imagine they will.' Her head swivelled back to Alyssa. 'Only the reason I ask if you're having a good time is that you and Jack seemed to be getting on well. *Very* well.'

And there was the reason for Belinda's sudden appearance on the clifftop. She must have spotted the two of them in their fake clinch – which hadn't felt fake at all.

'He's a nice man,' said Alyssa, keeping her eyes firmly fixed on the spring flowers bending in the breeze.

'A very nice man.'

'Probably.' Alyssa turned to Belinda. 'Things aren't always what they seem, you know.'

'Oh, I do know. Heaven's Cove is a hotbed of secrets, believe me. Even the bride has a few of her own, I reckon. But' – Belinda drew an imaginary zip along her mouth – 'my lips are sealed these days.'

That was unlikely, thought Alyssa, but it didn't really matter. If people were gossiping about what she was doing now, at least they weren't asking questions about her past.

'Aren't you going to have a dance?' asked Belinda. 'I see that Carey Wellings, who lives in that big house on the outskirts of Heaven's Brook, has nabbed Jack, but you could always cut in. I believe they used to call it an "excuse-me".'

Alyssa shook her head. 'I'm tired after being on my feet all day so I'm very happy to sit this one out.'

Belinda tutted. 'You work too hard. You need a nice young man to look after you.'

'That's not how it works these days,' said Alyssa with a grin.

'Oh, I know.' Belinda nodded quickly. 'Female empowerment, girl power and all that. I'm all for it. It's been a long time coming. But it's still nice, don't you think, to have someone to share your life with? Anyway, I mustn't hold you up when you're in need of a rest. I'm off to have a chat with Stan. He doesn't seem himself, and I noticed that he's started using a walking stick.'

'He's tired too,' Alyssa assured her, contemplating asking Bloodhound Belinda for her opinion on whether the marked paper from the old box could be a smugglers' map. The woman had a nose for uncovering secrets, but her habit of delving into other people's business made Alyssa decide to keep her at arm's length.

'Is there anything about Stan that I need to know?' Belinda persisted.

Alyssa shook her head. 'Definitely not.'

She wasn't lying. Belinda didn't *need* to know anything. It was up to Stan to tell people his devastating news as and when he wanted.

'Hmm.' Belinda didn't look convinced. 'Anyway, enjoy the rest of your day.' Then she added pointedly: 'You and Jack.'

As she bustled back into the marquee, Alyssa stole another

glance at the dance floor. It was crammed with people having fun, including Jack and Carey Wellings, but what she needed was some peace and quiet. Some time to gather her thoughts and relax.

Alyssa walked along the cliff, until the music dimmed to a distant thud. Then, she sat down on the grass, looking out to sea. The sun was still high in the sky and the water was a beautiful banded green. It was so peaceful here, in Devon: a world away from her old life and past mistakes.

She'd made a new life in this village, and she hoped that Charity and Josiah had been able to do the same, far from Heaven's Cove. It was strange. She felt close to them up here on the clifftop, as if they still existed and might wander along at any moment. What would they make of her smugglers' map notion? she wondered. Having lived when smuggling was rife in the village, they would know if she was barking up the wrong tree.

A small plane droned overhead as Alyssa pulled her phone from her pocket and clicked on the photo that she'd studied dozens of times already. That curved line definitely could be the cove, and the cross had to be the church, where Rosie and Liam had just made their vows.

Unless it marked the spot where treasure was buried. Alyssa gently cursed her overactive imagination and dropped the phone into her lap. Buried treasure? She could imagine what Jack would say about that.

'What were you staring at?' Jack's voice made Alyssa jump. He was standing behind her. 'Sorry. I didn't mean to startle you.'

'What are you doing out here?' asked Alyssa, thrown by Jack's sudden appearance. She remembered their kiss and her cheeks began to burn with embarrassment.

'Can I sit down?' he asked, and when Alyssa nodded, he sat on the grass beside her. 'Belinda said you were out here, and I wanted to have a word.' He cleared his throat. 'I wanted to say thank you, for doing what you did.' He shuffled round to look directly at her. 'Why did you do it? Why did you—?'

'—shamelessly snog you?' interrupted Alyssa, deciding that making a joke out of the whole thing was the best way forward. 'I heard you and Miri talking, and I thought you might want her to think I was still crazy about you.'

'Rather than her thinking our relationship was a figment of my poor, deluded imagination?'

'Something like that.' She grinned.

When Jack smiled back, he looked handsome, Alyssa realised, with his hair flopping across his forehead. And he'd been a much better kisser than Alyssa had anticipated. She'd expected precise, evidence-based moves – tried and tested pressure on lips, tongue here, hands there. Cool, calm precision. Whereas, in reality, once Jack had got over his surprise and relaxed into the whole deception, the kiss had been hot. Sexy, even.

Alyssa breathed out slowly as she picked a daisy and ran the petals through her fingers. 'From what I overheard, I got the impression that she didn't believe we were in a relationship.'

'Which we're not.'

'Which we're definitely not, but I figured Miri didn't need to know that.'

'But why?'

'Because... I don't know.' Alyssa threw the daisy into the wind. 'Because she was sitting there with her new boyfriend and being a bit...'

'A bit what?'

Should she say it? After all, Miri *was* still legally Jack's wife.

'What?' he asked again.

Alyssa went for it. 'She was being a bit of a cow. A bit unkind.'

'Well.' Jack swallowed. 'Whatever your reasons, it was kind of *you*. Thanks.'

Alyssa leaned sideways and bumped her shoulder against his. 'You're welcome. Did it work?'

'I think so. She's being very frosty with me.'

'Maybe she's not so keen on *Omen*-y Damian as she thinks she is.'

'Maybe.' He looked out to sea, his jaw tightening.

'However...?' There was something Jack wasn't saying.

He took a deep breath and laced his fingers together. 'What feelings she has or doesn't have for Damian probably don't come into it. Miri likes to be the woman everyone wants.'

'An alpha female?'

'That's not a term I've come across but, I suppose, yes.' He wiped a hand across his forehead. 'But I shouldn't talk about her behind her back with strangers.'

'Hardly a stranger! I just snogged you in front of half of Heaven's Cove.'

Jack threw back his head and laughed at that. 'This is very true. You do realise that Belinda saw us and is unlikely to let it drop?'

'Yep, she's already mentioned it to me.'

'Oh, good grief. We'll be engaged by next weekend.'

Alyssa laughed too, realising how nice it felt to be sitting here with Jack. Though kissing him, she now knew, had been a mistake. Because she'd quite like to do it again.

Helping Jack out had seemed like a good idea at the time – Miri's patronising sympathy towards him had been hard to stomach, and she'd felt sorry that he was sitting with the man who'd stolen the woman he patently still wanted.

It was only a kiss, she'd told herself when she pulled him into the clinch. She'd close her eyes and get it over with. But it hadn't turned out that way.

'What do you think of the view?' Alyssa asked, trying to distract herself. Sitting so close to Jack while thinking about kissing him was making her feel tense.

He squinted at the horizon. 'It's inspiring.'

When she gave him a sideways glance, he shrugged. 'Now what?'

'Inspiring? Is that all? Aren't you going to tell me what happens to all the water when the tide goes out, or why the sky's blue?'

He shook his head. 'Nope. I'm appreciating the view for what it is. It makes me feel... I don't know...'

Alyssa waited and, after a moment, he said: 'Small.'

She nodded. 'Me, too. The vastness of the universe puts our worries into perspective, don't you think?'

When Jack didn't reply, they sat in silence for a while, watching the sea rise and fall. A grey seal bobbed in the water before pulling itself onto a rock, its sleek body glistening in the sunlight.

'Actually,' said Alyssa, 'what *does* happen to all the water when the tide goes out? Does the sea get much deeper in the middle?'

Jack smiled. 'I can tell you if you really want to know. Oops!' He grabbed hold of Alyssa's mobile as she shifted and it tumbled from her lap.

The photo of the curious map was still on the screen, and he glanced at it before handing the phone back. 'What's that you were studying so intently before I interrupted you?'

Alyssa hesitated but it was too late. Jack had already seen it. 'It's a photo I took of something that was found in an old wooden box at Driftwood House, hidden in a fireplace. Rosie showed it to me.'

'Can I see?'

Alyssa reluctantly handed the phone back to Jack, who squinted at the screen. 'What is it?'

'A piece of paper. Old paper.'

'I can see that, but what are the marks on it?'

'I'm not sure, though...' She petered off, wanting to discuss her theory with someone, but not necessarily *this* someone.

'Though what?'

Alyssa shrugged. 'Don't mock me, but I think it could be an old map.'

'What sort of map?' he asked, staring at the photo and wrinkling his nose. He moved his thumb and finger across the screen to enlarge the picture. 'Is that cross supposed to depict a church in the middle?' He peered more closely at the pen marks. 'Hey, is this Heaven's Cove?'

'I think so.' Alyssa took a deep breath. In for a penny... 'I also reckon those lines there – the thicker lines that cut across the roads and merge into one near the cove – could be the route of old smuggling tunnels beneath the village.'

'Smuggling tunnels?'

She sighed, aware that she was probably inventing things. Just as she'd invented her new life in Heaven's Cove. There was no evidence or proof that the lines depicted smugglers' tunnels – and evidence and proof were what Jack cared about.

'It doesn't matter,' she said quietly.

But Jack wasn't going to let it lie. 'What, with treasure and pirates?' he scoffed.

'Probably no treasure and definitely no pirates. But—' She paused, but couldn't stop the words tumbling out. 'There *were* smugglers in the village, and, I've been thinking, what if this map was given to Charity by Josiah? It was found where Charity once lived. What if Josiah was a smuggler himself and that's why he had to leave without a word, when the customs men came?'

'So was Charity a smuggler too, in this reframing of history?'

Alyssa decided to ignore the jibe. 'No, she was the woman he loved.'

'So not the woman he brutally murdered, then?'

'Why are you so determined that your ancestor was a murderer?'

'Why are you so determined that he wasn't?' Jack pushed a hand through his hair and sighed. 'I hate to harp on about it, Alyssa, but life isn't always a fairy tale with happy endings.'

'Yes, I know that very well.' Alyssa's teeth were so gritted, she could hardly get the words out. 'My life hasn't been a bed of roses, I can assure you.'

They glared at each other until the sound of a distant cheer from the marquee broke the tension.

'Whatever,' muttered Alyssa, taking her phone back from him and shoving it into her pocket.

She felt bizarrely disappointed by Jack's reaction to the map, although she should have known he'd be sceptical. One kiss hadn't changed his entire personality, or his view of her.

She got to her feet and brushed grass from her backside, but Jack remained seated.

'What happened to them really matters to you, doesn't it. Why?' he asked.

Alyssa gazed at the seal, still stretched out on the rock like a sunbather without a care in the world. 'I think everyone deserves a chance of redemption, and the truth can provide that.'

She waited for Jack's derisive comments but, after thinking for a moment, all he said was, 'Maybe you're right and Josiah and Charity did run away together. They were ill-fated lovers.'

'Maybe.'

'Or perhaps they were dragged into the depths of the ocean by a sea dragon.'

Alyssa sighed but she realised that Jack was gently ribbing her, rather than mocking, when he looked up. His dark grey eyes were warm this time. He held out his hand. 'Let me have a proper look at this so-called map.'

Alyssa sat down again and handed over her phone. He

studied the photo again, a furrow appearing between his eyebrows.

'What do you reckon?' asked Alyssa after a while.

'It looks like it was drawn by Archie, when he was three.'

'Fair enough, but some of the lines have faded over the years.'

'Mmm.' Jack peered at it more closely. 'But I guess that squiggly outline there could be the cove, and the cross is the church, and perhaps that smudgy box there is supposed to be the castle? I'm just making stuff up now.'

Alyssa leaned closer. 'I thought it might be the castle, too. And those lines that converge at the cove could be the smuggling tunnels I mentioned.' She sat back and blew a strand of hair from her face. 'But even if this is a smugglers' map, I don't suppose there's anything left of the tunnels. All traces will have disappeared over the centuries.'

'Oh.' Jack, who'd been scrolling down the photo, suddenly sat up straight. 'What's this circle at the bottom, with a cross in it? I hadn't spotted that.'

'I have no idea. It's not a part of the map.'

'It looks familiar.'

'Familiar in what way?' asked Alyssa. She glanced around as she heard her name being carried in the wind. Magda was waving at her in the distance, from the marquee. 'Ah, I have to go because I'm needed to help again.' She got to her feet and waved back. 'But what do you mean, the circle with a cross in it looks familiar?'

'I don't know. I'm probably wrong,' said Jack. 'But meet me tomorrow morning at the shop.'

'Why?' Alyssa turned as her name was called again and shouted to Magda: 'Won't be a sec! I'm just coming!'

'It might be nothing but just meet me there, will you?' said Jack, handing back her phone.

Magda was still waving, so Alyssa nodded. 'All right. Ten o'clock?'

'Perfect.'

Alyssa hurried across the grass, wondering why Jack was being maddeningly mysterious all of a sudden. At least he seemed to agree that the marks on the paper could be a map of Heaven's Cove. Even if her theory about smugglers' tunnels had gone down like a lead balloon.

'So sorry to call you over,' said Magda as Alyssa got closer. People were spilling from the marquee behind her, including Miri and Damian. 'We need to get some tables cleared and moved to make more room on the dance floor.'

'Of course. I'll come and give you a hand.' She glanced at Miri, who'd just sidled up to her.

'There you are,' said Miri, her eyes sliding from Alyssa to Jack, who was still sitting on the cliff edge, with his back to them. 'We're heading off because I have a headache, and I was looking for Jack, to say goodbye.'

'He's over there, getting some fresh air.'

'Have you two made up?' asked Miri, linking her arm through Damian's.

Alyssa paused, tired of lying. 'I think that Jack and I are getting on better than we ever have,' she said carefully.

'Are you seeing him again?'

Mind your own business. Alyssa smiled sweetly. 'Yes, I am, tomorrow morning.'

'I'm delighted to hear it,' declared Miri, though her tight smile told a different story. 'Well, it was lovely to see you again.'

'You, too.'

Did Miri still love Jack or was she merely piqued not to be the centre of his attention? wondered Alyssa, heading back into the marquee. If she did still have feelings for him, perhaps witnessing the fake kiss with Jack that afternoon would give her the push she needed to give their marriage another go.

That was what Jack seemed to want and Alyssa would obviously be happy for him. She'd be delighted, in fact.

At least, that's what she told herself, as she worked with Magda to clear tables and move them away from the dance floor.

But if that was the case, why did the prospect of Jack and Miri reuniting make her feel so unsettled?

TWENTY-FIVE
MAGDA

Rosie and Liam's wedding party was still going strong. Dirty plates and glasses had been stacked into crates, with the help of Alyssa and a couple of girls from the ice-cream parlour. But there was no end in sight to the celebrations. The dance floor was heaving, the music was loud, and it seemed that most of Heaven's Cove were getting merry – Stan would sell out of paracetamol in the morning.

Magda waved at Belinda, who'd obviously had a few because she was making some very peculiar dance moves opposite her husband, Jim.

Jim and Belinda had been married for years, just like Stan and Penny. How Magda envied them.

She wouldn't want to be married to Jim, nice as he was, and living on her own was usually tolerable and often pleasant. But in her heart of hearts, she missed having a close relationship with someone who loved her – someone who knew everything about her but loved her all the same.

Magda glanced at Stan, who was sitting in a corner with Jack. No one looking at him would guess how poorly he was. But she knew, and she couldn't get it out of her head.

The years had taken their toll on Stan. But Magda, staring at him across the wedding marquee, remembered the man he was four decades earlier. She'd loved him then, and she loved him still.

How could she not tell him how she felt? Her resolve to stay quiet was disappearing as swiftly as the morning's sea mist.

While she was watching, Stan got up and walked unsteadily out of the marquee onto the clifftop. Now was the perfect time to talk to him. But was she brave enough?

Alyssa's words from the pub rang in her ears: *I let my fear win... and I've regretted it ever since.*

Time was running out for Stan – she'd thought of little else since his devastating news – and who knew what health calamity might befall her? Time was slipping through her fingers and the thought of going to her grave, not knowing if a brighter future had been there for the taking all along, was more than she could bear. And yet the prospect of telling Stan was terrifying because it risked their friendship that was so precious to her.

Magda took a sip of her drink, the rhythmic thump of loud music coursing through her. She could stay in here and keep her secret forever. Or she could be brave and say her piece.

The moment of decision had arrived. Magda pictured herself standing at a crossroads – one road offering the status quo and the other leading to change – because however Stan reacted to her profession of love, it would alter their relationship. But would it be a change for the better, or would it be disastrous?

'Enough of the ridiculous navel-gazing,' muttered Magda, necking the last of her Cava for Dutch courage and following Stan out of the marquee. She had to know, whatever the cost.

The man she loved was standing with his back to Driftwood House, staring out over the sea. Today the water was a beautiful shade of aquamarine, and the glistening waves were crested with white horses.

It was just the sort of cheerful spring day that Penny had loved.

Magda swallowed, her stomach churning, and walked over to stand beside Stan.

'It's beautiful, isn't it?' she said as brightly as she could. 'However many times I see this view, it still takes my breath away.'

Stan glanced around, leaning heavily on his walking stick. 'Magda! Hello.'

He didn't look overjoyed to see her, and Magda's resolve began to slip. But the sounds of happy couples in the marquee behind her spurred her on.

Maybe she could have a happy ending too. It might be brief. But it would be hers to remember until her last breath.

'You look done in, Mags,' said Stan, turning away from the view. 'You and Alyssa have been working non-stop all afternoon. You should take a break.'

'I'm not too bad, thanks to Alyssa, who's a marvel. She's been on her feet all day and has been a huge help. But how are *you* doing? It's been a long afternoon for you.'

In your condition hung unspoken in the air between them.

'There's no need to worry about me.' Stan went back to looking at the ocean. 'Your cake was magnificent, by the way. I've heard lots of compliments about it.'

'Rosie and Liam seemed happy with it.'

'I'm not surprised. It looked wonderful and it was delicious too. You've always been a cracking baker.'

'I learned at my mother's knee.'

'Back in the days when everything was made from scratch.'

Small talk. That's all she and Stan ever managed, even when his days were numbered. Magda took a deep breath. 'There's something I'd like to talk to you about.'

'OK.' He looked round and smiled. 'I'm all yours.'

If only that were the case. Magda swallowed, her unspoken words choking her. It was now or never – she couldn't bear to think of Stan dying with her words never said. She couldn't bear to regret her lack of courage on her own deathbed.

'Well?' asked Stan, warmth in his tired eyes. 'Spit it out, Mags. I'll need to go and sit down in a minute.'

'Right.' Magda glanced around to make sure she wouldn't be overheard. 'I have something to say. About us. Y-you know how much I cared about Penny.'

'Of course I do. You were great friends – best friends – and I know how much you miss her.'

'I do. But it's not just Penny I care... cared about. I care about you too.'

Stan smiled. 'I know that. You've been a good friend over the years, and I care about you as well. Especially when you bring me ice cream.'

He laughed and gave Magda a wink, but she remained stony-faced. She'd started now and had to finish what she'd wanted to say for so long. Always a careful woman, an unfamiliar recklessness was bubbling up inside her.

'No.' She shook her head. 'What I mean is, I *care* about you, Stan. *Really* care about you. In fact, I think... no, I know—' She swallowed again, hearing a buzzing in her ears. 'I know that I love you. I love you, Stan, I do. I love you. I'm *in* love with you.'

For goodness' sake! Not only had she said it, she'd said it several times. The unspoken words that had been eating her up for decades were definitely out in the open, and Stan now knew exactly how she felt.

She stared at him, blinking in the bright sunlight, and he stared back.

'I said—' she began, desperate to bridge the silence. But he interrupted her.

'I know what you said.' He frowned. 'Is this a joke?'

'Of course it's not a joke.' Magda was finding it hard to breathe. 'Why would I joke about something like that? It's the truth.'

'How *can* it be the truth? You were Penny's best friend.'

Magda clasped her hands together to stop them trembling – although there was nothing she could do to stop the tremble in her voice. 'I loved Penny. I still love Penny and I never said anything while she was here. I could never have done that. But I *am* in love with you, Stan, and I have been for years. I had to tell you.'

Did she have to tell him? Magda felt the fear that she'd suppressed, so that she could speak the truth, slide slowly up her spine. But it was too late now.

Stan opened and closed his mouth. He was still staring at her.

'I had to tell you because I didn't want to let my fear win,' said Magda. Which was ironic because her fear was winning right now. It was doing a victory lap around her head.

Stan shook his head, confusion etched across his face, but still he said nothing. Magda had laid her heart on the line, and he had nothing to say in return. A hot wave of humiliation shot through her, making her feel as if she were on fire. 'It doesn't matter,' she blurted out, turning so he wouldn't see the tears blurring her vision.

'I don't know what you want me to say,' spluttered Stan, and Magda's humiliation was complete. What did he *think* she wanted him to say?

'I mean, what would Penny think about all of this?' Stan asked.

What would Penny think indeed? Her best friend declaring undying love to her husband, when she was hardly cold in her grave. What kind of 'friend' had Magda become?

'Magda, look at me,' said Stan.

When she turned round, she saw confusion still on his face. And then she spotted it in his eyes: pity.

And that was when she knew for sure. She knew the truth.

'It doesn't matter,' Magda managed, her throat so tight she could hardly get the words out. 'Please forget I said anything. It's all ridiculous. I never could hold my drink and I've had far too much this afternoon. I didn't mean to be disrespectful to Penny's memory.'

Then she turned and started walking. She walked past the marquee and kept on going down the cliff path, towards home.

The sun was sinking lower, turning the sky from blue to gold, but Magda didn't stop. She kept on walking until she reached her cottage and let herself in. Then, she marched up the stairs, crawled into bed, still fully clothed, and lay on her back, staring at the ceiling.

'I'll be fine,' she murmured to herself. 'At least I told him, and I knew what he would say. Inside, I knew. It's done and I'm fine. I'm always fine.'

But today, right now, she wasn't fine at all. Magda buried her head in the pillow and sobbed – for her aching heart and the best friend she missed so much, and the man she loved who didn't love her.

TWENTY-SIX

ALYSSA

It had been a wonderful community wedding and it was fast turning into a fabulous community clear-up.

'Thanks, Fred,' said Alyssa as the Smugglers Haunt landlord dropped a pile of paper plates into a black bin bag.

The marquee's tables were almost cleared, and left-over wedding cake was all boxed up. Alyssa had feared a late night after Magda's text had pinged onto her phone two hours earlier: *Sorry, gone home with sudden migraine. Leave clearing up for later.*

But she hadn't reckoned on guests at the wedding pitching in to help.

There was no way Alyssa was going to leave the clearing up overnight, especially as Magda might not be better come morning.

'We can give you a hand,' Claude had told her, before spreading the word that she needed help. And everyone had done their bit – even Liam and Rosie, who were about to drive off on honeymoon.

Heaven's Cove was a special place, thought Alyssa as she

swept up crumbs from the dance floor. A place with history and heart, and she was grateful she'd chosen it as her refuge.

'I've found this,' said Belinda, bustling over. She was brandishing a walking stick. 'I believe it belongs to Stan. I can drop it in on my way home.'

'Don't worry. That takes you out of your way whereas I'll be walking right by his shop, so I can give it back.'

Alyssa took the elaborately carved wooden stick, less worried about Belinda's elongated journey home than Stan's ability to withstand more of her questioning about his health.

'He went home quite early. I saw Jack driving him away a couple of hours ago.'

'He did mention that he wouldn't be staying for too long,' lied Alyssa, trying to deflect Belinda's gossip radar. 'He said he had something to sort out in the shop.'

'I dare say. Always working, that man. He's trying to assuage his grief through keeping busy, don't you think?'

Alyssa mumbled noncommittally, though Belinda had a point. Idleness rarely led to peace of mind in her experience, whereas keeping busy kept the demons at bay. She began sweeping with extra vigour.

An hour later, Alyssa reached Stan's shop. It was closed but when she banged on the door Stan appeared and ushered her inside.

'Sorry to disturb you, Stan. How are you doing?'

'All right. The music was a bit loud so Jack and I came away early.'

Stan didn't look all right. His face was ashen-grey and his shoulders were drooped as if every step was an effort.

'You left this in the marquee,' said Alyssa, handing over his walking stick. 'Where's Jack?'

'Doing one of those video calls with Archie. The phone

signal's a bit hit and miss in here, so he's gone over to the village green where it's better.'

'In that case, let me get you settled upstairs and I can make you a cup of tea.'

'There's no need,' mumbled Stan, but he put up little resistance when Alyssa took his arm and helped him up the stairs.

She made him a hot drink while he settled into his chair in the comfy sitting room and sat staring out of the window, towards the sea. 'Kind of you,' he murmured when she set the steaming cup in front of him, not moving his gaze away from the view.

'You look tired, Stan. Is there anything else I can get you?' asked Alyssa, treading carefully because he was probably still unaware that she knew of his diagnosis.

'It's been a different kind of day,' he said quietly, turning to look at her. 'And you've been very kind to bring my walking stick back and make me a drink when you've had such a busy day yourself.'

'It's been even busier for Magda. Did you know she's gone home with a bad migraine?'

'I've hardly seen Magda all day,' said Stan, picking up his cup and saucer, the tremor in his hands making the china rattle. 'Has Jack finished his call yet?'

Alyssa walked to the window on the other side of the room – this window faced the church, and the village green where a woman in a yellow sweatshirt was walking her dog. Near to her was Jack, talking animatedly at his phone. 'It looks as if he's still chatting to Archie.'

'He misses that boy, and so do I. Archie was the apple of Penny's eye, you know. She'd be heartbroken that Jack and Miri are getting divorced.' Stan paused and took a sip of his tea. 'What do you make of Miri? I saw you this afternoon.'

Talking to Miri or kissing his son? When Alyssa hesitated, Stan added: 'You were talking to her outside the tent.'

'Well.' Alyssa chose her words carefully. 'She seems like an interesting woman.'

'Ha, you don't like her either.' The ghost of a smile played across Stan's lips. 'She brought her new man to the reception, which was very bad form in my view, and she hardly had two words for me.'

'Jack still seems very fond of her.'

'He's loved her for years, and she's not a bad woman. She's a good mother to Archie and she was a decent enough daughter-in-law, but now she wants to break up and Jack is finding it hard to accept. You can't always help who you love, I suppose.'

When he went back to staring out of the window, Alyssa decided it was time to leave Stan in peace. Jack was still chatting to Archie but would be back soon. She glanced at him again. He was pacing as he talked and appeared to be circling the Mourning Stone that marked Charity and Josiah's mysterious disappearance.

'I have a strange question to ask,' said Alyssa, picturing the old wooden box that had been hidden away at Driftwood House for years. 'It's a real long shot, but is there any way you might know if Josiah had red hair?'

Stan wrinkled his nose, looking taken aback. 'My murderous ancestor Josiah?'

Alyssa nodded. 'I wondered if any family stories you were told about his disappearance included any information about what he looked like?'

'I don't think so. But why does it matter? Have you found out something about him?'

'Maybe.' Alyssa shook her head. 'Probably not, actually.' Stan looked far too done in to cope with her suppositions and imaginings. 'Just ignore me. I think I'm a little obsessed with Charity and Josiah, which can't be good.' She laughed, but Stan didn't react. He'd closed his eyes and his mouth was falling open as he headed for sleep. The poor man was obviously exhausted.

Alyssa tiptoed to the door and was about to leave when Stan suddenly murmured, 'John had red hair.'

'John, your son?'

'And my great-grandfather's beard was the colour of straw-berries.'

Stan's breathing deepened as he slipped into slumber.

Lots of people had red hair, Alyssa told herself as she made her way back to her caravan, so the fact that red hair ran in Josiah's family didn't mean the lock found in the box at Driftwood House was his – the evidence was circumstantial, at best. Jack would immediately pooh-pooh it, and she wouldn't blame him.

But what if her suppositions and imaginings were right and the lock of red hair did belong to Josiah? And what if it had been lovingly hidden away by Charity? That might be a step towards the young man's redemption. It might indicate that he and Charity were in love, and had perhaps run away together.

Alyssa sighed. She'd first become interested in Josiah and Charity's story as part of her myths and legends tour. Her interest had snowballed alongside her research for a smuggling tour and now... now, as she'd confessed to Stan, she probably was obsessed with the young couple.

Why did the redemption of a man long gone matter so much to her? Alyssa wondered. Was she hoping for redemption herself? If so, it would take more than a happy ending for two people almost three centuries ago to achieve that present-day feat.

TWENTY-SEVEN

MAGDA

Magda opened the dishwasher and closed it again. It was jam-packed but she couldn't face unloading it. She couldn't face anything this morning. Especially not Stan. She couldn't face Stan again, not ever.

Yesterday, when she had stood at that crossroads, she had gone the wrong way and now everything was ruined beyond repair.

Magda sank onto a kitchen chair, set her elbows on the table and put her head in her hands. The words she'd said to Stan on the clifftop were running through her head in a loop.

They'd begun looping first thing that morning, when she opened bleary eyes as dawn light crept across her bedroom carpet. Seagulls were calling outside, and a salty breeze was ruffling the curtains. It was going to be another beautiful day in Heaven's Cove. But her head was filled to bursting with what she'd said to Stan: *I know that I love you. I love you, Stan, I do. I love you. I'm in love with you.*

Four declarations of love! Magda had never been one to do things by halves. Things were either done to excess or not done at all.

If only she'd plumped for the 'not done at all' option yesterday and had never opened her mouth. *I love you* were words she'd avoided saying for decades. Words that should never have been said out loud.

Dragging herself to her feet, Magda made a coffee so strong it would give her palpitations. Then she stood leaning against the sink, lost in thought.

Stan wasn't madly in love with her. She'd never been deluded enough to think he might be, but there had been a sliver of hope that she might mean enough to him. She didn't want to take Penny's place. She knew she could never measure up to the love of Stan's life. But she'd hoped she might be an acceptable second best.

Magda swallowed a sob and set her shoulders back. All hope was now extinguished. She would never forget the look in Stan's eyes which had delivered the devastating news: he didn't love her; he pitied her. Which somehow felt worse than his indifference.

'Hey, Magda.' Alyssa poked her head around the back door. 'I saw you were up. Is it all right if I come in?'

Heavy with misery, Magda said nothing but Alyssa came in anyway, shutting the door behind her. She'd walked across the garden with wellies on and a large knitted cardigan slung over her pyjamas.

Magda was usually pleased to see her. Alyssa brought life and laughter into her quiet cottage. But today, when she looked at the young woman who lived at the bottom of her garden, she felt stirrings of anger.

It was speaking to Alyssa, after all, which had prompted her to tell Stan about her secret devotion. Who did Alyssa think she was, giving advice when she kept her own secrets so close to her chest?

'Is your head OK now?' Alyssa asked, wrapping the cardi tightly around her. 'I'm sorry you had a migraine. That must have been a nightmare with the loud music and everyone whooping and cheering.'

'My head's fine today,' said Magda stiffly.

'That's good to hear. All of the crockery and glasses from the reception are back in their crates. Claude brought some back in his van yesterday, but there are still a few things left in the marquee. I can help you collect them later, if you like, and Claude's offered to pitch in again, once his van's unloaded.'

'Thank you but I'm sure I can manage.'

It might take half a dozen trips on her own but it would keep her busy, and she didn't want Alyssa's company.

'It's no bother.' Alyssa frowned. 'You look tired after such a busy day yesterday.'

'I am very tired. That's probably what brought on the migraine.' Magda took a scalding gulp of coffee. 'Anyway, I'd rather be on my own, if you don't mind.'

When surprise registered on Alyssa's face, Magda felt a flash of shame over her rudeness.

'Of course, I'll leave you to it.' Alyssa walked to the back door but turned, her fingers gripping the handle. 'Look, I don't mean to intrude and I'll leave you in peace, but are you sure you're all right now? You don't seem yourself today.'

Alyssa had hit the nail on the head, Magda realised. She felt like a different woman from the one who'd followed Stan out of the marquee onto the clifftop. That woman had been hopeful about the future, whereas this one didn't dare look ahead.

'I told Stan,' she said dully, part of her wanting Alyssa to understand the consequences of what she'd encouraged her to do.

'Oh.' Alyssa's eyes opened wide. 'That was brave of you. I didn't realise you'd changed your mind about telling him. How did it go?'

Magda clutched her coffee cup tightly in two hands, even though it was burning her palms. 'He doesn't feel the same way and he seemed appalled that I'd say such a thing. He felt it was a slap in the face for Penny, the dead wife he still adores.'

Alyssa stepped forward and stretched out her arms, as if she could dispense a hug from across the room. 'I'm so sorry.'

'Are you?' The anger building inside Magda was winning. It was making her feel hot and trapped in this small kitchen. In this tiny village.

'Yes, of course I am. I didn't think—'

'No, you didn't,' said Magda, slamming the coffee cup onto the drainer. Drops of scalding liquid burned her skin. 'You didn't think before you urged me to tell Stan exactly how I felt.'

Alyssa frowned. 'I didn't *urge* you to tell him. I was honoured that you shared with me how you felt, and I suggested you do what was best for you and Stan.'

'And then you said I should follow my gut feeling.'

'You pushed me into giving my opinion, Magda,' said Alyssa gently. 'If I remember rightly, I said it would be a shame if fear stopped you from telling Stan if that was what you really wanted to do. I thought you might feel better if you weren't keeping secrets any longer.'

'Secrets?' Magda gave a hollow laugh. 'I had one secret, Alyssa. One secret that I should have kept. But what about you?'

'What do you mean?' Alyssa had gone pale.

'What about the raft of secrets that you're keeping? Why are you living in a caravan at the bottom of my garden and getting mysterious brown envelopes through the post?' The words were spilling out of her now, as if she could rid herself of her pain by throwing it at this mysterious young woman who'd arrived out of the blue. 'Why don't you ever talk about your past life? What's so awful that you have to keep it quiet?'

'I don't—'

'Oh, it doesn't matter.' Magda sank back onto the kitchen chair, her anger vanishing as swiftly as it had arrived. In its place was a bone-numbing weariness. 'Keep your secrets, just as I should have kept mine.'

'I'm so sorry, Magda.'

Alyssa's eyes were shiny with tears but Magda hardened her battered heart.

'It's too late to be sorry, I'm afraid. The damage is done.'

'Stan cares about you. That's obvious whenever the two of you are together. And you're an amazing woman.'

'Not amazing enough,' said Magda bitterly. 'I've wasted my life in many ways, Alyssa, yearning for someone who would never choose to be mine. So let me give *you* some advice. Whatever you're running from, run faster. I wish I'd run fast and far and had never come to live in Heaven's Cove.'

'You don't mean that,' said Alyssa in a shaky voice.

'But I do,' Magda replied, her shoulders suddenly relaxing as she realised the answer to her dilemma. 'So, I'm going to move on. It's time for me to leave the village.'

Alyssa's jaw dropped. 'Surely you don't have to go? You're a huge part of Heaven's Cove and you'd be missed so much.'

Maybe she would be, but Magda's certainty that leaving was the answer to her problems was growing. She loved this village by the sea, with its soaring cliffs and the wild moors so close, and the people here had become dear to her. But she couldn't see Stan every day and pretend that nothing fundamental had changed.

She shook her head. 'I'm leaving, as soon as I can.'

'What about your businesses?'

'I can sell the parlour. I've had a couple of offers recently from people looking to buy a going concern in the village. And I might move up country to be nearer my sister. She gets lonely sometimes, like me.'

'And what about Stan?' asked Alyssa quietly. Magda winced: the thought of not seeing him every day felt sharp and raw. 'Even though it didn't go as you'd hoped with Stan, he needs you.'

'He doesn't need me, and he has enough to cope with, without an embarrassing, love-struck friend hovering in the background. He has people around him who love him and will look out for him. And I'll stay in touch with Jack, obviously, to see how his dad's doing. That's what Penny would want.'

She paused because, in truth, she had no idea what Penny would want. How sad that the one woman who might give her wise counsel after yesterday's debacle was the one woman to whom she could never speak again.

Though perhaps it was just as well that no counsel could come from beyond the grave. Magda could only imagine her best friend's disappointment and sense of betrayal. 'I'd like you to go,' she said loudly to Alyssa, feeling any self-control she still possessed beginning to slip. 'Now, please.' Magda buried her head in her hands again, despairing at the mess in which she found herself.

When she looked up again, Alyssa had gone.

TWENTY-EIGHT
JACK

Alyssa hadn't turned up. Jack glanced again at his watch. It was quarter past ten and she wasn't here, even though he was ready to humour her wild imaginings about smuggling maps and his murderous ancestor.

He poked his head out of the shop door and looked down the lane. Alyssa was punctual for her shifts in the shop but this morning, when she was calling round to see him, there was no sign of her.

Her no-show felt like being stood up, which was ridiculous because this wasn't a date. But he had been looking forward to seeing her, he realised. The two of them had little in common but maybe her positive, gung-ho attitude was starting to rub off on him.

He snorted at the thought of him ever being described as 'gung-ho' and glanced again along the street. He hoped Alyssa hadn't cried off because she was embarrassed, or even mortified, after kissing him. But mostly he hoped that she was OK.

Jack wasn't one for catastrophising, not unless there was sound evidence to back up his fears. But what if Alyssa had walked to the marquee earlier this morning, to start clearing up?

The cliff path could get crumbly close to the edge. Locals knew where the path could be treacherous, if you weren't concentrating. But Alyssa wasn't from around here and her head was often in the clouds.

When an image of Alyssa's broken body lying at the foot of the cliffs swam into his mind, Jack called out to his father: 'Do you mind if I nip out for a bit? Can you manage?'

'Of course I can. How do you think I've been managing all these years you've been in London?' was his dad's curmudgeonly reply.

Jack sighed, concerned that yesterday's wedding had been too much for his father, who'd been like a bear with a sore head all morning.

'Actually,' Stan added, 'I might go out myself for a bit. I could do with a break.'

'Then you need me to hold the fort while you're out.'

'No, I don't. I'm not sure how long I'm going to be, so I'll close the shop for a while.'

Jack frowned. His father never closed the supermarket during the day. During yesterday's wedding, he'd arranged for friends from Heaven's Brook to mind the store.

'Where are you going? I can come with you.'

'No, thank you,' Stan shot back. 'I'm still perfectly capable of going out without a minder, and where I'm going is my own business.'

'Please be careful and remember to take your walking stick.'

When his father grunted in reply, Jack sighed. His father's bad mood was another reason he'd looked forward to seeing Alyssa's wide, bright smile that seemed to light up the space around her. Maybe she could cheer up the old man, because he certainly couldn't.

He stuck his head around the front door and looked up and down the lane again, but there was still no sign of her. He'd invited her here on what was probably a wild goose chase so, in some ways, it was probably better she hadn't turned up. But he was still worried that she hadn't.

'See you later, Dad,' he called, slipping out of the shop and setting off towards Magda's cottage. He'd check Alyssa's caravan first, in case she'd slept in, and, if she wasn't there, head for Driftwood House.

She'd simply forgotten their rendezvous, he told himself, hurrying along. Though that was surprising, when she was so curious about the map and what it might mean. She seemed determined to add to her working repertoire with a new smuggling tour, so she was hardly likely to pass up on a chance to find out more.

She can't stomach spending time with me after that pathetic kiss. Jack did his best to squash the thought flat and walked on, past men hauling baskets of fish across the quayside and tourists gazing into gift shop windows.

After nipping round the side of Magda's cottage, he knocked on the door of Alyssa's caravan and then peered through the window.

'She's out,' said a voice behind him. 'Gone for a walk on the beach.' When he turned around, Maisie, one of the teenagers Magda employed part-time in the ice-cream parlour, was watching him. As the parlour was next to Magda's cottage, staff members sometimes sat in her garden during their breaks.

'If it's Alyssa you're looking for, she's out,' repeated Maisie slowly, as if he, around twice her age, couldn't be relied upon to grasp her meaning. 'She said she was walking to the cove when I bumped into her earlier. To clear her head, or something. She looked upset.'

'Upset about what?'

Maisie sniffed and reached into her jeans pocket for a packet of cigarettes. 'I dunno. But Magda's in a right mood, too.' Her lighter flared when she lit the cigarette she'd pushed between her lips. 'Personally,' she mumbled, 'I think people should keep their bad moods to themselves.'

Jack wondered if he should list the scientifically proven risks of smoking but decided that Maisie wouldn't take kindly to his interference. Instead, he said, 'Thanks for the info,' and left Maisie to her cigarette break. The good news was that Alyssa was alive and well – albeit in a bad mood, like everyone else that morning.

Back in the lane that ran past Magda's cottage, Jack stood on the pavement, hardly aware of people stepping into the road to avoid him. It made sense to head back to the shop. That was the logical, sensible thing to do, and what the Jack of a few weeks ago would have done.

But, instead, he found himself walking towards the beach. Maybe Alyssa didn't want to see him, after yesterday's embarrassing kiss, but the truth of it was, he wanted to see her.

He walked past the castle ruins and along the lane that led out of the village, until he reached the cove. The morning was so grey and blowy, tourists had given the beach a miss. Their loss, thought Jack. This place was beautiful in all weathers. Low tide had exposed a wide expanse of sand, dotted with water-smoothed boulders, and rock pools fed by the retreating waves. A few dog walkers were out on the sand, and Jack paused for a moment to watch their pets careering around and barking at birds who flew too close. Where was Alyssa?

By the cave at the corner of the cove, Jack suddenly spotted a flash of daffodil-yellow. There she was, sitting on the sand with her knees drawn up under her chin. She cut a solitary figure, staring out to sea.

Now that he'd actually found her, Jack hesitated. Alyssa had chosen not to come to the shop, even though yesterday she'd agreed that she would. Instead, she had walked to the beach, to be alone or to avoid him. Either way, it probably wasn't a good idea to disturb her – except that Maisie had said she was visibly upset.

Why? he wondered. He wasn't egocentric enough to believe that kissing him had sparked such an extreme reaction hours later. He was hardly Brad Pitt.

Jack walked across the beach and, without a word, sat down beside Alyssa on the cold sand. Waves were lapping close to their feet and the dark mouth of the cave yawned behind them.

She looked around, alarm sparking in her blue eyes before she realised it was him.

'You stood me up,' he said, over the sound of waves crashing and seagulls screeching.

'I did what?'

'We arranged that you'd come to the shop at ten o'clock this morning.'

'Oh no, I'm sorry.' Her hand flew to her mouth. 'I totally lost track of time.'

She looked so pained, he nudged her arm with his. 'It doesn't matter.' He smiled at her. 'Are you sitting here hoping a sea dragon will lumber out from the cave?'

'That would be marvellous,' said Alyssa, her tone strangely flat. 'Why are you here? Were you out for a walk?'

'I came to find you because I was worried.'

'You were worried about me? Why?'

'When you didn't turn up, I thought you might have done an accidental nose-dive off the cliff.'

Or stood me up on purpose.

'As you can see, I didn't fall off the cliff, though some people might wish I had.'

'Which people?'

Alyssa picked up a handful of sand and let it trickle through her fingers. 'Magda.'

Jack hadn't been expecting that. Surely, Magda and Alyssa

were thick as thieves? They'd been amicably working together only yesterday.

'What's happened with Magda?' he asked.

'We had a row. Well, not a row, exactly.' Alyssa puffed out her cheeks. 'Let's just say she's not very happy with me at the moment, and I don't blame her.'

Jack frowned, finding it hard to imagine placid Magda rowing with anyone. 'She wasn't bothered that you and I...? I mean, you only kissed me to make a point to Miri and I can't see Magda being upset about that, even if she saw us.'

'I don't think she saw us.' Alyssa turned her head to look at him. Her cheeks were damp with sea spray – or tears: he wasn't sure which. 'No, it's nothing to do with what happened between you and me at the reception. It's about something else entirely.'

'Do you want to talk about it?'

'Not really, but thank you for offering.'

Jack dug the toes of his trainers into the sand. Miri had stored up resentments and slights and would never discuss them, even when it was patently obvious that she was upset or annoyed. And that, with the benefit of hindsight, had been a nail in the coffin of their marriage.

In fact, it was only after she had decided she wanted a divorce that his perceived failings had come to light. She'd never stopped talking about them after that. But it was too late by then. She'd made up her mind and he didn't have a chance to address her irritations.

He had his faults. There was no doubt about it. But, more and more, Jack was coming to realise that Miri hadn't been the easiest of people to live with. The reasons for the failure of their marriage weren't as one-sided as Miri, or he, had believed.

'I'm thinking of leaving Heaven's Cove,' said Alyssa suddenly. She pulled her feet back from the edge of the incoming tide.

'Why's that?' Jack asked, noting an uncomfortable sensation, as if his stomach was sinking into the sand. *I should have eaten breakfast this morning,* he thought, not wanting to explore why the prospect of Alyssa leaving the village might unsettle him so much. After all, he'd be off himself soon, heading back to London.

Alyssa hugged her arms across her chest. 'I don't think the caravan will be available for much longer.'

'Has Magda asked you to leave?'

'Not exactly.'

Why did she talk in riddles, as if her whole life was one of her fantastical stories? wondered Jack. Being straightforward was so much less confusing.

A sudden gust of wind carried the scent of Alyssa's perfume. She smelled of summer roses and patchouli. And freedom.

Jack gave himself a mental shake. Freedom indeed! Alyssa was a free spirit, whereas he was a buttoned-up individual. He knew it, but what was the problem with that? Being buttoned-up kept everything under control. And who knew what would escape if the buttons were undone?

Jack moved on the cold sand, slightly away from Alyssa. 'Even if you have to leave the caravan, couldn't you move somewhere else in Heaven's Cove?' he asked.

'Do you know how much I earn from my tours and part-time work in your dad's store?'

Jack shook his head. He imagined it wasn't very much, and rental prices in the village were steep. Lots of people wanted to live in such a beautiful place, and many properties were rented out, year-round, to tourists at eye-watering prices. Far more than Magda would charge for a rundown caravan at the bottom of her garden.

'I'll be sorry if you leave,' he said, before he could stop the words tumbling out.

'Are you sure?' Alyssa turned her head and looked into his eyes. 'I'd have thought you'd be glad to see the back of me.'

'What, and lose my devoted girlfriend?' said Jack, all fake jollity, even though it felt like the sand beneath him was shifting as the conversation veered back towards dangerous territory. 'I guess you've got under my skin.'

'Like an infection?' asked Alyssa, the corner of her mouth lifting.

Jack laughed. 'Yeah, exactly. Like ringworm.' He blinked. Had he just compared this vibrant young woman to a fungal infection? He really was hopeless at anything approaching banter but, to his relief, Alyssa smiled at his useless joke.

'Look.' He got to his feet, deciding to be direct. 'Do you want to come and see my cellar or not?'

'Is that why you want me to come to the shop?'

'I have something to show you.'

'In the cellar?' she asked, raising an eyebrow.

'There's something down there, something that your map reminded me of, that you might find interesting.'

Alyssa stared at him for a moment before standing up and brushing sand from her backside. Her hair was blowing around her face and she pulled it into a ponytail that she secured with a band from her pocket. 'I will come to see your cellar,' she announced, 'but you're going to have to improve your chat-up lines considerably. Showing me your cellar ranks only slightly higher than inviting me in to see your etchings.'

Jack laughed again. She was funny. Once you got past the airy-fairy exterior, and if you ignored the secrets she was obviously keeping about her past, Alyssa was funny. And fun to be around.

Three point one four one five... he began to recite in his head, as they walked across the beach together. His life seemed to have switched to fast forward and he was being carried on a wave, no longer in charge.

Nine two six five three five...

He continued reciting the mathematical constant while they walked back towards the shop. The mental gymnastics meant his mind was only half on their conversation. But that was a small price to pay for feeling more grounded and less all at sea in this unusual woman's company.

TWENTY-NINE
ALYSSA

Walking across the sand, in step with Jack, felt strange. Alyssa was touched that he'd been worried about her and had come to find her. Though she still couldn't work him out.

He was as tight as a guitar string – the rigid way he held himself when he walked, his serious approach to life and his closed mind. Yet sometimes it was as if the walls he'd built around himself were breached and she glimpsed someone else. When he looked at Miri with hurt in his eyes. When he laughed at Alyssa's stupid jokes.

When he kissed her.

Though, of course, she was no better. Presenting one side of herself to Jack – to everyone – and hiding a different side away.

That was one reason why Magda had been so angry with her this morning, and that anger was warranted, thought Alyssa. She'd encouraged Magda to show Stan the hidden side of herself, while she herself stayed in the shadows. Her 'advice' had been tainted by her own shortcomings.

If only she could go back to their conversation in the Smugglers Haunt and give a different opinion: *Guard your secrets well, because bringing them into the light causes pain.*

Alyssa pictured Magda's furious, heartbroken face as she'd recounted Stan's rejection, and blinked away tears as she and Jack strode along the lane, after leaving the beach behind.

Magda wasn't right that Alyssa was fully responsible for loosening her tongue because, ultimately, it had been her own decision to tell Stan. But Alyssa understood her anger. Battered and bruised, Magda had needed to lash out at someone, to release the hurt she was feeling. And it was undeniable that Alyssa had played a part in the whole sorry mess.

'Are you quite sure you want to come back to mine?' asked Jack. They'd hardly said a word to each other since leaving the beach.

Alyssa tried to concentrate on what was happening. All around them, Heaven's Cove was gearing up for a busy Sunday. Shops were open, the streets were filling with visitors, and a queue was forming on the quay for a boat trip around the headland.

Jack glanced at her. 'It doesn't matter if you'd rather not.'

Did she want to spend time in his cellar, even if there was something in the map that had sparked a memory in Jack? There was no point in pulling together a smuggling tour, or finding out more about Charity and Josiah, for that matter, if she was considering leaving Heaven's Cove.

'I mean,' Jack continued, 'I don't mind if you'd rather go straight back to the caravan.'

He said the words lightly, but the disappointment in his eyes implied that he would mind very much. It was strange, thought Alyssa, that, right now, Jack seemed to care more about the mysterious map than she did. Strange, and quite sweet.

'Yes,' she answered. 'I mean no. I don't want to go straight home, and I do want to come back with you. I'm intrigued about what you have to show me.'

'It might be nothing,' he answered, frowning as they

reached Gathergill's Mini Mart and found a large 'Closed' sign on the front door.

'Has your dad shut the shop?'

'It seems so. He said he was going out and would shut up shop for a while, but I wasn't sure he really would.'

'Where's he gone?'

'He wouldn't say.'

'Do you think he might have gone to see Magda?'

'Maybe.' Jack fumbled in his pockets for his keys. 'Why? What's going on? You and Magda have had some sort of argument and Dad's been horribly grumpy all morning. Have he and Magda had a fight too?'

'Um.' Alyssa bent to retrieve the keys that had slipped through Jack's fingers. 'I'm not sure but, if they have, perhaps they're having a chat and making up.'

Perhaps Stan, after having second thoughts, was declaring his love to Magda at that very moment, and their story would have a happy ending. Alyssa crossed her fingers behind her back.

'I have no idea what's going on in my life any more,' muttered Jack, opening the door and beckoning Alyssa inside.

'Do you need to open the store? I can stay and help if you'd like.'

Jack hesitated with his hand on the 'Closed' sign but then he stepped back, leaving the sign in place. 'No, people will have to cope without eggs and milk for ten minutes. It won't kill them. Just come and see what I wanted to show you, which, I warn you, might be a wild goose chase.'

That might be the case, thought Alyssa, following Jack towards the back of the shop. But at least a wild goose chase would distract her from worrying about what might or might not be going on at Magda's.

The stone steps to the cellar were narrow and worn and, Alyssa knew, would soon be quite unsuitable for Stan. What would happen to him then? she wondered. Would he have to move and give up this cottage that had been home to his family for generations? A cottage that had once been home to Josiah, who, in her mind's eye, sported a thatch of flaming red hair?

'Well, here we are,' said Jack, switching on a bare lightbulb that hung from the low ceiling. It swayed drunkenly, filling the space with shadows that danced across the stone walls. 'Can I have your phone?'

'I doubt you'll get a good signal down here.'

'I don't want to call anyone. I want to see your photo of that map again.'

When Alyssa found the picture, Jack squinted at it in the poor light while she looked around. The small cellar was crammed with boxes of tinned goods, which made it more claustrophobic. And it smelled of damp, as if the sea was lapping against the other side of the wall, waiting to burst in and drown them both.

Alyssa breathed out slowly, silently cursing her over-active imagination. This cellar had given her the shivers from day one. 'What are you looking at?' she asked.

'This symbol, or whatever it is.' Jack enlarged the photo and peered at it. 'The circle with a cross in it looks so familiar.' He handed the phone back to Alyssa. 'Could you help me to move the cupboard?'

'The big one filled with baked beans?'

Jack nodded.

The tall cupboard in the corner held boxes of imperishable food, including a tower of tinned beans. The inhabitants of Heaven's Cove seemed to get through a huge amount of them every week.

'That cupboard didn't always stand there,' said Jack. 'When I was a kid, it used to be over there, by the steps.'

Alyssa shrugged. 'OK.'

'Can you give me a hand?' asked Jack, pulling out one of the boxes and placing it on the floor.

Alyssa joined in and, when the cupboard was empty, Jack put his shoulder against the piece of furniture and gave it a shove. It scraped little more than an inch across the flagstones, the noise putting Alyssa's teeth on edge.

'I need your help again, I'm afraid.'

When Alyssa started pushing and shoving the cupboard, Jack stopped and wiped a hand across his face. 'Aren't you going to ask me why we need to move it?'

She shook her head. 'I figure you must have a good reason.'

'Miri would have refused to help until she'd heard the whys and wherefores behind my request. But you just rolled up your sleeves and got stuck in.'

Why did he have to bring up his estranged wife and compare the two of them? Alyssa sniffed, not sure if getting stuck in was a good thing in Jack's mind or more proof of her own lack of evidence-based reasoning. 'Miri and I are very different types of people,' she said in the end, and Jack didn't disagree.

Together, they pushed and heaved the heavy cupboard across the stone floor until it stood a few feet away from the wall.

'Phew!' Alyssa put her hands on her hips, her face burning and her arms aching. She must look a sight.

Jack's face was flushed too. He looked healthier with more colour in his cheeks: far less like a scientist forever stuck in a lab. After pulling his phone from his jeans pocket, he turned on the torch and shone the beam onto the wall, where the cupboard had stood. 'There it is. I was right.'

'Right about what?' Alyssa stepped closer to him and peered at the wall. 'What am I looking at?'

'That,' said Jack, pointing. 'Can you see it there? It's very faint.'

Alyssa moved forward until her nose was almost touching the wall. And then she saw it, carved into the old brick at shoulder height. Her heart seemed to suddenly speed up; she could hear it pounding in her ears. 'Oh, my. Do they match?'

She opened the picture of the map again and enlarged it. The drawing at the bottom, the curious circular symbol with a cross inside it, was exactly the same as the indentation in front of her. 'It *is* the same symbol. That's amazing!'

Alyssa breathed out slowly, as the past and present collided. She could almost feel Josiah's hand on her shoulder as a piece of the puzzle slotted into place – not that anything was any clearer. It was like putting together a jigsaw puzzle when there was no picture on the front of the box to guide you.

She glanced at Jack, who was peering at the lines scraped into the brick. 'How on earth did you notice this symbol on the wall as a child? It's so small and faint, it's hardly visible.'

'I spent a lot of time down here,' he said, scuffing his feet across the flagstones.

'Why? You weren't shut down here for bad behaviour, were you?'

'Definitely not.' Jack grinned at her. 'One, I was a very well-behaved child, and two, my parents weren't monsters. You know my dad. Can you imagine him doing such a thing?'

Alyssa couldn't. Stan was so kind he didn't always ring up the full price when Heaven's Cove's least well-off families came in to top up their larders. 'No, sorry. But I don't understand why you'd be in the cellar so much.'

'It was quiet down here when John was ill,' said Jack softly, his face in shadow. 'Upstairs, there were always visitors or medical staff, and Mum and Dad were either busy looking after John or, when he was in hospital, trying to pretend they weren't devastated. This cellar was peaceful, and somewhere I could be alone with my thoughts. That's all.'

Alyssa could imagine young Jack down here in the gloom

trying to make sense of an impending tragedy spinning out of his control. Her heart ached for the child he once was and the serious adult he'd become – an adult who still found refuge in cold, hard facts. 'I'm so sorry. That must have been awful to cope with.'

She stepped towards Jack and lifted her hand to touch his face. It was an automatic gesture, made, without thinking, in a bid to bring some comfort to the child she could still see in him. But he moved away before her fingers made contact with his skin.

'It was a long time ago,' he said, his voice suddenly brisk. 'And at least being down here so much meant I noticed the mark on the wall.'

'That's true,' said Alyssa, matching his brisk tone to mask her embarrassment. Had she really almost touched his face? The fall-out with Magda, followed by Jack's display of vulnerability, must have really jangled her emotions. She ran her raised hand through her hair, as if she'd never meant to touch him at all, before tapping the torch icon on her phone. A beam of light spilled across the wall in front of her. 'Do you think the bricks look a little unusual here, just below the marking?' she asked. 'They're a slightly different shade.'

He looked closely at the wall. 'Possibly.'

'It's as if the bricks don't quite match. As if this bit of the wall was built, or rebuilt, later than the rest of the cellar,' said Alyssa, her imagination beginning to run away with her.

Jack whistled softly through his teeth. 'From what I've come to know about you, Alyssa, I assume you're implying that there was once a gap here? Or the opening to a tunnel?'

'You never know.'

'And the symbol – what? Marks the spot?'

'Perhaps in 1753 the bricks could be removed to reveal the tunnel.' Alyssa gave them a gentle push to check her theory, but they didn't budge. 'What do you think the symbol means?'

'I have no idea and I must admit that I'm curious. That's why I wanted to show it to you but' – Jack shook his head – 'you're leaping ahead again. Let's look at the evidence. All we have is a piece of paper with some scrawled lines that look vaguely map-like, and a weird symbol that happens also to be on our cellar wall.'

'The cellar of the cottage where Josiah, a smuggler, once lived.'

'He might not have been a smuggler.'

'OK, but he disappeared on the same night as a smuggling gang in Heaven's Cove was rounded up. And then there's the hair.'

Alyssa briefly screwed her eyes shut. She hadn't meant to mention that particular piece of the puzzle, concerned it might prove to be a leap too far for Jack.

He leaned against the wall and folded his arms. 'What hair?'

Alyssa took a deep breath. 'The box that held the map – possible map,' she corrected herself. 'It also contained a lock of red hair in a piece of paper that had "beloved" written on it. And...' She hesitated because Jack was staring at her as if she'd completely lost her marbles. 'And red hair runs in your family,' she said in a rush. 'Your dad said.'

When Jack continued staring, without saying anything, Alyssa added: 'So maybe that means Josiah gave the map to Charity.'

Jack pushed himself away from the wall, his arms still folded. 'And I suppose he gave her a lock of his hair because it fits with your theory that he and Charity were lovers?'

'Well, probably not lovers. Not in the seventeen hundreds, when sex before marriage was taboo. But they might have been *in* love.'

How had it come to this? wondered Alyssa. Talking about sex in a cellar with a man who made her feel... She shook her head, not knowing quite how she felt about this reserved, uptight man whose flashes of vulnerability touched her heart.

'Hmm.' Jack gave a wry smile. 'It's all totally circumstantial and would never stand up in a court of law, you know.'

'But we're not detectives making a case. We're people trying to make sense of an ages-old mystery and I, for one, in light of the circumstantial evidence and adding a big dollop of wishful thinking, believe this cellar could have once housed the entrance to a smuggling tunnel. Those bricks close to the symbol definitely look a little lighter to me.'

She stopped to take a breath and looked expectantly at Jack, who was watching her from the gloom.

'There's not likely to be a tunnel behind that wall,' he replied.

'You're right, and even if there were, it's probably fallen in by now. But wouldn't you like to find out for sure?'

Jack wrinkled his nose. 'If there is an old tunnel, it'll be dark and dangerous, and you're not going to find a sea dragon living in it.'

'You never know,' said Alyssa with a grin. 'There's more to life than facts and figures, and not everything can be explained. It's good to do something spontaneous and non-evidence-based sometimes. So come on, Jack. Live a little.'

She thought she'd gone too far when Jack stared at her, a line between his eyebrows. But then he started laughing.

'What?' asked Alyssa. Was he laughing at her?

'Nothing. It's just that you're irrepressible, Alyssa Jones.'

Her made-up name from his lips sounded so wrong: it was jarring, and Alyssa felt her excitement begin to wane.

But Jack was rooting around in a large metal box in the corner and turned suddenly, brandishing a sledgehammer. 'Dad's tool box. I thought he had one of these. Let's sort this out, once and for all.'

'What are you going to do?'

'Bash a hole in the wall to see if anything is behind it. Mind out of the way.'

Alyssa's mouth fell open. 'What will your dad think about that?'

Jack rested the head of the hammer on his foot. 'With any luck he'll never know. I'll knock out a couple of bricks to show there's nothing there and then we can patch it up before he gets back from wherever he's gone. And, hey, at least I'm being spontaneous!'

Was that sarcasm or excitement in his voice? Alyssa wasn't sure but she stepped back and covered her ears as Jack swung the hammer at the wall at waist height. He swung the hammer again and, after a third wallop, two bricks fell to the ground. There was a sudden waft of cold air and a stale aroma of damp and earth and rotting leaves.

Alyssa bent over, shone her torch into the gap and gasped. 'Wow, there's definitely some sort of cavity there.'

Jack bent down beside her and looked for himself. Then he straightened up. 'Step back,' he ordered, before swinging at the wall again with the hammer.

The noise was enough to wake the dead. Alyssa glanced nervously at the cellar steps, but Stan didn't come to investigate. Hopefully, he was still with Magda, making up and declaring his devotion.

Alyssa coughed when splinters of brick flew in all directions and dust rose into the air. Physical labour suited Jack, she decided, as his self-control disappeared and he bashed hell out of the wall.

A few minutes later, the floor was littered with old bricks and Jack had made a hole large enough for a person to squeeze through.

He knelt down and shone his torch inside. He paused for a moment before saying quietly: 'You'd better come and see this.'

Alyssa knelt beside Jack, so close their thighs were touching, and peered into the gap.

'There really is a tunnel,' Alyssa whispered, her breath turning to clouds of condensation in the icy draught.

As far as Alyssa could see – as far as Jack's torch beam reached – the tunnel they'd uncovered was lined with brick and had a dirt floor. A wooden prop was wedged against the roof, to provide additional stability.

'There's a tunnel leading from our cellar!' said Jack, sitting back on his heels. 'An actual tunnel.' He shook his head in amazement. 'So, what do we do now?'

Alyssa stared into the darkness, imagining Josiah and his colleagues moving along the enclosed space, smuggling goods under the authorities' noses. Perhaps the tunnel was also a clandestine meeting place for Josiah and Charity.

'I guess we'd better let somebody know,' said Jack. 'The council, maybe?'

'That sounds like a good idea. But first,' said Alyssa, excitement taking over, 'I could squeeze inside and have a quick look.'

'No, you couldn't,' said Jack firmly, putting the hammer down on the floor. 'I just had a go at being spontaneous, which is fine, but going into the tunnel is taking spontaneity too far.'

'Just a little way,' urged Alyssa. 'Think what I might find inside.'

'I *am* thinking. I'm thinking about what I've read regarding the degradation of wood and brick. It's not safe.'

'That's why I'll only go a little way.' Alyssa smiled at him reassuringly. 'You can stay here and sound the alarm if a dragon appears.'

'Very funny.'

'It's just that the council will probably block the tunnel off and we'll never properly find out anything about it.' Alyssa shone her torch into the darkness again, feeling bizarrely drawn to the place. Something on the floor a few metres inside glinted like a jewel, reminding her of the brooch that went missing on the night that Charity and Josiah disappeared.

'I know you're being sensible and science-y,' she told Jack. 'But my instincts are telling me that it'll be fine to go a little way inside.'

'Your instincts?' Jack sighed. 'Come on, Alyssa, face it. On this one, I'm right and you're wrong.'

Alyssa's breath caught in her throat as Jack's turn of phrase brought back painful memories. Her mind reeled back fourteen months, to another man who'd stood in front of her and told her exactly the same thing. But she'd learned a painful lesson that day: just because someone said they were right, it didn't mean that they were. Sometimes it was better to trust your instincts.

'Let's cover the hole for now and think about who we need to tell,' Jack continued.

But Alyssa wasn't listening. Instead, she dropped forward onto her knees and wriggled through the small gap.

THIRTY
JACK

'Alyssa, come back, please,' said Jack as firmly as possible. But the infuriating woman took no notice whatsoever.

'It's fine, Jack,' she called back. 'The ceiling's pretty low – it's touching the top of my head when I stand up – but it's amazing in here. Don't worry. I'll only go a little way and then I'll be back. Something's glinting and I want to see what it is.'

Jack sat back on his heels. What was Alyssa thinking, heading into a centuries-old tunnel with no idea what lay beyond the torch beam? He was partly to blame for bringing her down here, to chase a ridiculous story. But the main problem was that she had a head full of myths, legends and happy-ever-afters.

He stared up at the strange indentation on the wall. There was no denying that the symbol on the brick – the symbol that had fired up his curiosity – matched the one on the map. And it was exciting that he'd had a part to play in uncovering an old smuggling tunnel. Young Jack, who'd once sat here in the dark as John lay dying, would have been thrilled at the thought of it.

But now he was older and wiser. And though part of him was desperate to check out the tunnel and share in Alyssa's optimistic beliefs, he knew that he was doing the right thing by staying back.

He bent down and shouted into the darkness: 'Are you still all right?'

'Fine,' she called back. 'This is fantastic. I'm going a bit further but I won't be long.'

'Not too far,' he called, worried that her torch beam was dimming as she got further away. Soon, he wouldn't be able to see her at all. He shouldn't have let her go into the tunnel alone.

Jack got to his feet and began to pace up and down the cellar. He couldn't help feeling that Alyssa was off having an adventure while he, as usual, was standing back and doing the sensible thing.

He'd always been sensible, ever since his brother's death had made him realise that losing control could be dangerous. Life had a tendency to veer off in unexpected directions if you weren't always on top of things: always aware of what was real and what wasn't. Always looking for evidence to guide your path.

The consequence of being determined to lead a controlled existence had been a smaller, tighter life. That was a price he'd thought worth paying. But was it too costly when bad things were happening anyway? Miri wanted a divorce, he hardly saw Archie these days, and his father was unwell. Everything was falling to pieces and the harder he looked for answers and sought control, the worse it seemed to get.

Maybe, he thought, still pacing, it was time to be different. To take a leaf out of Alyssa's bonkers book and live more for the moment.

Moving into a caravan and telling tales of dastardly dukes and monsters of the deep was taking it too far. But perhaps being more spontaneous from time to time, like enjoying a sunset for the wonderment of it all, would do him good. Bashing hell out of the wall with the hammer had felt surprisingly good.

Jack crouched down and stared into the tunnel. In any case, he had no choice, really, because he should never have let Alyssa go in there on her own.

Taking a deep breath, he wriggled through the gap, cursing as his hips scraped against the bricks, and stood up – remembering, too late, what Alyssa had told him about the height of the tunnel.

'Damn!' he exclaimed as the top of his head hit the low ceiling and dirt tumbled around his shoulders. Smugglers in the olden days must have been tiny. Bending his neck, he began to make his way along the tunnel, sweeping his torch beam in front of him. 'Alyssa,' he called out. 'I'm coming. Wait for me.'

The air was damp and freezing cold as he picked his way slowly through the tunnel, towards the glow of Alyssa's torch beam. And as he moved along the dirt path, Jack realised to his surprise that excitement rather than fear was his over-riding emotion. Exploring an old smugglers' tunnel that had been bricked up for hundreds of years – this was all the longed-for adventures of early boyhood rolled into one: a chance to be brave and redeem himself; a chance to be one of the cool kids. The cool kid who got the girl.

He smiled in the darkness and called again to Alyssa, who was a shadow ahead of him.

She turned to him as he caught up with her. 'You decided to join me then,' she said with a grin, her teeth shining white in the torchlight. 'Actually, I was about to turn round and come back. You know, be a little more sensible about the whole thing.'

Jack hesitated. For once, he wasn't being sensible and there was a thrill in that. He dimly remembered taking risks as a child, before John had died and his parents' mantra of 'Be careful' had seeped into his brain. It had been said with love because they couldn't bear the thought of losing another child. But their fear had constricted him then, and was constricting him still, he realised.

'Are you coming?' asked Alyssa, her dark hair a glowing frame around her face. 'We can give the council a call.'

Jack drew back his shoulders. 'In a minute but... let's go a little bit further. I'll take the lead.' He moved past Alyssa and walked on, feeling brave.

* * *

Something about Jack was different, thought Alyssa, flattening herself against the wall of the tunnel so he could squeeze past, his body pressing briefly against hers. He'd been so against her exploring the tunnel and yet here he was, striding ahead like Indiana Jones on a mission.

She watched him walking off into the gloom. He was hard to figure out – one minute he was pooh-poohing everything she said about smuggling, or Josiah and Charity, and the next he was inviting her into his cellar to see a symbol that he'd vaguely remembered. She'd never have found the tunnel without his help.

'Keep up,' Jack called, ahead of her.

'Hold on, wait for me.' Alyssa hurried after him, not sure why he'd changed his mind but glad of his company. Truth be told, the excitement and bloody-mindedness that had propelled her into the tunnel had started to dissipate. The jewel-like glinting that had caught her eye and encouraged her into the tunnel had turned out to be nothing more than a scattering of old nails, and then there were the silver threads of cobwebs that hung thickly from the ceiling. She rubbed her hands across her shoulders to dislodge any spiders that might have hitched a ride, and shivered.

'I can't believe you're exploring this place with me,' she said, when she'd almost caught up with Jack.

'Me, neither,' he said over his shoulder. 'But I couldn't let you hurtle into the darkness on your own.'

There wasn't much hurtling going on, thought Alyssa, stumbling as her foot hit a brick that had fallen from the ceiling. It was quite worrying that a brick had fallen from the ceiling, actually.

She noticed how much chillier the tunnel had become and wondered if the sharp right-angle they'd taken a while back meant they were now heading towards the ocean.

Jack suddenly stopped dead and asked: 'Can you hear that?'

'Hear what?'

'That strange booming noise.'

Alyssa breathed out slowly, the warm air from her lungs turning to mist in the torchlight. There was definitely a noise in the distance: a faint boom followed by a roar. It sounded like the mythical sea dragon that had dragged Charity and Josiah to their deaths.

'Could that be the sound of waves hitting against rock?' asked Alyssa.

'It might be. Perhaps there's a hidden entrance to the tunnel in the cave somewhere.'

Jack sounded animated, which was ironic seeing as her excitement was fading in direct proportion to Jack's new-found sense of adventure. Instinct had led her into the tunnel, and instinct was now telling her to get the hell out.

'I really think we should go back,' said Alyssa, putting her hand on Jack's arm. 'I should never have encouraged you to follow me in here, though it's really sweet that you did. And surprising too, to be honest.'

Jack glanced down at her hand. 'I'm not always a dull, sensible stick-in-the-mud, you know.'

'I know that,' said Alyssa, suddenly very aware that they were completely alone, with darkness pressing in around them. 'You wouldn't have followed me in here if you were.'

'It's strange,' he said, staring into her eyes as the boom and roar echoed faintly around them. 'I thought you brought out the worst in me, Alyssa Jones, but I'm starting to wonder if you sometimes bring out the best.'

'I'm not sure what you mean.'

'I'm not sure I do either, but I just...' He tailed off, as if his words were being absorbed by the walls enclosing them.

Alyssa knew they should be heading back to the safety of the cellar, but her legs didn't want to move as Jack bent his head towards her. Was he going to kiss her, for real this time? She stopped breathing and waited, her eyes never moving from his face. But then he took a sudden step backwards.

'Did you hear that?'

Alyssa breathed out slowly, forcing herself not to sigh.

'What?' she asked, her stomach trembling. Or was her whole body moving? She looked around in alarm, sweeping her torch from side to side.

'There was a different noise.'

And then she heard it: a low groan that seemed to seep up from the ground and make her legs shake. Then there was another sound: a louder, tearing noise as if the world was ripping in two; and then the walls of the tunnel began to shake and bricks began to fall.

'Watch out!' yelled Jack, grabbing hold of Alyssa and pushing her to the floor. He threw himself on top of her, shielding her head with his arms as bricks and earth rained down and the world went black.

THIRTY-ONE

MAGDA

Almost three hours had passed since Magda had taken Alyssa to task for encouraging her to bare her soul to Stan. And those three hours had been exhausting.

Magda had cried and paced and eaten far too much cake and decided that it would definitely be impossible to face Stan again.

This meant a move was inevitable because how else could she avoid bumping into him? And even when he was no longer in this world – though even thinking about that made Magda's heart hurt – she would never come back to Heaven's Cove. There would be too many bittersweet memories here.

'I should have kept my mouth firmly shut,' she said out loud, ignoring the tiny part of herself that would never truly regret telling the truth to the man she loved.

Magda stopped pacing and stole a glance at herself in the hall mirror. Never a raving beauty, she looked particularly unappealing today: unbrushed hair and red-rimmed eyes were far from flattering, and there were cake crumbs around her mouth.

There was a sudden tremble beneath her feet – a particularly large wave crashing into the harbour wall, presumably – and she adjusted the mirror, which had tilted slightly on the wall.

Then, she brushed the crumbs from her lips, wiped her eyes and ran a brush through her hair. This would be her new normal, her new life, and she needed to get used to it: a life without Stan, without Penny, and without the community in Heaven's Cove.

She walked into the kitchen and gazed at the caravan sitting at the end of her garden. What was Alyssa doing now? she wondered, stabbed by guilt as she remembered how upset the younger woman had looked three hours earlier.

Magda went over her conversation with Alyssa in the Smugglers Haunt, when she'd spoken of her love for Stan. But the anger that had consumed her earlier had gone for good and the truth was plain to see: Magda had taken out her despair on Alyssa, who had troubles of her own, because blaming her was less painful than blaming herself.

Magda sighed. Not only was her heart broken; she was now riddled with guilt for wrongly blaming Alyssa, who had done nothing more than try to help her.

She leaned against the window watching the leaves on the trees rustling in the breeze. Beyond them stood Driftwood House, sitting high on the clifftop where Magda had made a total hash of her life.

A sudden knock on the front door made her jump. She wasn't expecting anyone, so she stayed quiet and still in the kitchen, hoping they'd go away. If there was a problem at the ice-cream parlour, the girls would have to sort it out for themselves this time.

But the rapping at the front door began again, louder this time. And when Magda didn't move, someone began thumping on the door.

'Wait!' called Magda, hurrying into the hall. It had to be Maisie, who she'd only hired as a favour to her aunt. Unfortunately, the girl was turning out to be a bit of a nightmare.

'What's the problem?' she demanded, yanking open the front door.

'Hello, Magda,' said Stan, his walking stick raised as he was caught mid hit.

'What are you doing here?' Magda meant to sound inquisitive but, in the shock of seeing Stan, her tone was combative. She ran a hand through her hair, aware that she looked a sight.

Stan lowered his walking stick. 'I was hoping to see you.'

'Why?'

Stan cleared his throat, his knuckles whitening as he clenched and unclenched his fingers. 'I've been thinking about what you said and I wanted to make sure that you're all right.'

'Just forget what I said,' said Magda quickly. 'And there's no need to check up on me, Stan. I can look after myself. I have done for years.'

'I know that.' Stan hesitated, his face pale. 'Can I come in anyway? I hate to play the illness card, but I'm not sure how much longer I can stand up. I've been sitting by the sea for a while and my muscles appear to be seizing up.'

Magda sighed quietly and opened the door wide. 'Of course. Come on in and sit down.'

Stan walked slowly into the kitchen, leaning heavily on his stick, and lowered himself into a chair at the table.

'Is that chair comfortable enough? Do you need a cushion?' asked Magda. It was hard to break the habit of wanting to look after him.

'This is fine, thanks, and I'm not staying.' Stan wiped a hand across his face. 'Look, Magda, let's not beat about the bush. About yesterday, I—'

'Like I said,' interrupted Magda, her face growing hot with the memory, 'just forget what I said. Too much drink was taken.'

She tried to smile, but her lips were wobbling. She clamped them together, aware that Stan was staring at her.

He took a deep breath. 'I've been thinking about this all night and it needs to be said, Magda. The truth is, I was taken aback by what you said to me on the cliff and I'm aware that I didn't react well.' He held up a hand when Magda went to interrupt. 'Please, I need to say this because I've realised something important. Something that I need to say to you.'

Had Stan had a change of heart and realised that he did have feelings for her, after all?

I am in love with you, Magda. I was thrown by your declaration of devotion, but later the truth hit me like a bolt from the blue. Of course I'll always love Penny, but I've realised that I'm in love with you, too.

Magda held her breath, hope flickering in her battered heart.

'Well.' Stan cleared his throat again. 'I'm a man of few words when it comes to emotions. You know that. Penny was always the one who dealt with the emotional side of things, so I don't know how best to say this.' He paused, breathing heavily. 'What I'm trying to say is I care a great deal about you, Magda. You were Penny's best friend, and you've been dear to me since I was a young man. You've always been an important part of my life and I've realised that I need you in it forever, especially as my life comes to an end.' He blinked, pain in his eyes. 'The truth is, I'm scared, Magda, and I can't imagine leaving this world without you by my side. But I know that what I can offer you isn't fair.'

He swallowed and studied Magda's kitchen tiles, unable to meet her eye. 'What I'm saying, very badly, is that I'm terribly flattered that you feel so strongly about me. And so very sorry that I don't feel the same way. I can't, you see. Penny was the only woman for me – always was and always will be.'

The last vestige of hope flickered and died in Magda's chest.

'But I can't bear the thought of us falling out,' Stan went on, 'and I'm hoping that, when I'm gone, you'll be there for Jack, because he'll need you. You've always been like a second mum to him. But I understand that it might be too difficult for you to be with me, now we've had our chat.'

He stood up slowly, shuffled across the kitchen and took hold of Magda's hands. He'd never held her hand before and the feeling of his skin warm against hers took her breath away.

'I've made an idiot of myself,' she whispered, tears running down her cheeks.

Stan squeezed her hands. 'Not at all. You told me something very precious that has touched me deeply. I'm just sorry that I can't...' He petered off, still holding on to her hands, and took a deep breath. 'I do love you, Magda, but I'm not *in* love with you. And I quite understand if that's not enough for you.'

Was it enough? Magda wondered, tears dripping off her chin.

She looked at him, the man she'd secretly loved for so long. He'd been young and handsome and energetic when she'd first known him; now, he was old and tired, his body increasingly ravaged by an illness that didn't care. His hair had turned from brown to silver and his face was lined. But he was still the same Stan who was so precious to her.

It felt – rather dramatically, she acknowledged – as if her whole life had been leading up to this moment.

The years of watching Stan and Penny together and the nights she'd cried herself to sleep scrolled through her mind. The chances of romance with other men – good men – that she'd turned down, and her move to Heaven's Cove to be closer.

But she'd always known, in her heart of hearts, that her love for Stan was unrequited – it had had to be.

And now the man she'd known in his prime, when he was afraid of nothing, was terrified of what was to come.

She couldn't leave him. Not when he needed her.

Magda nodded. 'Yes,' she told him, gently pulling her hands from his grasp. 'It's enough for me.'

It would have to be.

The tunnel fall seemed to go on forever. Alyssa couldn't move and was finding it hard to breathe. Your life flashes before your eyes just before you die. That's what she'd heard. But as bricks and earth thundered down, all she could think was, *I'm sorry, Jack. You were right and I was so very wrong.*

Not the most comforting of final thoughts to have. But, fortunately, when the rumbling and thudding stopped, Alyssa realised she was still very much alive. She couldn't move but that was because Jack had thrown himself on top of her – however, he wasn't moving either.

Why had she dragged him into the tunnel? He'd been perfectly fine before she came on the scene, with her ridiculous romantic stories about people long gone and her gung-ho 'trust your instincts' attitude.

She'd been so sure, after what had happened in her life before Heaven's Cove, that it was a good idea to follow her gut feelings all the time. But now Magda was heartbroken after following her advice. And Jack was terribly hurt, or maybe even dead.

Alyssa began to sob but her breath caught in her throat

when Jack groaned and moved on top of her. He groaned again and rolled off her body, onto the ground.

'You're alive,' she cried, flinging her arms out into the inky blackness. Her fingers touched skin and she felt herself being pulled into an embrace. She hugged Jack on the dirt floor and snuffled into his chest, clinging on tight. Her ear was flat against his body and she could hear his heart thumping. 'Are you OK?'

'I think so,' he mumbled into her hair, coughing in the dust that was turning the air to soup. He shifted beside her and she heard his fingers scrabbling in the dirt.

'Got it,' he said hoarsely, as a beam of light hit their faces. 'I dropped my phone but it's not broken, thank goodness.'

He swept the beam in a circle revealing a wall of rubble behind them. A pile of bricks and dirt had fallen where they were. But if they'd been just a few feet further back, almost the whole lot would have landed on their heads. Alyssa shuddered, trying not to imagine their buried, broken bodies. They'd had a lucky escape.

Jack slowly got to his feet, put out a hand and pulled Alyssa up. Her legs were wobbly, like Bambi on ice, and her wrist was aching where she'd fallen.

'Are you sure you're OK?' she asked, tasting brick dust on her tongue. She screwed up her eyes which felt gritty and sore.

Jack rubbed his scalp and moved his neck from side to side. 'Just a bump on the head and a few bruises, I think. What about you?'

Alyssa gingerly pressed her hands to her abdomen before flexing her arms and legs. 'Nothing but a sore wrist, as far as I can tell.'

'I think we've been very fortunate in the circumstances.' He held his phone high and stared at the screen. 'There's no signal down here. I didn't think there would be, but it was worth a try. What about yours?'

Alyssa pulled her phone from her pocket. The screen had

cracked but she could still make out the signal icon. There were no bars showing. 'Nope, it's the same as yours.' Her legs were still shaking, and she sank back down to the floor. 'So, what do we do now?' she asked, the two of them staring at the wall of brick and earth that blocked their way back to the safety of Stan's cellar.

'I guess we go on and hope there's another way out,' said Jack, brushing dust from his hair.

'Could we try digging our way through the rubble and going back the way we came?'

'The wooden struts are damaged,' said Jack, sweeping his torch beam across the roof. 'If we start digging, we could bring even more down on our heads. The remaining struts are bearing a huge weight, but I don't know the specifics of axial force to understand their load-bearing capacity.' He paused. 'Is that too sensible and science-y for you?'

There was a sardonic edge to his voice, which Alyssa thought was fair enough in the circumstances.

'Sensible and science-y is what we need right now,' she told him. 'I don't think a sea dragon is going to help us out of this mess.'

'Probably not.' Jack held out his hand and Alyssa grasped it firmly. 'So, let's see where this goes, shall we?'

They started walking, Alyssa trailing behind because the tunnel was narrow, but still keeping a tight hold on Jack's hand.

There would definitely be another way out, she told herself as they moved slowly along. Jack obviously had a large, logical brain and if he wasn't panicking, there was no need for her to have a meltdown either. All tunnels needed an exit as well as an entrance, and the smugglers who'd built this one had clearly known what they were doing. Except, obviously, for the day they were caught by the king's customs men. The day Charity and Josiah disappeared.

Jack suddenly came to another abrupt halt and she barrelled into his back.

'What is it?' she asked.

In reply, Jack swept the beam of his torch ahead of them. There was another huge pile of bricks and earth, completely blocking their way — and this pile was even more substantial than the one they'd just left behind. As well as blocking the tunnel from floor to ceiling, it also extended along the walls of the tunnel, narrowing the passageway to little more than a metre.

'Another cave-in,' murmured Jack, letting go of her hand and crouching down to inspect the rubble.

'Has this fall just happened, do you think? At the same time as the other one?'

'I don't think so. There's far less brick dust and dirt in the air back here. This one could have happened years ago, which means the tunnel's been unstable for some time.'

'I'm starting to rethink my plans for a smugglers tour,' said Alyssa, her attempt at brightness undermined by the wobble in her voice. She was trying so hard not to give in to the panic that was clutching at her throat. Trying so hard not to focus on the fact that she and Jack were trapped far beneath Heaven's Cove and it was her fault. She would be responsible for another tragedy.

Jack gave a hollow laugh and sank down onto his haunches. 'The evidence available does seem to indicate that abandoning your new tour would be a very good decision.'

A trickle of blood was snaking down his cheek, Alyssa noticed. She pulled a tissue from her pocket and knelt down beside him. 'You're bleeding.' She dabbed gently at his face, the tissue catching slightly on the stubble on his chin. 'Are you sure you're OK?'

'Apart from being stuck in an unstable tunnel deep underground?' Jack pushed his fingers into his hair and winced.

'Falling debris has left a bump and what appears to be a small cut on my head. I'm sure I'll live.'

He caught Alyssa's eye and swallowed hard, the evidence for that declaration being in short supply. He looked away and began to sweep his torch beam across the rubble again.

'I'm sorry that I dragged you into this,' said Alyssa quietly.

'You didn't. It was my decision to follow you.'

'Yes, but if I hadn't— wait, what's that over there?' She put her hand over his to guide the torch light. 'I thought I saw a chink in the stones, at the side there.'

'Where?' Jack stood up, bending his neck to avoid banging his head on the roof, and squinted at the fallen bricks and earth.

'Over there, where the tunnel narrows at the side.' Alyssa pushed her fingers into the small gap she'd noticed, and almost cried with relief when her hand went straight through. 'There's not so much rubble here. Maybe we can move some of it and get through without destabilising everything.'

Together, they began to move the bricks and stones to one side. Cold damp earth wedged itself under Alyssa's fingernails as they carefully shifted the rubble, keeping an eye on the roof above, until there was a gap just wide enough for a human body to fit through.

Jack scrambled through the hole first and Alyssa followed, thanking her lucky stars that they had found a way out. They would both live, and she could apologise to Magda and to Jack and start to turn her life around.

There was something about being in mortal danger far below ground, she realised, that brought one's existence into sharp focus and shone a spotlight on everything that was wrong with it.

She'd run away. She'd made a terrible mistake and run away. But the mistake would always follow her, however far she ran. She could see that now. And it was time to take a different path. Being trapped down here had been traumatic but it would turn out to be a blessing in disguise.

Alyssa got to her feet and brushed dirt from her knees as Jack arced his torch around them. 'What the hell?' he said, his deep voice echoing as he illuminated their surroundings.

Alyssa blinked as she followed the light with her eyes – and her heart sank: it turned out that there would be no second chances at life after all.

'Where are we?' she asked dully, squinting to see through the gloom.

They were in some kind of enclosed room. There was rotting wood on the floor, and the place smelled of damp and something Alyssa couldn't place at first. Then it hit her. Alcohol. Down here, far beneath Heaven's Cove, it smelled faintly of the Smugglers Haunt on a Saturday night.

'We can't get out this way,' said Jack, the beam of his torch showing up nothing but brick walls. 'This must have been where they kept smuggled goods before they were moved on... We've basically gone sideways out of the tunnel into a storeroom.'

'Which means the way ahead, the way out, is still blocked.'

'That's about the size of it.' He sighed. 'Let's see if there's anything in here that might help us.'

Alyssa wasn't sure what they were looking for, but she began to circle the storeroom, until her torch beam caught a flash of white in a corner.

'What the hell is that?' she muttered, moving towards it. Then she realised. 'Oh my God!' Her phone fell from her hand and slapped down onto the dirt floor.

'What have you found?' Jack came to join her, and she heard his sharp intake of breath.

What Alyssa had found was bones. Lots of bones, gleaming white in the light of Jack's torch.

'Is it an animal?' she whispered.

Jack moved to stand over the bones, training the light directly on them. 'I'm afraid not. I think they're human remains.'

'It must be another person who got trapped.'

'People,' said Jack quietly. 'Two people.'

When two illuminated skulls suddenly yawned out of the gloom, Alyssa gasped and stumbled backwards.

She and Jack were trapped in a tomb.

'Are you all right?' Jack's voice sounded odd, as if he could hardly get the words out.

'I think so,' said Alyssa, trying to slow down her breathing. She was hyperventilating and her head was swimming. 'It's bones. Just bones,' she muttered to herself. 'Bones, just bones.'

Jack had squatted down beside the remains and Alyssa forced herself to kneel beside him. She could see it was two people now. Some of the smaller bones had become displaced over time and lay alone on the dirt. But where the long arm and leg bones intertwined, two people had become one jumble of collagen and calcium.

'Poor things,' murmured Alyssa. 'Do you know anything about... about—?'

'—about dead bodies?' Jack swallowed. 'Not much. I work in a lab analysing data from living, breathing people. But if I had to hazard a guess, I'd say that these two have been here for quite a while.' He pointed at a thigh bone that was pitted and marked, but shone white as chalk. 'I'd also guess that one skeleton is male and the other female. Her bones are much shorter than his. And what's that in her hand?'

Alyssa leaned in closer to take a look and suddenly she knew.

'It's Charity and Josiah,' she whispered, her heart hammering.

'That's a stretch,' said Jack, getting to his feet. 'I know I'm lobbing in a few guesses but at least mine are based on reasoned deduction.'

'So is mine.' Alyssa reached across the bones and, with only the slightest of hesitations, gently moved the woman's hand. 'Sorry,' she whispered to the dead as she picked up the sparkling object that had lain partially hidden beneath the woman's fingers.

Jack's torchlight sparked off the gold and jewels resting in Alyssa's palm.

'I can reasonably deduce that these are the remains of Charity and Josiah because this is the brooch that Josiah was supposed to have run away with after murdering Charity.'

'Are you sure?'

Alyssa ran her fingers across the exquisite piece of jewellery. It felt heavy in her hand. She traced the ruby at its centre, red as blood, and the glittering diamonds and emeralds that surrounded it. The seed pearls she'd sketched into her notebook at Driftwood House hung from the bottom of the brooch, brushing her skin. 'I'm quite sure. It's exactly the same as the brooch described in the history book that belonged to Rosie's mum. Have a look.'

She passed the brooch to Jack, who studied it for a while in silence before handing it back.

'I have to admit, that is quite compelling evidence.' Jack whistled through his teeth. 'I can't get my head around it. This is Charity Hawkins and Josiah Gathergill.'

'You thought he'd murdered her and fled, and I hoped they'd run away together. But it seems they've been here in Heaven's Cove all this time.'

'So, no happy-ever-after then,' said Jack gruffly.

Alyssa shook her head as tears trickled down her cheeks. It was all too much: being trapped in what was basically a tomb, and now discovering that Josiah and Charity had suffered a tragic end.

Jack knelt down again beside the skeletons. 'What do you think happened to them?'

Alyssa scrubbed her cheeks with the back of her hand. 'I think that Josiah was a smuggler and, if Charity was close to him, she probably knew these tunnels well. She found out that the customs men were planning a raid and came down here to warn him and to give him something precious, her mother's brooch, so he would have the funds to flee. But part of the tunnel collapsed and they were trapped.'

Alyssa waited for Jack's alternative theory about what had happened to these two poor souls. But all he said was: 'I wonder why they weren't rescued after the cave-in.'

'What if no one knew they were in the tunnels?' said Alyssa, very aware that no one knew she and Jack were down here either. 'The rest of the smuggling gang was arrested so never came back, tunnel entrances were bricked up or blocked off by the customs men, and Josiah was thought by local villagers to have murdered Charity and made his escape.'

'So, no one came looking,' said Jack, the shake in his voice betraying that he was thinking the same thing as Alyssa.

'Your dad will look for us, won't he?'

'Of course. But I'm not sure where he's gone or how long he's going to be, and he won't think to look for us in the cellar anyway.' Jack ran a hand through his hair. 'Let's just hope there aren't any more rock falls before he does eventually get round to checking the cellar. That last one could have made the whole tunnel unstable.'

Alyssa shuddered, hoping that she and Jack weren't about to join ill-fated Charity and Josiah in their final resting place.

Jack took in a deep breath and sighed. 'I thought he'd murdered her,' he said quietly. 'I never gave him the benefit of the doubt.'

'Everyone thought he was a murderer.'

'Everyone, except you.'

Alyssa's shrug went unseen in the gloom. She wanted to tell him why Josiah's redemption meant so much to her, explain how it had become tied to her own, but she didn't know where to start. So she picked up her dropped phone instead and said nothing.

As the roof supports creaked and groaned, Jack glanced up nervously before searching around the pile of bones. 'I can't see a lantern anywhere so they must have been in darkness after the rock fall.'

'But at least they were together,' said Alyssa, trying to salvage some comfort from that fact. The smaller skull was resting on the larger rib cage, as though Charity and Josiah were embracing. It was unbearably romantic and unutterably sad.

'It's such a shame they weren't rescued.'

'Not really,' said Alyssa into the darkness. 'I mean, what would they have faced if they had been discovered in time? Josiah would probably have been hanged as a smuggler, and Charity's reputation would have been trashed for being found alone with him. She'd have ended up married off to any man who would still have her.'

No, it was better this way because they'd rather have died, thought Alyssa, tears snaking down her cheeks again. Died together, in each other's arms.

THIRTY-THREE

JACK

The skeletons were entwined. Jack stopped studying the bones as if they were exhibits in his lab and tried to picture them as people: Charity, small and slight with a precious brooch clasped in her hand as a gift for her lover; and Josiah, taller and broader – with a mop of bright red hair, if Alyssa's theory was correct. And it probably was. Alyssa, with her wild flights of fancy, seemed to be right about a lot of things.

Charity and his ancestor Josiah had lain together, undiscovered in the dark for almost three hundred years. And now they'd been found, and the mystery of their disappearance was solved, thanks to Alyssa.

Though what was the point of solving an ages-old mystery if they were about to become a present-day one: two more people who disappeared, without trace, from Heaven's Cove? No, Jack corrected himself, that wouldn't happen because he and Alyssa would be found eventually – once his dad realised they were missing and the fallen piles of rubble had been carefully removed.

But it would likely be too late by then.

Jack slid down to the floor, his back to the wall and, after a moment, Alyssa eased down beside him.

He breathed deeply, trying to quell his rising panic. He'd managed to stay calm until now, mostly by pretending he was in a superhero movie. But being trapped in an underground tunnel, with a risk of the roof falling in at any moment, was actually way outside his comfort zone. It was absolutely terrifying.

'Three point one four one five nine—'

It was only when Alyssa murmured 'What did you say?' that he realised he was muttering his mantra.

'It's pi,' he said, not caring any more what Alyssa thought of him. What did it matter when they were trapped underground with no way out? 'It's a mathematical constant which represents the ratio of the circumference of a circle to its diameter.'

'I know what pi is.' She paused. 'Kind of. We did it at school. But why are you reciting pi right now? Are you coming up with some clever scientific way of getting us out of here?'

Jack sighed, feeling more useless than ever. He was a supernerd, not a superhero. And supernerds never saved the day; they were never one of the cool kids; and they never got the girl.

'I'm afraid I'm all out of clever, scientific ideas. I'm actually reciting pi to as many decimal places as I can remember because, when I feel stressed, it helps.'

Alyssa was quiet for a moment. 'Because of the familiarity of it? The unbending logic and order of it when life seems chaotic?'

'Yes.' He was surprised she got it. 'When my brother was dying...' His voice caught and he stopped and took a deep breath to gather himself. 'Do you mind if I switch off the torch, to save the phone battery?'

'Yeah, that makes sense.'

It did make sense, but the truth was Jack knew it would be

easier to say what he wanted to say into the darkness. He turned off the torch and the room went black. 'When John was dying,' he began again, 'everything around me was in chaos. My parents, my life, everything I'd ever known. Nothing made sense any more, and nothing felt safe. We happened to be learning about pi at school and it was the most comforting example of constancy that I'd ever come across. I started to recite it in my head and I found it helped to block out all of the madness. And I guess it's become a habit over the years. Whenever life gets stressful, it grounds me.'

'How old did you say you were you when your brother died?' asked Alyssa, and he felt her hand move on top of his. Her warm skin felt soothing, and his shoulders dropped as the panic building inside him began to fade.

'I was twelve, and John was fourteen. That's no age to die, is it?'

'No age at all. What was wrong with him?'

'He had ALL, which is—'

'—acute lymphoblastic leukaemia.'

'That's right.'

Alyssa breathed out slowly. 'Poor lad. There's a high recovery rate these days, but twenty years ago not so much, I imagine.'

'Do you know someone who's had ALL?'

Alyssa hesitated. 'A few people, yes. Did John have a bone marrow transplant?'

'Yes, but it didn't work as well as they'd hoped.'

Jack felt Alyssa's fingers tighten around his hand. 'I'm so sorry that you lost your brother and for all that you had to go through.'

He swallowed, grateful for her sympathy. 'It was a long time ago now.'

A long time ago that sometimes seemed like yesterday. It was strange, thought Jack. It felt as though John was with him, here in the dark. He hadn't felt his presence for so long because he always pushed him away – with his pi mantra, with hard work, with throwing himself into his marriage.

And it was only now that he allowed himself to acknowledge how much he'd missed John over the years, and how much he still grieved for his older brother. If only the existence of heaven wasn't, in his view, so scientifically invalid, the prospect of being reunited with John if the roof caved in might provide some comfort.

Jack took a few steadying breaths and rested his head against the cold bricks behind him. 'What about you?' he asked. 'How do you keep the madness at bay?'

Alyssa paused for so long he thought she wasn't going to answer him. But then she said in a rush: 'I run away. That's what I did last year, anyway. I run away and then I cock up other people's lives – Magda's life, yours.'

'What are you talking about?' asked Jack gently.

Alyssa continued as though she hadn't heard him. 'I've been running for so long. Trying to be completely different from how I was back then. But the irony is, I've ended up just like him, wrongly thinking I know what's best.'

'Just like Ben?'

That stopped Alyssa in her tracks. She paused and he felt her hand slide from his. 'You saw the letters and the note in my caravan, then? I wasn't sure that you had.'

'They were on the table as I left, so I couldn't help seeing them. "I miss you, Baby. Love Ben",' Jack recited from memory. 'Is Ben your husband?'

Alyssa gave a hollow laugh into the darkness. 'No, I've never been married.'

'Is he your partner then?'

'No. Ben's my brother. It's just me and him.'

'But he calls you "Baby"?'

'It's an in-joke. He sends on any letters that have arrived for me, and he calls me Baby in his notes because he's ten years older than I am. I was always the baby of the family.'

Jack frowned. 'Then I still don't have a clue who or what you're running from.'

A thick, soupy silence filled the cold storeroom. Then Alyssa said quietly: 'I killed someone.'

As her words hung in the air, Jack felt a shiver run down his spine. He was trapped in the dark with two ancient skeletons and a woman who'd just confessed to a deadly crime. He should be scared and appalled, horrified even – but he couldn't quite believe it of the cheerful woman who fed tall tales to tourists.

'Who did you kill?' he asked, switching his torch back on. Ghostly shadows danced in the corners of the room.

'A man, younger than you,' said Alyssa, her face and voice strangely emotionless. 'I am called Alyssa, but Jones isn't my surname. If you search online with my real name, you'll find that I worked as a nurse and that I was implicated in the death of a patient.'

'What happened?' Jack asked, exhaling slowly.

'I haven't talked about it for so long.' Alyssa sighed. 'I worked with young adults who were seriously ill, and I was good at it. My work was sad sometimes because not everyone survived – just like John. But we had our fair share of triumphs. People got better and went on to have good lives. But then there was Ollie.'

She took a deep breath. 'He was very ill but he could have got better. At least, he might have got better, if I hadn't been too scared to stand up to him.'

'Stand up to who? To Ollie?'

'No, to the consultant who prescribed double the dose of drug that Ollie should have received.'

Jack paused, trying to get his head around what Alyssa was telling him. 'But if it was the consultant who prescribed the drug, surely it wasn't your fault that—'

'But it was.' Alyssa's voice rang out around the ancient, shadowy storeroom.

'How could it be when it wasn't you who got the prescription wrong? Wasn't there an inquest or enquiry or something?'

'Yes, and the consultant was sanctioned.'

'Were you?'

'Not really.'

'Well, then—' began Jack, but Alyssa cut him off.

'But it wasn't the consultant who actually gave Ollie the drug that killed him, was it?' Her voice was almost a whisper now and flooded with emotion. 'It was me. I had misgivings about the dose he'd prescribed. I thought it was a high dosage for a man of Ollie's build and I tried to say that, but the consultant didn't listen. He told me that I was only a nurse whereas he had far more training and experience, so I should just do my job.'

'He sounds like an arrogant piece of work.'

'He was, and when I tried again to voice my concerns, he warned me that if I didn't give Ollie his medication at once he would report me. He said' – Alyssa's voice wobbled but didn't break – '"I'm right and you're wrong," and I believed him.' The anguish in Alyssa's voice was unmistakable. 'Even though my instincts were telling me that I was right, I ignored them and believed him and gave Ollie the medicine. I could tell almost straight away that I'd made the most disastrous mistake.'

She took a deep breath, and her voice shook when she said: 'Ollie died. He was already in a fragile state and was unable to tolerate the dosage of medication he received.'

Jack wanted to reach out his hand and touch Alyssa but he was frightened she would stop speaking. So he sat still and asked: 'What happened next?'

'The consultant apologised and was sanctioned for his mistake.'

'A mistake that wasn't yours.'

'But it was. The mistake was also mine because I didn't listen to my instincts and I allowed myself to be cowed by a man who thought he knew everything about medicine. So much so, he didn't listen to anyone who might have spotted that he wasn't infallible after all.'

Alyssa was taking on far too much responsibility for a dreadful error. But Jack knew that telling her so right now would be pointless. She needed to get her story out and telling it here, into the darkness of this subterranean storeroom, was easier than facing up to it in the bright light of day.

'So,' he asked. 'What did you do after the investigation was over?'

'I ran.' Alyssa stifled a sob. 'I ran from my job and my life and came back to Devon, which had felt safe as a child, and feels safe now. This village gives me the same sort of comfort that reciting pi gives to you. It provides stability and order amidst the chaos.'

'And you've turned to myths and legends while you're here, rather than nursing or science.'

'Yes, there's a comfort in the distant past, in the stories that have been passed down for generations and the ways in which those stories have interpreted the truth and made it... magical.'

'More magical than cold, hard reality?'

'Exactly.' Alyssa paused, her face pale. 'So now you know the truth about me.'

Jack nodded. He not only knew the truth about Alyssa's past, he could also now understand why she was so inclined to follow her instincts – whether her instincts told her Charity and Jeremiah's story wasn't as it seemed, or encouraged her to rush headlong into a dangerous smugglers' tunnel.

Though he had played a part in landing them in this dire situation, with his newly found sense of adventure. Alyssa had wanted them to turn back, but he'd been keen to press on.

When he sighed, Alyssa asked quietly: 'Are you shocked and horrified about me?'

'God, no.' Jack leaned towards her until their arms were touching. 'I feel terribly sad about what happened to Ollie and sorry that you've had to deal with such a terrible situation on your own. What about your family and friends?'

'My parents are wrapped up in their own lives and I've lost touch with my friends and everyone really, apart from Ben. I stopped talking to anyone after what happened.'

'But now you've talked to me,' said Jack softly, trying to ignore the creaks and low rumbles that constantly laced the air around them. It sounded as if the tunnel was shifting.

Alyssa gave a wry smile. 'There's something about being stuck underground, with your life in peril, that loosens the tongue.'

'So you'd have told anyone who happened to be stuck down here with you,' said Jack, feeling bizarrely disappointed.

'No, I don't think so,' answered Alyssa quietly. 'Only you.'

She was blinking, trying not to cry, and even by the shadowed light of his mobile phone she looked so done in, so vulnerable, Jack put his arm around her shoulder and she sank against him.

He felt honoured that she'd told him her secret, although he knew that she felt safe confiding in him because of their dire situation: he couldn't ever spill the beans if they weren't discovered down here until it was too late. After all, dead men didn't tell tales.

Jack rested his cheek against Alyssa's soft hair and glanced at the bones nearby. He shivered, wondering if Charity and Josiah had shared secrets as they lay dying.

'We will get out of here,' said Alyssa, sounding suddenly fierce.

'Yes, we will,' said Jack, pulling her closer and hoping he sounded more confident than he felt.

THIRTY-FOUR

ALYSSA

Alyssa had lost track of time. They'd been sitting like this for a while, with Jack's cheek resting against her hair, and it felt so comforting, she didn't want to move.

The harsh truth was she was trapped underground and wrung out after confessing her darkest secret. But here, with her head against Jack's chest and his arm around her shoulders, she felt strangely at peace. The torchlight gloom seemed less threatening somehow, and the bones in the corner less indicative of how limited their future might be.

Ironically, with the roof likely to cave in at any moment she felt as if a weight had been lifted from her shoulders. She'd told Jack why she was in Heaven's Cove, and he hadn't recoiled in horror. He hadn't blamed her, even though she'd done little else for the last fourteen months. He was a good man.

Alyssa felt his arm tighten around her and she leaned into him, feeling horribly guilty for dragging him into such danger. He had a father and a son who loved him and would miss him if everything went even more pear-shaped than it currently was. An estranged wife, too, who didn't seem ready to let Jack go, even though she'd brought her new man to Rosie's wedding. It was all a complete mess.

'I'm sorry,' she said. 'So sorry for getting you into all of this.'

When she moved her cheek against Jack's chest and looked up at him, he was staring down at her.

'You didn't make me follow you into the tunnel. It was my decision.'

'I know but I shouldn't have—'

Alyssa blinked in surprise when Jack placed his finger briefly against her lips.

'Stop. We can't change anything that's happened so there's no point in beating yourself up.'

'But that's what I do best.' Alyssa's game attempt at a laugh sounded more like a sob. 'I really am very sorry.'

'I know you are, and I'm sorry, too.'

'For what?'

He hesitated before answering. 'For turning out to be a supernerd rather than a superhero.'

Alyssa wasn't quite sure what he was going on about, but she tried to make him feel better anyway. 'I reckon superheroes are overrated. Superman never did it for me.'

When she smiled at him, Jack placed his finger on her lips again, but this time let it rest there as he traced the shape of her mouth. His touch was unexpected and gentle, and incredibly sexy.

'Alyssa,' he said gruffly. 'Alyssa Jones, or whatever your name is.'

He really was going to kiss her this time, thought Alyssa, wondering what it would be like to kiss Jack for real. The kiss in the marquee had been pretty special and that one was merely make-believe.

Her breathing became shallow as Jack pulled her closer and lowered his mouth towards hers.

This kiss would be real and wanted, as long as – the thought popped into her head – as long as it wasn't simply motivated by trauma.

Trauma could heighten the emotions; she knew that from her nursing days. And perhaps Jack figured half a ton of rubble dropping on his head wouldn't be quite so bad if he was locked in a smooch at the time.

Dying mid-kiss sounded better to Alyssa, too. Far nicer than dying as she sat in the dirt, telling herself she was a bad person. But they were going to be rescued. Alyssa had to believe that.

And there was one major issue with the no-doubt delightful kiss that was heading her way: traumatised Jack didn't really want to kiss her at all. The woman he did really want to kiss was Miri.

Alyssa sighed, jerked her head away from Jack's and sat up straight. 'What about Miri?'

'What about her?' asked Jack, sounding confused.

'I've told you my big secret and now you need to share yours.'

'What are you going on about? What secret?'

'That you're still in love with your wife.' Alyssa's words echoed around the dark storeroom.

'No, I'm not,' retorted Jack. 'Why do you think that?'

'Because of the way you look at her and you're totally gutted by the fact she's seeing someone else. You pretended I was your girlfriend, for goodness' sake!'

'Don't remind me.' Jack sighed. 'I'm not sure how I feel about Miri, to be honest.'

'That's not surprising because everything's muddled, but I'm sure. You lied about going out with me because you still love her,' said Alyssa, feeling a sharp stab to her heart. 'You wanted to make her jealous so she'd realise what she was throwing away. I get it. I really do. And it's OK, because I'm sure she's still in love with you.'

She expected Jack to react. To ask her why she thought that.

To cry with frustration that he was trapped down here while his estranged wife was up there, still crazy about him. But he didn't say a word.

Alyssa filled the silence. 'Miri was very put-out by me being your girlfriend, and you should have seen the look she gave me when I came back to the marquee, after we'd been chatting on the cliff. I don't think that can all be due to her inner alpha female. I reckon poor old Damian's days are numbered, so your ploy – having me as your pretend girlfriend – totally worked.' She took a deep breath because her voice was shaking. 'I know I'm not who you'd ever choose in real life, Jack. You think I'm ridiculous with my myths and legends. But Miri totally fell for the make-believe. So, well done and you've got to get out of here so you and she can have a happy reunion. For your sake, and for Stan's and Archie's.'

Alyssa clamped her lips together, afraid she might cry as Jack turned off his torch and the room was plunged back into darkness.

'We'd better save the phone battery,' he said, his voice thick with emotion.

They sat apart in the darkness for a while, the air charged with their kiss that never was. It felt like static electricity, thought Alyssa, starting to shiver in the cold. A crackling energy that divided them.

Her fingers were going numb but she didn't dare huddle up to Jack for warmth. She didn't dare because of her heart. Because she was envious of Miri, and the truth of that had knocked her sideways.

She had feelings for Jack, which were utterly pointless. They were either about to die, which would put the kibosh on any chance of romance; or, if by some miracle, they got out of this tunnel alive, he and Miri would have a beautiful reunion and live happily ever after – while she lived a half-life in the caravan in Magda's garden.

Actually, she couldn't even live there, she remembered, picturing Magda's angry face. She would have to move away and start again, somewhere new.

Which wasn't the worst of ideas if Jack and Miri were going to make up and walk hand in hand through the village. She didn't want to spend her life trying to avoid them.

Alyssa closed her eyes, replaying in her mind what had just happened – almost happened – between her and Jack. Perhaps she should have just gone with the kiss, even if it wouldn't really have meant anything to him. But the problem was it would have meant something to her, and if – when – they were rescued, that kiss would have made Jack and Miri's reunion even harder to bear.

Jack's voice suddenly sounded in the darkness. 'Do you feel weak at all?'

'No.' The spikes of adrenaline coursing round her body were making sure of that.

'Do you have a headache?'

Alyssa opened her eyes. 'No, why?'

'We're in a relatively confined space, trapped between two cave-ins, which, while not completely airtight, must be drastically limiting the flow of fresh air.'

Alyssa winced. 'That's not making me feel any better.'

'About twenty per cent of air is made up of oxygen,' Jack continued, switching his torch on. 'When we breathe, we take in oxygen and give out carbon dioxide. Too much carbon dioxide causes symptoms including, if I remember rightly, weakness and headache – initially.'

'And then?'

'Ultimately, suffocation.' Jack frowned.

'Feel free not to be so blunt.'

Surprised flitted across Jack's face. 'I'm only telling you the facts.'

'And you're telling me them because...?'

'Because I'm surprised we've not started feeling any effects yet of carbon dioxide levels rising.' He tapped his chin. 'Can you show me the photo you took of the map again?'

Alyssa fished the phone from her pocket and found the picture, which Jack studied intently for a few moments. Then he stood up, shaking the cramp out of his legs.

'Come with me.'

'Why?'

'I don't intend to end up like poor Charity and Josiah, or have people claim we were eaten by a sea dragon. There's no way I'm becoming part of a myth. I'd never live it down. So, follow me.' He wriggled back through the pile of rubble into the main tunnel. 'Are you coming?' he called.

Alyssa pushed her hand into her pocket and ran her fingers across the precious brooch nestling there. 'I'll be with you in a second.'

Kneeling down beside Charity and Josiah, she slipped the brooch back into Charity's skeletal hand. 'Here you go,' she whispered. 'I'm returning this to where it belongs.'

With one last look at the entwined skeletons, Alyssa scrambled through the hole in the rubble and stood beside Jack, who was still studying the photo. She listened for the sound of a rescue party or, at the very least, Stan calling out their names. But all was silent. Perhaps no one knew they were even missing.

'It must be somewhere around here,' said Jack, sweeping his torch beam across the wall.

'What's where?' asked Alyssa, trying to look over his shoulder at the photo without their bodies touching. 'What are you doing?'

'I'm looking for this.' Jack enlarged the map and traced his finger along the lines. 'If this line is the tunnel, I think we must be here' – he pointed at the screen – 'because we'd gone past this right-hand bend, and I think this shaded area here could be the storeroom we've just come from. Do you agree?'

Alyssa peered at the map. 'That makes sense.'

'And if that's the case, what's this?' Jack pointed at a faint line running off the tunnel, close to where they were standing.

'A slip of the pen?'

'Perhaps, if our luck's run out. But I've been thinking, what if it's some sort of ventilation shaft that's topping up the oxygen levels down here? That might explain why we don't seem to be suffering from carbon dioxide build-up.'

'Would they have bothered building ventilation shafts if the tunnel was open at both ends?'

'I don't know. Maybe they would, to keep the air down here as fresh as possible.'

'And a ventilation shaft would lead to the surface.'

Jack only gave a tight nod, but it was enough to spark hope in Alyssa. This could prove to be their way out, if the shaft existed and they could find it. It was a long shot, but they were all out of other ideas.

'We'd better get searching, then,' she said, already digging her hands into the rubble.

If the map was to be believed, the shaft lay on the opposite side of the tunnel from the storeroom. Part of the roof had collapsed there, probably years ago, and she and Jack began carefully to pull away fallen stones and earth, trying to see what lay behind.

It was hot and heavy work, and after a while Alyssa's hopes began to fade. Nothing but brick walls lay behind the fallen rubble that she was moving.

She stopped and wiped her forehead with the back of her hand, craving a glass of clear, cold water. And space – the walls down here seemed to be folding in on her, making her feel claustrophobic and panicky. She closed her eyes and imagined that she was standing on the beach, her bare feet sinking into the sand and the wide, bright sky above her. She pictured the sun rising out of the sea, its golden rays lighting the cliffs that soared to the heavens, and she felt her shoulders drop. She would see the sky again. She had to hold on to hope.

'Are you doing OK?' Jack's voice cut through her thoughts. Turning her hot face towards him, she opened her eyes. He'd stopped digging in the rubble and was watching her, his dark shadow looming behind him like a monster. 'Do you need to take a break? We don't want to get too dehydrated.'

But Alyssa had stopped listening because something was different. 'Can you feel that?' she asked, turning her face from side to side.

'Feel what?'

'There's a draught coming from somewhere. It's cold on my skin, on my cheeks.'

He moved to her side, bumping into her in the gloom, and held up a hand in front of her face. Then he smiled. 'You're right. I can feel it too.' He began to move his hand along a section of the tunnel wall that they'd almost cleared of rubble. 'It's here!' he said triumphantly, grabbing hold of Alyssa's hand and holding it where his had been.

Alyssa grinned at him as a stream of cold air began winding round her fingers. 'Let's get the rest of this section cleared.'

Together, they began to move the rubble that remained piled up against the tunnel wall, until a loud *clang* echoed around them. A metal grille was set into the wall, at waist height.

'Well, will you look at that?' said Jack, laughing with relief.

Alyssa resisted an urge to throw her arms around him in celebration. The mark on the map hadn't been a slip of the pen at all. The smugglers, bless them, had had the foresight to build a ventilation shaft – though Alyssa doubted they'd imagined it being used as an escape route almost three hundred years later.

'Give me a hand getting this off,' said Jack, his jaw straining as he pulled at the grille.

Alyssa hooked her fingers around the edge of the metal and

began to pull with him. Sharp slivers lodged under her nails but she kept on pulling until the grille began to shift and suddenly it came free, sending her and Jack tumbling backwards.

'Ouch!' Alyssa rubbed her shoulder as she helped Jack to his feet. The metal grille lay on the ground and a strong, cold draught was snaking out from the hole in the wall.

'Abracadabra! A ventilation shaft!' Jack grinned broadly and shouted 'Hello' into the opening. 'Can anyone hear me? Help! We're trapped!' His words disappeared into the void and were met with silence.

Alyssa shone her torch into the opening and the hope that had flared in her heart dimmed a little. The ventilation shaft was basically another tunnel, but this one was little more than a body-width wide, and it climbed at a steep angle.

'Hello!' Jack shouted again. 'We need help!' But there was still no reply. The cavalry wasn't coming any time soon. If at all.

Alyssa flinched when a dusting of earth dropped on her head from the roof. The tunnel had been destabilised by the latest cave-in, not to mention her and Jack moving fallen rubble around, and she didn't fancy waiting to see how unstable the whole thing had become.

She took a deep breath. 'There's only one way to find out where this tunnel goes, and to get help.'

'You're right.' Jack inspected the narrow entrance to the shaft. 'I think I'll fit into it.'

'Not you. Me. I can climb up and raise the alarm when I get out.'

'No way.' Jack put his hands on his hips and shook his head. 'It's too dangerous.'

'I doubt it's more dangerous than waiting for the roof to fall in. And I'm smaller than you, so I'll fit into the space easily.' Alyssa shivered because 'easily' was pushing it. The thought of crawling through that small opening made her feel light-headed. But the creaking of the roof supports nearby made up her mind. 'You know it makes sense for me to climb up, rather than you, Jack. We could wait around for your dad to realise where we are and raise the alarm, but what if he comes in, opens the shop and doesn't go into the cellar for hours? He'll think you're still out somewhere, and I don't know about you, but I don't think I can stay down here much longer, waiting for the roof to cave in, without losing it completely. So, this is worth a shot.'

'You don't have to do this,' said Jack, putting his hands on her shoulders and turning her to face him, his grey eyes black in the low light. 'You really don't.'

'Yes, I really do,' said Alyssa, determined to make up for getting Jack into this mess in the first place. Poor Stan had suffered too much over the years to face another tragedy, and Archie needed his dad.

Before she could change her mind, Alyssa pulled away from Jack, crouched down and pushed her shoulders through the opening in the tunnel wall. She dragged herself fully inside and began to crawl, sweeping the torch ahead of her.

Almost immediately, she realised how bad an idea this might have been. The walls of the ventilation shaft were inches from her body and the roof was only a foot above her head. Bubbles of panic started to rise into her throat. 'My life has to change,' she muttered to herself, crawling slowly along the incline, her knees scraped by rough stones. 'If I get out of here alive, my whole freaking life has to change.'

'Are you all right?' Jack's voice echoed along the shaft. 'Alyssa, speak to me!' His apparent paucity of panic had vanished. He sounded almost as fraught as she felt.

'Yeah, I'm OK,' Alyssa shouted over her shoulder. 'And the draught is getting stronger.'

She crawled on up the incline, singing a Taylor Swift song under her breath to push down the panic; singing, and picturing the faces of the people she'd left behind when she fled: Ben, her parents, friends – she'd hardly seen any of them during the last six months. She'd been too busy running from a tragedy she could not escape.

What would smugglers have sung to themselves as they'd built this infernal tunnel? she wondered. What might Charity have sung to herself as she rushed to give Josiah the brooch that could help to secure his freedom? 'Greensleeves' was the only old song she could remember, and she only knew the chorus, but she sang that as she climbed ever higher.

The rush of air gradually turned into a strong breeze and Alyssa began to hear booming sounds ahead of her. But the cramped ventilation shaft was still dark, and she found out why when her fingers hit something hard: the way ahead was blocked. And it was at that precise moment that her phone ran out of battery and the torchlight died.

'You have got to be kidding me!' she shouted into the blackness, wondering if she could slide back down the way she'd come. Physically turning around would be impossible, and even trying such a risky move might result in her getting stuck. 'You are in *big* trouble,' Alyssa muttered, trying not to panic, though that was nearly impossible seeing as she was now even more trapped than she had been in the tunnel with Jack.

'Alyssa!'

Jack's voice, sounding like it was miles away, brought tears to her eyes. She so wanted to see his face again, to feel his fingers on her lips, to kiss him senseless. Who cared if he still loved Miri? She should have kissed him while she had the chance.

'Stupid! Stupid!' she berated herself, hitting out at the blockage ahead of her in frustration. Her hand hit cold, hard stone and she ran her fingers across it. A huge rock was blocking the ventilation shaft.

But, when she squinted into the darkness, a faint sliver of light caught her eye. A sliver of daylight.

Alyssa hadn't come this far – braving collapsing tunnels, bones and disclosing her darkest secret – to give up at the final hurdle. She put her shoulder against the rock and pushed with all her might. Nothing happened, so she tried again and again until it shifted a little.

'Yes!' she yelled, pushing until her muscles began to cramp and she felt hot enough to burst into flame. But the rock was moving and, as it shifted a little more, the ventilation shaft was suddenly flooded with light. Soil was falling on her head, and she yelled again as bugs and spiders cascaded down around her shoulders.

Jack's voice sounded from far below. 'That's it. I'm coming to get you.'

'I'm all right,' she shouted back but she could hear Jack grunting and groaning as he started crawling along the narrow tunnel.

He's going to get stuck, thought Alyssa. *At least Charity and Josiah died in each other's arms. There's no way we're dying apart, rammed into this shaft like trapped peas in a pod.*

She shoved the rock again as hard as she could and, though the boulder didn't move very far, it was enough. Through the gap she'd created, Alyssa glimpsed the most wondrous sight she'd ever seen: sky the colour of cornflowers and pillows of white cloud. One more almighty push, with every last ounce of energy she possessed, and the gap was big enough to squeeze through.

She emerged, blinking, into pale sunlight and gasping in deep breaths of fresh air as she tried to get her bearings. She was above the beach, where the land rose, and the booming noise she'd heard while she crawled was the sound of waves crashing against the cliffs.

Alyssa scrubbed at her cheeks as tears streamed from her eyes. She was safe and Jack soon would be too. She could hear his voice as he crawled along the tunnel, getting closer. He was calling her name, sounding frantic.

'I'm here! I'm out!' she shouted into the mouth of the opening. She could just see the top of his head coming towards her. 'Keep going. You're almost there.'

With a lot of grunting and swearing, Jack pulled himself out of the ventilation shaft, into the daylight. He jumped to his feet and, grabbing hold of Alyssa, pulled her tightly against him.

'For goodness' sake!' he whispered. 'I thought you were badly injured when you yelled. I thought the tunnel had fallen in on top of you.'

'It was spiders,' said Alyssa, relishing the comfort of Jack's embrace.

'Spiders?' He held her at arm's length and frowned.

'A load of spiders fell on my head when I was trying to move the rock and get out.' She'd forgotten about them in the euphoria of not dying, and she ran her hands through her hair in case any were still lurking. 'Are you going to tell me every scientific fact about spiders now, and how, seeing as there are no deadly species in England, I totally overreacted?'

'God, no. I'd have screamed the place down. I hate the bloody things.'

His face creased into a smile and Alyssa felt her heart quicken. Maybe it was the joy of being alive and free, but she still badly wanted to kiss him. However, in the beautiful but cold light of day, knowing that neither of them were about to die, what was the point? She was very obviously not Jack's type, apart from in traumatic situations when choice was limited. And, anyway, he was still in love with Miri, and Alyssa had to safeguard her heart.

Jack was staring at her, his face streaked with dirt.

Alyssa looked away. 'So, where have we come out?'

Jack let go of her arms. 'Close to the beach, which isn't surprising.' He bent down to study the small opening they'd both squeezed through. 'Whoever built the ventilation shaft wanted this opening well hidden.' He ran his hand across the large boulder that had blocked it from view for generations. 'I'm very impressed that you managed to shift this, but we'd better push it back, don't you think? So that no one else gets trapped down there. Have you got any energy left to give me a hand?'

Alyssa nodded and, together, they pushed the boulder back into place and rearranged the brambles that had grown up around it.

Afterwards, Jack rolled his shoulders and looked out across the ocean. 'It's so good to see that beautiful view!'

Below them, on the curve of sand, people were walking dogs and a few hardy sun-worshippers had stripped off to their swimsuits. Sunbeams were dancing on the waves, making them glisten.

'It's glorious,' Alyssa agreed, drinking in the blues of sky and sea, the yelp of dogs barking and the scent of wild flowers scattered among the grass. Her senses were heightened, making her feel more alive than she'd felt in a long time.

Jack glanced at her. 'What about Josiah and Charity? Down there, together, in the dark.'

He sounded concerned and Alyssa marvelled at how much had changed in the few hours they'd been trapped underground. Jack's view of his ancestor had done an about-turn, and she had solved the mystery that had been haunting her. She'd got to know more about Jack's traumatic childhood and understood him better. And he knew everything about her, now she'd shared her secret. Would he tell? Alyssa smiled because she knew that he wouldn't. He was a trustworthy man.

'We can't just leave them there,' Jack added. 'It doesn't seem right.'

'I agree. It would be good to bring Josiah and Charity into the light after almost three hundred years.'

'It's only because of you that they've been found.'

'Because of my bloody-mindedness?' Alyssa asked, raising an eyebrow.

'Because of your determination and persistence,' said Jack. 'You should be proud of yourself.'

It had been so long since anyone had said that, since she'd felt any pride in herself at all, Alyssa's eyes filled with tears.

'It's all right now. We're safe.' Jack brushed his thumb across her cheek, to wipe away a tear that was trickling over her skin. And it was such an intimate gesture, Alyssa held her breath as seagulls wheeled overhead and a crescendo of barks rose from the beach. 'Please, don't cry,' urged Jack, cupping her cheek in his hand.

Suddenly, Alyssa wasn't sure where this was going to end. If he kissed her now, would that be trauma-induced? Or would he really mean it?

She was destined never to find out because the shrill tone of his mobile phone broke the spell, and he dropped his hand to fish his phone from his pocket.

'Hello,' he said, his eyes still locked on to Alyssa's. 'Dad. Are you all right? ... Yeah, I'm on my way home right now. Sorry. I've been out for longer than I expected.' He raised an eyebrow at Alyssa and grinned. 'OK, see you soon. Oh, and by the way, the cellar's a bit of a mess so please don't go down there until I get back.'

Jack shoved his phone back into his pocket. 'I don't want him finding the tunnel and trying it out for himself.' Then he breathed in slowly and held out his hand. 'It's been quite an interesting few hours, Alyssa Jones, or whoever you are. Shall we go home?'

Alyssa took his hand and his fingers wrapped around hers as they walked down the grassy slope and past the beach. Neither of them spoke – and it should have felt awkward, holding his hand. But it felt totally natural, Alyssa realised, as they walked along the lane and past the castle ruins. Just as

Jack brushing a tear from her cheek had felt as if it was meant to be.

Alyssa wasn't sure who let go first, but they'd stopped holding hands by the time they reached the first shops in Heaven's Cove. The village was just the same as it had been when she'd woken up that morning – picturesque, historic, the beating heart of the local community – but so much had changed for her since then.

She'd lost a friend in Magda, along with her home. She'd been trapped in an underground tunnel, discovered the truth about Josiah and Charity, and told Jack her secret.

It felt good to have spoken it out loud at last, but it wasn't the only secret she was carrying. Her feelings for Jack had completely changed since they'd first met, but she was confused now about how he felt. She was almost sure he'd *really* wanted to kiss her when they'd emerged into the sunshine from the ventilation shaft. She'd seen it in his eyes. So where did that leave her?

Alyssa didn't want to play games. There were enough of those going on with Miri and Jack. It was better to find out the truth. She stopped walking and said quietly, 'Before you go home... can we have a quick word? There's something I need to ask you.'

He stopped and turned to her. 'Of course.'

What about Magda and Stan? The thought popped into her head. *Magda told Stan how she felt and look how that turned out.*

But when Jack smiled at her, crinkles appearing around his eyes, Alyssa's heart flipped and she knew that she had to speak up. However this turned out, she couldn't stay silent.

THIRTY-FIVE

JACK

Jack waited for Alyssa to speak. A line had appeared between her eyebrows and there was a smudge of dirt on her nose.

He had an urge to brush the dirt away but that seemed too intimate, here in the middle of Heaven's Cove. That's why they were no longer holding hands. He wasn't sure why he'd taken Alyssa's hand as they'd walked past the beach, but it had felt natural and nice, and she hadn't seemed to mind.

The two of them walking along, side by side, had reminded him of Charity and Josiah and the way their bones were inter-mingled and entwined. They must have held hands almost three centuries ago, just as he and Alyssa were doing – until the shops of Heaven's Cove had come into view, and he'd suddenly felt awkward and let go.

In spite of Alyssa opening her heart to him in the tunnel, and telling him her secret, he was still finding her hard to read. He was attracted to her, that was indisputable. But he couldn't work out what she felt about him. The kiss in the marquee had been mind-blowing but it had all been for show. Then, when he'd almost kissed her while they were trapped in the dark with

Charity and Josiah, she'd moved away and started talking about how much he loved Miri.

Alyssa took a deep breath. 'The thing is, there's something I'd like to say. Well, I say "like" but it's more that I *need* to say it. Though it's probably not a good idea.'

Jack gave in and brushed the dirt smudge from her nose. 'Just say it, Alyssa. Whatever it is.'

'OK.' She swallowed and opened her mouth to speak.

'Hey, there you are!'

Jack jumped when Miri's shout rang out across the street. 'I was on my way to your dad's shop to find you.'

'Miri,' said Jack, his stomach doing a flip as he took a step back from Alyssa and shoved his hands into his pockets. 'I didn't expect to see you. I thought you and Damian would have left by now.'

'Damian's gone on ahead. I had something to do first.' She looked him and Alyssa up and down, and her eyes narrowed. 'What on earth have you two been up to? You're both filthy.'

'It's a long story. What do you want, Miri?'

He sounded off-hand. He knew he did. But after being trapped in a tunnel, discovering Alyssa's darkest secret, and scrambling his way to safety, the last thing he needed was to be blindsided by the sudden appearance of the woman who wanted to divorce him.

Though Alyssa reckoned Miri was actually still in love with him. Was she? Jack should be able to tell, surely. He knew her so well. They'd shared bringing up Archie, for goodness' sake, and yet these days she seemed like a stranger.

'Can we talk?' she asked, flicking her fair hair over her shoulder. She was wearing it long, which suited her. She glanced at Alyssa, who was standing next to him. 'Can we talk alone, I mean? Without Alice.'

Was she using the wrong name deliberately? Jack wondered. Deliberate or not, it got under his skin. 'You can say whatever you want to say here,' he told her, squaring his shoulders.

Alyssa shifted beside him. 'Don't worry. I'll go.'

'No.' Jack's voice was louder than he'd meant, and a group of tourists on the other side of the street glanced over. He lowered his voice and spoke to Alyssa directly. 'No, please stay. This won't take long.'

Miri frowned, her mouth pulled into a pout. 'OK. If that's what you want.' Taking hold of Jack's arm, she pulled him to one side.

Jack was now standing so close to Miri he could smell her perfume. She was wearing the scent he remembered – a heady mix of exotic flowers, which brought back memories: the first time they'd kissed, her delight at his proposal, their honeymoon in France, sitting next to her proudly at Archie's nativity play.

'What was it you wanted to say?' he asked, steeling himself for another blow.

Perhaps she wanted to limit his time with Archie even further, or announce that Damian was moving in. It was only a matter of time, he supposed.

'I need to tell you how I feel,' she said quietly, but not so quietly that Alyssa couldn't overhear. 'Being here with you this weekend, at Rosie's wedding, has made me realise that I gave up on our marriage too early.'

Jack opened his mouth and closed it again.

'What I mean,' Miri said, moving even closer, 'is that I'd be up for giving our marriage another go.'

'What about Damian?' Jack asked, his mind whirling.

Miri shrugged. 'Damian's a good guy but he's not you. I know this is difficult and you're with someone else now' – she shot a glance at Alyssa and grabbed his hand, the hand that Alyssa had been holding ten minutes earlier – 'but you still love me. I know you do, Jacky. It's obvious. And I want us to get back together, back to how it was. So, what do you think?'

'I think—' Jack began, not sure how this sentence was going to end. He was finding it hard to think straight.

But he didn't have a chance to say any more because Miri suddenly looped her arms around his neck and was kissing him.

This was everything he'd dreamed about. He and Miri back together, as if the last few months had never happened. Damian was toast and everything was good again. Miri still loved him, and he still loved his wife. Alyssa had been right.

Alyssa... Surely he shouldn't be thinking about Alyssa when Miri was kissing him?

Jack drew back from her and wiped the back of his hand across his mouth. A trace of Miri's red lipstick smeared across his knuckles.

'I know this is what you want,' Miri insisted. 'And I know you don't really love anyone else. Not like you love me.' She glanced at Alyssa, who was now walking away without looking back. 'So, let's be together, Jack. As we should be.' When he said nothing, she added: 'For Archie's sake because he misses you so much.'

Was she right? wondered Jack. Whatever had happened between them, surely he and Miri should make a go of their marriage for the sake of their son? That was what good parents did, and he so wanted to be a good dad to Archie.

'Well?' Miri asked, a faint smile on her lips, as if she knew what his answer would be.

THIRTY-SIX

ALYSSA

Alyssa walked at top speed through Heaven's Cove until her legs were aching and her lungs were fit to burst.

She would go home and rest. She should definitely go home and have a good clean up. A shower at Magda's was out, but she could fill the tiny basin in the caravan and wash away the grime that coated her skin.

But the thought of being alone with her thoughts was unbearable.

First, there was the trauma of being trapped in the tunnel to process, along with finding two skeletons, which would freak anyone out. Although, actually, it hadn't been so scary once she'd realised who they were. It was odd, but Charity and Josiah felt like old friends – people Alyssa liked and cared about – and realising it was them had swiftly turned her fear to sorrow. But there had also been the trauma of crawling up through the ventilation shaft, which had been awful. Memories of her phone dying and everything going black still made her shiver... and then, there was Jack.

He'd seemed more vulnerable, more accessible, when they were trapped together in the dark. That was why she'd opened her heart to him. And they'd seemed close when they walked into the village, hand in hand, which was when she'd really begun to wonder if she'd been wrong about his feelings for Miri.

Miri was still keen on him, she'd told herself as they walked. That was obvious enough. But perhaps Jack was ready to move on, after all? Would a man still in love with his estranged wife have cupped Alyssa's cheek in his hand as they stood in the sunshine and stared at her with such... longing?

Once they'd reached the village, she'd been about to tell him that she liked him – *really* liked him – and ask if he had any similar feelings. It meant putting her heart on the line, which was scary. But she was psyching herself up to do it nonetheless, when Miri had gate-crashed – and she'd got her answer.

Alyssa pictured Miri and Jack locked in an embrace and wiped away tears.

If Jack was still in love with Miri, it was best for him and for Archie that they were back together. Even if the disappointment made her heart hurt. But she still couldn't shake the feeling that this was all a game to Miri: a game that she was determined to win.

Alyssa shook her head, her mind a jumble of emotions, and let herself into her quiet caravan.

One very thorough wash later, Alyssa pulled her suitcase from the top of the cupboard and started folding clothes into it. Once again, she'd made a total hash of her life and she needed to get away from Heaven's Cove.

She should never have gone along with Jack's claim that she was his girlfriend. Upping the ante at Rosie's wedding by kissing him had been, frankly, ridiculous. And as for dragging him into a dangerous tunnel once roamed by smugglers... what had she been thinking?

She'd been so desperate to follow her instincts and distance herself from the woman she once was. But the fact was her life had been out of control from the moment when, under someone else's orders, she'd administered too large a dose of medication to Ollie. She'd been running ever since, and punishing herself – cutting herself off from family and friends, scraping a living by running tourist tours, and never getting close to anyone.

Until she met Jack, that is, and let down the guard she'd spent months building up.

That was why the sight of Miri kissing Jack had felt like a knife to the heart.

Alyssa sighed, crammed her toiletries bag into the suitcase and zipped the case shut. Running away again wouldn't make anything better because, however far she ran, she could never escape herself. But she couldn't stay in Heaven's Cove. It would be impossible with no home, and with Jack and Miri wandering around, all loved up, during visits to Stan. It was time to move on.

Alyssa slid onto the floor with her back to the window bench, trying not to think about how much she was about to lose. She would go and visit Ben for a few days and decide what to do next. That was the best idea and, who knew, perhaps one day this wouldn't all feel so raw?

She traced a circle in the dirt she'd tracked into the caravan and sat there, feeling miserable, until a tentative knock on the caravan door made her jump. The door creaked open and Magda poked her head inside. 'Would you mind very much if I came in for a minute? I promise I won't get angry.' She spotted the suitcase and her mouth fell open. 'Are you going somewhere?'

'Yes, for a while,' said Alyssa, wearily getting to her feet.

'You can't.' Magda stepped into the caravan, shaking her head. 'Are you leaving because of what I said this morning?'

'No, not really. There's other stuff going on and I need to get away.'

'But I'll miss you.'

When Magda's face crumpled, Alyssa stepped forward and led her to the window seat. 'Sit down. Do you want some water?'

Magda gulped and nodded. 'Yes, please.'

While Alyssa was fetching water from the fridge, Magda suddenly blurted out: 'I'm sorry I was bad-tempered this morning. I shouldn't have blamed you for the total mess I made of things with Stan. That was down to me and me alone. I asked for your opinion and you gave it, but it was me who decided to speak out.'

She stopped speaking and nodded to herself, as if she'd been rehearsing what to say and was pleased that she'd managed to do it.

'That's all right,' Alyssa assured her, closing the fridge.

'Only it's so much easier to blame other people rather than yourself, don't you think?'

'Always. But you honestly don't need to apologise, Magda. You've been brilliant to me since I arrived in Heaven's Cove, and me leaving is not just about what happened this morning, I promise you.'

Alyssa handed over the glass of water, feeling relieved that their spat was being resolved. She'd grown very fond of Magda over the last few months and didn't want to leave while they were on bad terms.

'He came to see me, you know.' Magda stared at the glass, which was catching the light and projecting rainbow colours around the caravan. 'This morning, after our little bust-up, Stan came round and told me that he loved me.'

'Wow, Magda, that's brilliant! I'm so happy for you. Does—'

Alyssa stopped speaking when Magda held up her hand. She didn't look like a woman whose passion had been requited.

'He told me that he loves me but he's not *in* love with me, and never will be. He still loves his wife, you see.'

Alyssa nodded. She did see. Like father, like son.

'So, what are you going to do,' she asked gently, 'now that Stan has laid his cards on the table? Are *you* still leaving Heaven's Cove?'

Magda gave a sad smile. 'No, I don't think so. Stan needs me, you see, and what kind of love would I have for that man if I deserted him in his hour of need?'

Her selflessness took Alyssa's breath away. Her willingness to put aside her own heartbreak to help a man who could never give her the affection she craved was admirable, and perfect proof of true love.

Alyssa crouched down beside her. 'I'm sure that Penny would approve of you being here to look after him.'

'Yes, I rather think that she would.' Magda sniffed back tears. 'But what about you, Alyssa? You can stay in Heaven's Cove now that I'm staying too. The caravan is yours for as long as you'd like it.'

'Thank you, and I do appreciate all of the kindness you've shown me since I turned up, out of the blue. You've been amazing.' Alyssa's eyes were suddenly full of tears and she gulped, trying not to sob. It had been a difficult day of trying to hold herself together, and Magda's kindness and generosity were about to push her over the edge.

'Ah, bless you.' Magda pulled Alyssa onto the seat beside her. 'I don't know what's going on in your life but you're very welcome here. You're good for me – and for Stan too, I think. You seem to understand the challenges he'll face, and he needs all the support he can get.'

Magda took a sip of water while Alyssa weighed up whether to tell this remarkable woman the truth about her own past. The truth had been a weight around her neck for so long but now, having told Jack, it seemed to have lost some of its power.

She took a deep breath. 'Actually, I know quite a lot about

what Stan's facing because I used to be a nurse, and I've come across his condition before. I've cared for patients badly affected by it.'

Curiosity sparked in Magda's eyes. 'You were a nurse?'

'Yes, I worked in a hospital as a nurse for about ten years.' Much to Alyssa's surprise, Magda said nothing but went back to sipping her water. 'Aren't you going to ask me why I've given up nursing to run myths and legends tours in Heaven's Cove?'

'No,' replied Magda, shaking her head. 'Fortunately, I'm not as inquisitive as Belinda. I assume you have a very good reason for your change of circumstances, and you'll tell me if and when you're ready.' She patted Alyssa's hand. 'We all have very good reasons for the actions that we take, even if, with hindsight, they're not always such good reasons after all.'

They sat in silence after that, both women preoccupied with thoughts of what they'd done that could never be changed, what they'd lost, and what might have been.

'So, are you still leaving Heaven's Cove?' Magda asked after a while.

Alyssa breathed out slowly, her mind still elsewhere. 'We found the bones of Charity and Josiah today.'

Magda sat up straight. 'What did you say? Who found what bones?'

Everything that had happened during the last few hours already seemed like a story – a myth she should tell to tourists, because it felt so far removed from her quiet little caravan. But Alyssa outlined the day's adventures: 'Jack and I discovered an old smugglers' tunnel leading from the cellar in his shop. We went inside it – long story, and my fault – and we found them in there: two skeletons, the bones of Charity and Josiah, the couple who disappeared from the village almost three hundred years ago. It turns out that Charity wasn't murdered by Jack's ancestor or dragged into the ocean by a sea dragon. She did die that day in 1753, but she died beneath Heaven's Cove alongside Josiah, after a part of the tunnel collapsed.'

Magda's mouth had fallen open but she snapped it shut. 'Are you quite sure it's Charity and Josiah?'

'As sure as I can be. A beautiful brooch disappeared at the same time that Charity did, and one of the skeletons – the smaller one – had the brooch in her hand.'

Magda's jaw had dropped again. She breathed out slowly. 'So, where's the brooch now?'

'Still with Charity. It didn't seem right to leave her in the dark without it. Not when it's been with them for so long.'

Magda nodded as if she agreed with Alyssa's reasoning. 'Have you told anyone else about this?'

'Not yet. Maybe Jack has, although he's probably too busy right now.' Alyssa brushed a hand across her face, trying to wipe away the thought of Jack and Miri making up.

'But this is absolutely amazing!' Magda was on her feet. 'No one has known what happened to that poor couple for almost three centuries and you've been in Heaven's Cove for a few months and have solved the mystery. Did you say you found them in a smugglers' tunnel?'

'Yes, I guess Josiah was a smuggler and Charity was trying to help fund his escape from the authorities with the brooch. But then the roof of the tunnel fell in and they were trapped.'

'Poor loves.' Magda shivered. 'I would imagine smugglers' tunnels were very unstable.'

'They still are,' murmured Alyssa, but so quietly that Magda didn't hear her.

'You said you found these bones with Jack. So where is he now?'

'I have no idea,' said Alyssa, staring at her fingers. She'd washed off the worst of the dirt, but dark soil was still trapped under her nails. Proof that she really had been trapped underground with Jack, even though it was all starting to feel like a dream: darkness, bones and an almost-kiss.

Magda's eyes narrowed. 'I know you're a private person, Alyssa, but I have to ask, what's going on with you and Jack?'

'I told you. We found the tunnel together and discovered the bones.'

'No, love.' She sat down again beside Alyssa and took hold of her hand. 'I mean, what's *really* going on with you and Jack?'

'He and Miri are back together.' Alyssa tried to sound upbeat as she shared the news, but failed miserably.

'Ah, I see.' Magda tapped the toe of her trainer on the caravan floor. 'That's a shame.'

'I thought you'd be pleased.'

'Not really. I want Jack to be happy, of course, and I don't have anything in particular against Miri. She's nice enough, but I don't think she's the right sort of person for Jack, and I know that Penny thought the same.' Magda gave Alyssa a sideways glance. 'I thought that you and Jack were becoming good friends. I saw you talking at Rosie's wedding reception.'

'Only talking?'

'Yes, why? What did I miss?'

'We kissed,' said Alyssa, not caring who knew any more. Jack had probably confessed all to Miri by now anyway. 'We were trying to make Miri jealous, which sounds ridiculous now. He told her I was his girlfriend, and I played along.'

'I see, and your deception appears to have worked very well. Rather better than you'd have liked, perhaps?' When Alyssa nodded, her throat too tight to answer, Magda sighed. 'We both appear to be in love with men who are in love with other women. Which is rather unfortunate.'

Magda's words brought Alyssa up short. She knew she really liked Jack, but as she remembered Jack's arms around her in the dark tunnel, the way his eyes crinkled when he smiled, and the pain in her heart when Miri had kissed him, she admitted the truth.

She couldn't be sure when it had happened – when dislike had turned to friendship and then to much stronger feelings – but Magda was right.

They were both in love with unsuitable men, and there was nothing that either of them could do about it.

THIRTY-SEVEN
JACK

Jack sat with his knees pulled up beneath his chin. Behind him, Driftwood House was empty of guests while Rosie and Liam were away on their honeymoon. He turned and studied the handsome house, perched so high on the cliffs above Heaven's Cove, and wondered about Josiah Gathergill.

Did his seven-times great-uncle walk up this cliff path in the hope of catching sight of Charity and enjoy this same view? Had he been the sort of man who marvelled at the whole grand 'wonderment' of a sunset, or who dissected it into smaller chunks to be better understood?

Whatever sort of man Josiah was, he wasn't a murderer, and that made Jack's heart sing. His pleasure was entirely illogical, seeing as he'd never been worried that criminality was inherited. But he felt it all the same. He was happy that Josiah's reputation had been redeemed and that he and Charity might soon be released from their dark tomb.

And their release was all due to Alyssa, who'd never given up in her bonkers quest to uncover the truth. Unpredictable, chaotic, intriguing Alyssa, who had been in his arms deep beneath Heaven's Cove just a few hours ago and who, he'd since found out, was now leaving the village.

He'd never met anyone like Alyssa before, but he understood her better now. She had craved redemption for Josiah, just as she craved it for herself.

Jack looked back at the sunset spread out before him and drank in the scene. Pillows of cloud near the horizon were violet jewels in a sky banded pink and gold, and the sea was a rippling palette of translucent blues.

Alyssa was right, he thought, his heart heavy. It didn't always matter why the sky was breathtakingly glorious. Sometimes it was simply enough that it was.

He glanced at Heaven's Cove to his left, far below him. It wasn't dark enough yet for people to switch on the lamps in their cottage windows, but the low sun was reflecting off panes of glass and making the whole village twinkle.

Was Alyssa still down there or had she set off already, to who knew where? Jack sighed and began to recite pi, but he couldn't think straight and the numbers wouldn't come.

A flash of yellow caught his attention and he squinted at the cliff path, then groaned. Another walker like him, keen to enjoy the sunset from on top of the world, was making their way up the path, and he was in no mood to make polite conversation.

Getting to his feet, he stretched his legs, ready to move off. But he did a double take when the walker got closer. He would recognise those impractical yellow trousers anywhere, and the streaks of peacock-blue in her hair.

Jack sat back down on the grass, trying to appear nonchalant as Alyssa approached him. He wasn't sure which posture would best communicate this, so he leaned back on his elbows, smiled and hoped for the best.

'Hello,' she said, standing in front of him. She pushed hair from her eyes, a serious expression on her beautiful face. 'What are you doing?'

'Watching the sunset.'

'Nice.'

He cleared his throat. 'I thought you were leaving Heaven's Cove.'

'Why did you think that?'

'Magda told me. She came round – I thought to see Dad – and said you were going. She went out of her way to tell me, actually. I was sorting out some stuff in the loft and she climbed the loft ladder to find me.'

'Is that right?' The hint of a smile played on Alyssa's lips.

'I went to your caravan to try and find you, to say goodbye, but you weren't there.'

'I've been out walking for ages, trying to clear my head after everything that happened today. In the tunnel, I mean.' She wrinkled her nose and fell silent.

'And you decided to come up here?'

'Only when I bumped into Magda and she told me you'd gone out for a walk to watch the sun set.'

Jack sat up, a puzzled expression on his face. 'I came down from the loft and told Dad where I was going. She must have overheard.'

'And she then passed that information on to me.' Alyssa raised an eyebrow. 'Actually, she didn't so much bump into me in the street as pursue me along it until I stopped to listen to her.'

'Mmm.' Jack shook his head. Magda's conniving to get the two of them together was worthy of his mother's matchmaking efforts in the past. But her efforts had been wasted.

It was nice that Alyssa had climbed up here, presumably to say goodbye to him after all that they'd shared deep underground. But the inkling he'd had at times that she might feel something for him was nothing but his ego giving him a boost. He was, and always would be, a nerd in Alyssa's eyes. A nerd with a closed mind.

Perhaps their play-acting for Miri's benefit had spilled over into real life for a moment or two. But that's all it had been on Alyssa's part – play-acting. He was sure of it.

He turned his face towards the sun and found comfort in the warmth of the day's final rays.

'Where's Miri?' Alyssa asked, sitting down beside him. Before he could answer, she added: 'I'm pleased that you're back together. I knew you still cared about her and I hope you'll both be very happy.' When he glanced at her, she was staring at the sunset, her face expressionless. 'I thought you might be out on a walk together.'

'No. Miri's on her way back to London, I imagine.'

'I didn't realise she'd be going back on her own.'

'Oh, she's not on her own.' Jack breathed out slowly. 'She's with Damian.'

Alyssa turned to him, her forehead furrowed in confusion. 'Damian? But I thought you two... I mean, I saw you two...' She puffed out her cheeks. 'I have no idea what's going on.'

'Me, neither,' Jack admitted. 'But one thing I do know is that Miri and I aren't right for each other. Not any more.'

Alyssa shifted round on the grass until she was fully facing Jack. 'But you kissed her, in the street. I saw you.'

'I think the evidence would show that she kissed me, actually.'

He remembered Miri's passionate kiss, and the petulance that had crossed her face when he hadn't leaped at the idea of the two of them getting back together. *But I don't understand it,* she'd told him, pouting prettily. *You want me. This is what you want.* She'd almost stamped her foot in the street.

But after watching Alyssa walk away from him, Jack had realised that *this* wasn't what he wanted any longer. He had changed his mind, though he wasn't sure exactly when.

'What happened?' Alyssa asked gently.

'I realised that our marriage won't work, and Miri knows it

too, deep down.' He gave a hollow laugh. 'She just doesn't like to lose.'

'So is it definitely over?'

'Yes, my marriage is most definitely over.'

It was strange how saying those words out loud just a short while ago would have killed him. Yet now, although it would be challenging at times, he knew that he would survive. Life would go on and he would make the best of it.

But when Alyssa asked, 'What about Archie?' sorrow speared Jack's heart. He would do anything to make the boy happy but living with two parents whose relationship had run its course would ultimately make him miserable. He could see that now.

'Archie will be all right because he still has two parents who love him. I'll give Miri every support I can in raising him and I'll see him as often as I'm able. It is hard, though.' When he scrunched up his eyes so he wouldn't cry at the thought of his son's trusting face, he felt Alyssa's arm press up against his. 'Anyway,' he said, opening his eyes wide and focusing on the heavenly colours in front of him, 'Miri didn't take it well. She informed me that she'd been having an affair with Damian for weeks before we split up and she'd rather be with him anyway.'

'Ouch!' Alyssa nudged her shoulder against his. 'But what she said isn't necessarily true, you know. She wasn't happy that you'd rejected her, and she was lashing out. Plus, my statement that your estranged wife is a bit of a cow stands.'

'You're... irrepressible!' spluttered Jack, feeling his misery lift a little.

Unpredictable Alyssa, with her secret past and her interest in the fantastical, was soothing to his soul.

What a terrible shame that the two of them would soon be leaving Heaven's Cove and going their separate ways.

THIRTY-EIGHT
ALYSSA

Irrepressible. Alyssa slowly rolled the word around her mind.

She couldn't imagine a man like Jack being interested in an irrepressible woman, even if he had moved on from Miri. He was a man rooted in evidence and science, and she could understand why, now that she knew him better. She knew the value of both these things herself, after a career in nursing: a career she'd loved. But the last year had shown her there was more to life than facts and figures.

'Why are you really leaving Heaven's Cove?' Jack asked suddenly, his dark hair streaked with rays of violet and gold from the setting sun. 'It's not because you told me why you came here, is it? I won't say a word to anyone about it.'

'I know you won't. I trust you.' She trusted him implicitly, Alyssa realised. And she couldn't bear the thought of never seeing him again. 'Oh, my,' she muttered. She was in deep trouble.

'Trauma takes a while to heal.' He said the words so quietly, Alyssa wondered if they were to himself. 'And guilt too. You can't turn off feelings like a tap. I felt guilty, you know, after John went.'

'Siblings sometimes do when a brother or sister dies.'

'I felt it should have been me because John was the first child, the first son, the brainy one. He excelled at all subjects, especially science, whereas I had to work at it. And I worked at it so hard after he died.'

'Studying for the two of you?'

His eyes met hers. 'Maybe. John wanted to be a research scientist and I followed where his footsteps would have been. But now, after meeting you, I look at this sunset and I see something different from the nuts and bolts of it. I see life in colour.' He groaned and stood up in one fluid movement. 'I can't believe I said that. I see life in colour? I'm a total idiot.'

'No, no, you're not.' Alyssa jumped up and stood in front of him. 'I know what you mean, and I feel flattered if you think I've had any hand in that. But I don't see how when you think I'm ridiculous.'

'And you think I'm a nerd.'

'Only sometimes,' said Alyssa, grinning. 'Mostly, I think you're a lovely man who's had a lot to cope with.'

She stopped grinning, her heart hammering, when Jack stepped forward until his body was almost touching hers. His face was so close, she could see the tiny lines around his eyes and the dark bands circling each iris.

'I know that *I'm* ridiculous,' he said, hair flopping across his forehead. 'I recite pi at the most inopportune moments and I find life chaotic and confusing. I'm not always an easy person to be with.' The muscles in his jaw were working overtime.

'Three point one four one five nine,' said Alyssa softly.

'Ha!' He let out a gentle chuckle. 'Have you been practising?'

Alyssa grinned up at him. 'I read up about it while I was sitting by the sea, before I walked up here. It's a pretty cool mathematical constant, actually, and if it helps you to cope with life's challenges without going crazy, then that is all that matters.'

'And what works for you, Alyssa Jones, or whatever your name is? What keeps the demons at bay?'

Heat flooded Alyssa's body when Jack brushed his fingers across her cheek.

'Sunsets, the wind in the trees, white-tipped waves rolling into shore, videos of kittens.'

She was burbling nonsense now, but all coherent thought had fled with Jack's touch on her skin.

'Videos of kittens?' He raised an eyebrow.

'YouTube,' she managed, staring into his eyes. 'You should try it.'

'I think maybe kittens are a step too far, but you've changed me, Alyssa.' He swallowed. 'I was sitting here, before you came, looking out to sea and watching the sunset and I can see the wonderment of it. I see the... the...' The words caught in his throat and he tried again. 'I see the wonderment of you.' Then he groaned again. 'I've excelled myself there. That is *so* cheesy.'

'Actually' – Alyssa stood on tiptoes – 'it's perfect.' She leaned forward and kissed the tip of his nose. Then his arms were around her and she was pulled hard against him as they kissed, their entwined bodies lit by the glorious rainbow light of the setting sun.

EPILOGUE

It had rained earlier, and a rich peaty smell rose from the earth. It curled around the gravestones and hung in the summer air as a small group of people stood by the open grave.

'Taken too soon.' Belinda sniffed and shook her head. 'Taken far too soon. Life can be very unfair.'

Alyssa nodded and wiped away a tear before putting her arm through Jack's and pulling herself against him until their hips touched. They seemed almost inseparable these days.

'Are you all right?' she asked Magda, who was standing so close to the edge of the yawning grave, she looked as if she might topple in at any moment.

Magda nodded, blinking back tears. 'I was so moved by the funeral service. It was a real celebration of life.'

'Life cut short,' intoned Belinda, who was determined, it seemed, to make a sombre occasion as tear-jerking as possible. She'd certainly dressed for it, from her black hat and dress to her charcoal gloves and shoes. The sun had come out from behind the clouds, the temperature had leaped up, and she was probably quietly boiling.

Jack looked down at Alyssa and squeezed her arm against his side. 'Are you doing OK?'

She nodded. 'This was always going to be a sad day.'

'Sad, but proper,' said Stan from his wheelchair. 'Those two deserve a decent burial after lying alone in the darkness for nigh on three hundred years.' He glanced past the churchyard wall to the village green where the Mourning Stone stood, its inscription now updated:

In memory of Charity Hawkins, aged eighteen years and three months, and Josiah Gathergill, aged twenty-two, who died together on the 15ᵗʰ of October in the year of our Lord 1753.

Now Charity and Josiah were being buried together. And, before long, it would be his turn to be lowered into the cold, dark earth.

Stan shivered and tried to turn his thoughts away from his inevitable demise. He was already fading fast, his limbs increasingly deaf to his brain's demands and his swallowing becoming more difficult and laboured.

But at least he was here, to witness ancient bones finally being laid to rest.

The two skeletons had been released for burial after weeks of being examined and investigated, and they would be placed in the same grave, here in Heaven's Cove.

It would be wrong to part them now. They would lie together for all time, in the village's peaceful churchyard, their names engraved on a single headstone. Just as he, one day soon, would join his beloved Penny, whose gravestone was just visible beyond the yew tree that spread its branches wide.

And Alyssa and Jack and Magda would gather once more, to mourn a life cut shorter than he would have liked. But not so short that anyone would particularly comment on it.

Stan sighed, but his heart was warmed by Jack and Alyssa standing so close together in front of him.

Jack was a different person these days, with Alyssa in his

life – more spontaneous, less guarded, more at ease... happier. Stan could see in him again the boy he'd once been, before his brother had become so sick. John's death had closed him down but Alyssa was opening him up again, a feat that Miri had never managed.

Stan thought fleetingly of his former daughter-in-law, now living with Damian, her fiancé. But his thoughts flitted past her to Archie. His bright, funny grandson was coming to stay next week, and Stan would enjoy every moment of his energy and optimism.

Jack, too, would benefit from spending time with his son. He saw as much of him as he could, even though that was more challenging now that Jack had moved to Heaven's Cove – a move purportedly to be with Alyssa but, just as much, Stan suspected, to look after him.

The bond between Archie and Jack still seemed strong. They spent ages talking on Facefit, or whatever it was called. And Jack had wangled a few days away from his new job at a nearby university, to spend time with him next week. No doubt, one of their trips out would be to Heaven's Cove cultural centre to see the precious brooch, guarded by Charity for centuries, that was now a celebrated exhibit.

Alyssa, too, had taken leave from her new nursing job so she could build a bond with Archie. She and Jack appeared to be in it for the long haul, which made his battered heart glad.

And then there was Magda. Stan watched her wipe away a tear as the coffin bearing Charity's and Josiah's bones was lowered into the grave. That woman had a warm heart and a shining soul.

Stan had sometimes been a selfish man. He knew that, and he knew he was being selfish with Magda now. He couldn't change the way he felt about her. He couldn't be the companion she wanted. However, he also knew that he wouldn't manage the end of his life's journey with dignity without her by his side.

Penny had once described Magda as 'one of a kind', and she'd been right. Magda was one of a wonderful kind. He hated that he'd unwittingly caused her pain over the years. But he felt blessed to have been loved by two such magnificent women.

That wasn't a bad epitaph for a little life spent in a tiny village on the Devon coast, he mused, smiling at Magda as she walked towards him. He coughed, his body wracked with spasm, knowing that, even as his life slipped away, he was a fortunate man.

A LETTER FROM LIZ

Dear reader,

Thank you so much for reading *The Path to the Last House Before the Sea*. I thoroughly enjoyed writing about Heaven's Cove and its inhabitants – and I hope that you've enjoyed spending time in the village, too.

If you did, and you'd like to keep up to date with all my latest releases, just sign up at the following link. Your email address will never be shared and you can unsubscribe at any time:

www.bookouture.com/liz-eeles

I'm back in Heaven's Cove at the moment, writing the next book in the series, and having a lovely time imagining the village in the depths of winter. There's plenty of snow... and, of course, lots of romance, family intrigue, and secrets to uncover. That book will be out in late 2023.

Before I go, if you've read *The Path to the Last House Before the Sea* and enjoyed it, I'd be really grateful if you could write a review. Your review might encourage other readers to visit Heaven's Cove. Thank you.

And finally, there are links below to where you can find me on social media. I love hearing from readers so do pop by and say hello, if you get the chance.

Liz x

www.lizeeles.com

facebook.com/lizeelesauthor
twitter.com/lizeelesauthor
instagram.com/lizeelesauthor

ACKNOWLEDGEMENTS

Thank you, as always, to the wonderful, hard-working team at Bookouture. And a special thank you to my talented editor, Ellen Gleeson, without whose encouragement, wise words, and plot-wrangling skills, Heaven's Cove would not exist. Thank you to my family and friends who, as well as being supportive, are understanding if I'm distracted (and, occasionally, ever so slightly tetchy) when a writing deadline is approaching. And I'm so grateful to everyone who takes the time to blog about my books or post a review.

Ingram Content Group UK Ltd.
Milton Keynes UK
UKHW011052020623
422771UK00004B/132